THE MYSTERY OF
MRS. CHRISTIE

THE MYSTERY OF MRS. CHRISTIE

MARIE BENEDICT

THORNDIKE PRESS
A part of Gale, a Cengage Company

GALE
A Cengage Company

Copyright © 2021 by Marie Benedict.
Thorndike Press, a part of Gale, a Cengage Company.

ALL RIGHTS RESERVED
The characters and events portrayed in this book are fictitious or are used fictitiously. Apart from well-known historical figures, any similarity to real persons, living or dead, is purely coincidental and not intended by the author.
Thorndike Press® Large Print Core.
The text of this Large Print edition is unabridged.
Other aspects of the book may vary from the original edition.
Set in 16 pt. Plantin.

LIBRARY OF CONGRESS CIP DATA ON FILE.
CATALOGUING IN PUBLICATION FOR THIS BOOK
IS AVAILABLE FROM THE LIBRARY OF CONGRESS.

ISBN-13: 978-1-4328-8485-7 (hardcover alk. paper)

Published in 2021 by arrangement with Sourcebooks, Inc.

Printed in Mexico
Print Number: 02   Print Year: 2021

THE MYSTERY OF
MRS. CHRISTIE

THE BEGINNING

The letter flutters on the desk, almost keeping time with the footsteps thundering across the floor. Back and forth, back and forth, the feet pace, and the thick writing paper quivers to the same rhythm. The black, spiky words that possess the ivory page seem to come alive and pulsate with each heavy tread.

How do you want this story to end? It seems to me that there are two paths from which you can choose, the first involving a softer landing than the second, though neither are without bumps and bruises, of course. These small injuries are simply a necessary consequence of this entire exercise, as I'm sure you must understand by now. Or have I overestimated you and you haven't guessed? No matter. My goal — which you will undoubtedly find utterly unacceptable — will be met regardless of your awareness. Freeing myself of the shackles of your judgment and your malfeasance will be a delightful result of your duplicity, a result you never intended. Because you only ever intended to serve your own needs and satisfy your own desires. I was never in the forefront of your mind, not even in the early days, even as I was told that you should always be at the forefront of mine.

The room, already dark despite the morning hour, grows even blacker. Seconds later, a gust of wind blows open the lightly closed but unlatched window, and the pages of the letter blow off the desk and onto the carpet. Darkness blankets its words until a crack of thunder sounds — *how very fitting and typical that it is a dark and stormy night,* the letter's recipient thinks — and lightning suddenly illuminates the room. And the words make themselves known again.

Read on and follow my instructions closely if you wish the safety of the first path and the security of its conclusion. It will not be easy. You will have to be stalwart, even when the road is rocky and you suffer from doubts and shame. Only by following my directions at each crossroads in this journey will the story end well for us all.

PART ONE

PART ONE

CHAPTER ONE:
THE MANUSCRIPT

October 12, 1912
Ugbrooke House, Devon, England
I could not have written a more perfect man.

"Lose your dance card," a voice whispered to me as I passed through the crowd and onto the dance floor. Who would dare say such a thing? Particularly since I was on the arm of Thomas Clifford, distant relation of my hosts, Lord and Lady Clifford of Chudleigh, and quite the focus of the unattached ladies at the Ugbrooke House ball.

Impertinent, I thought to myself, *even rude.* I imagined the scene if my dance partner had overheard him. Even worse, imagine if my dance partner was the one — our Fate, as my friends and I liked to describe prospective husbands — and had been distracted from his attentions. Still, a frisson passed through me, and I wondered who would hazard such impudence. I turned in the direction of the voice, but strains of

Elgar's Symphony No. 1 began to play, and my partner pulled me out to dance.

As we waltzed, I tried to identify the man from among the throngs lining the vast ballroom floor. Mummy would chastise me for not focusing my attentions upon the young Mr. Clifford, but from rumors, I knew that the eligible, well-connected gentleman needed to marry an heiress and could have no legitimate interest in me anyway. I was nearly penniless with only the inheritance of Ashfield villa to offer, an estate many would consider a curse rather than a blessing, particularly since I had no funds to support it and the villa was in constant need of repair. A lost opportunity Mr. Clifford was not. But I had no doubt that opportunity would indeed present itself. Wasn't that the destiny of all us girls? To be swept away by a man and then swept into the tidal pull of our Fate?

Dozens of men in evening dress stood in the corner of the gilded ballroom, but none seemed a likely candidate for such a brash invitation. Until I saw *him*. A fair, wavy-haired man stood on the fringes of the dance floor, his eyes on me. Never once did I see him engage in conversation with any of the other gentlemen, nor did I see him attempt to escort any of the ladies onto the floor. His only movement occurred when he walked over to the orchestra and spoke to the conductor, after which he returned to his spot in the corner.

The last chords of the orchestra sounded, and Mr. Clifford returned me to my post next to my dear friend Nan Watts, who was breathless from a quick turn around the floor with a red-faced acquaintance of her parents. As the orchestra began the next song and a florid young gentleman swooped in to fetch Nan, I glanced at the dance booklet dangling from my wrist by a red silk cord to see with whom I was paired.

A hand appeared on my wrist. I looked up into the intense blue eyes of the man who had been staring at me. Instinctively, I pulled my hand away, but somehow, he slipped my dance card off my wrist and entwined his fingers in mine.

"Forget your dance card for just one song," he said in a low, gravelly voice that I recognized as belonging to the brazen young man from a few minutes ago. I couldn't believe what he was asking, and I was shocked he'd taken my card. Allowing another man to cut into your dance card lineup simply wasn't done, even when that dance card had gone missing.

I thought I heard the distinctive chords of

a famous tune by Irving Berlin. It sounded like "Alexander's Ragtime Band," but I knew I must be wrong. Lord and Lady Clifford would never have requested this modern song from their orchestra. In fact, I guessed that they'd be irate at this deviation from standard protocol; classical, symphonic pieces — paired with sedate dances certain not to inflame the passions of the young — were the order of the day.

He watched the expression on my face as I listened to the music. "I hope you like Berlin," he said with a small, self-satisfied smile.

"*You* arranged this?" I asked.

A sheepish smile spread across his face, displaying his dimples. "I overheard you saying to your friend that you longed for some more up-to-date music."

"How did you manage it?" I was astonished not only at his audacity but at his determination. It was, well, flattering. No one had ever made such a grandiose gesture for me. Certainly none of the ragtag suitors with whom my mother tried to match me in Cairo for my coming out two years ago, a necessary endeavor because the cost of coming out in London — the numerous fashionable gowns, the parties attended and hosted, the price of renting a town house

14

for the season — was too high for Mummy's reduced circumstances. And not even dear Reggie, whom I'd known my whole life as the kindly older brother of my dear friends the Lucy sisters but who only recently became much more than a family friend, had undertaken a similar effort. Reggie and I had formed an understanding — between each other and our families — that our lives and our families would one day be linked by marriage. An amorphous future marriage, but matrimony nonetheless. Although now, viewing that union in the context of this splashy wooing, it seemed a placid affair, albeit a comfortable one.

"Does it matter?" he asked.

I suddenly felt quite overwhelmed. Looking down at the floor, a fierce blush overtaking my face, I shook my head.

"I hope you'll dance with me." His voice was low and firm.

Even though I could hear Mummy's voice in my head cautioning me against dancing with a man to whom I had not been properly introduced, never mind that he had somehow wrangled an invitation to the Ugbrooke House ball and laid waste to my dance card, I said, "Yes."

Because really, how dangerous could one dance be?

CHAPTER TWO:
DAY ONE AFTER
THE DISAPPEARANCE

Saturday, December 4, 1926
Hurtmore Cottage, Godalming, England

The precision of the Jameses' breakfast table setting inspires in him a sense of rightness and contentment that he has rarely felt since his return from the war. The gleaming cutlery lies adjacent to the Minton porcelain, each utensil lined up exactly with the next. The delicately etched plates, a Grasmere pattern he believes, are an impeccable two inches from the edge of the table, and the floral centerpiece — a restrained yet elegant seasonal spray of winterberries and greens — is placed at the center. *By God,* he thinks, *this is the sort of order that can put a man at ease.*

Why doesn't his home bear this level of perfection? Why must he be constantly assaulted by its lack of household rigor and the emotions and needs of its inhabitants? With these thoughts, a sense of righteous

16

indignation blooms within him, and he feels perfectly justified.

"I do believe that a toast is in order," his host, Sam James, announces with a nod to his wife, Madge. She in turn signals to the uniformed housemaid, who reaches for a bottle of champagne that has been chilling in a crystal bucket on the sideboard.

"Archie, we had wanted to toast your plans last evening, but the unexpected visit by Reverend —" Madge starts to explain.

A soft pink hue begins to spread across Nancy's cheeks, and though she looks lovely with her cheeks aflame, Archie understands that the Jameses' focus on their situation is the cause of her discomfort and wants to placate her. Raising his hand, he says, "The gesture is much appreciated, my dear Madge, but not necessary."

"Please, Archie." Madge holds fast. "We are well pleased with your plans. And you will have little enough opportunity to celebrate."

"We insist," Sam echoes his wife.

To protest further would be impolite, which Nancy implicitly understands. This sense of decorum is a quality they share, and he relishes it in her. It obviates the need for the firm guiding hand toward properness that he must exercise elsewhere in his

17

life. His home, in particular.

"Sam and Madge, thank you. Your support means the world," he answers. Nancy nods in agreement.

The crystal flutes sparkle with the honey-colored champagne as the maid fills each of their glasses in turn. Just as she finishes pouring the final glass, a knock sounds at the dining room door.

"Pardon the interruption, sir," a woman's voice, thick with a country accent, calls through the closed door, "but there is a telephone call for the colonel."

He exchanges a quizzical glance with Nancy. He hadn't expected a call so soon, if at all, particularly since he'd kept his weekend whereabouts as quiet as possible. For the obvious reason. Nancy sets her glass down and gently touches his elbow over the crisp linen tablecloth. It is a silent acknowledgment of their shared concern about the call.

"Pardon me," he says with a nod to their hosts, who place their flutes back down on the table. Standing, he buttons his suit jacket and nods to Nancy with a confidence he does not feel. He strides out of the dining room, quietly shutting the door behind him.

"This way, sir," the maid says, and he follows her into a tiny room tucked under the intricately carved main staircase of Hurtmore Cottage, a misnomer for the grand home. There, the candlestick telephone, its receiver sitting on the desktop, awaits him.

Sitting down at the desk chair, he places the receiver to his ear and the mouthpiece to his lips. But he will not speak until the maid has closed the door behind her.

"Hello?" He hates the uncertainty he hears in his voice. Nancy prizes his self-assurance above all else.

"My apologies, sir. This is Charlotte Fisher."

What in the devil is Charlotte thinking, ringing him here? He had entrusted her with the Hurtmore Cottage information with the gravest of admonitions. Even though he'd gone to great lengths in recent months to curry favor with the family secretary and governess — necessary, he believes, to effectuate the smooth transition for which he hopes — he makes no effort to coddle her now by keeping the anger from his voice. Damn the consequences. "Charlotte, I thought I instructed you not to contact me here except in the case of an extreme emergency."

"Well, Colonel," she stammers, "I am standing in the foyer of Styles next to

19

Constable Roberts."

Charlotte stops speaking. Does she really think that the mere mention of the presence of a police officer in his home should explain all? What does she want him to say? She waits for him to speak next, and in the quiet, dread fills him. He can find no words. What does she know? More importantly, what does the constable know? Every word seems a trap he'll spring.

"Sir," she says when he does not respond. "I do believe that this qualifies as an extreme emergency. Your wife is missing."

CHAPTER THREE:
THE MANUSCRIPT

October 12, 1912
Ugbrooke House, Devon, England

A murmur of surprise rose up from the revelers as the Irving Berlin tune became more recognizable. While the older guests seemed uncertain about the propriety of dancing to such a modern song, my partner did not hesitate to pull me onto the dance floor. He led me directly into the bold one-step, and the younger set followed in our wake.

Without the intricate dance steps of the waltz to place distance between us, our bodies felt awfully close. It almost made me wish for the old-fashioned gowns with their armor of corsets. In an effort to create some sort of barrier between myself and this very forward stranger, however artificial, I kept my gaze fixed firmly over his shoulder. His eyes, however, never moved from mine.

Normally, my dance partners and I fell

into easy chatter, but not this time. What could I say to such a fellow? Finally, he broke the silence. "You are even prettier than Arthur Griffiths described you."

I could not say which part of his remark astonished me more: the fact that I shared an acquaintance with this unusual man or that he had the audacity to call me "pretty" when we hadn't even been formally introduced. My set had firm rules governing our behavior, and although those unspoken guidelines had relaxed in recent years, commenting on my appearance right out of the gate broke even the loosest conventions. If I were honest with myself, I found his candor refreshing, but girls like me weren't supposed to like directness. He'd left me with two choices — either to stomp away at his effrontery or to ignore it entirely. Given that this man intrigued me despite his gaffes, I chose the latter and benignly asked, "You know Arthur Griffiths?" The local vicar's son was a friend.

"Yes, we are both with the Royal Field Artillery, and I'm stationed with him at the garrison at Exeter. When he found out that he couldn't attend tonight because of his official duties, he asked me to come in his stead and look out for you."

Ah, well, that explained something, I

thought. I met his gaze and discovered that his eyes were a remarkable bright-blue shade. "Why didn't you mention him straight off?"

"I didn't know I needed to."

I did not state the obvious, that any young man from a good family knows how to make proper introductions, including a reference to your acquaintances in common. Instead, I fished around for a bland response and said, "He's a fine fellow."

"Do you know Arthur well?"

"Not very well, but he is a lovely friend. We met when I was staying with the Mathews at Thorp Arch Hall in Yorkshire, and we got on."

My dance partner — who still had not introduced himself by name — didn't respond. The silence bothered me, so I got chatty. "He's a good dancer."

"You sound as though you're disappointed I'm here instead of him."

I decided to see if this young man's mood could be lightened. "Well, sir, this is our *first* dance. And since you've liberated me from my dance card, you may yet have the chance for another to prove *your* dancing skills."

He laughed, a deep, rich sound. As he spun me around the floor, past the familiar

23

faces of the Wilfreds and the Sinclairs, I laughed along with him, feeling quite different from those around me. Freer somehow. More alive.

"I intend to do precisely that," he said.

Emboldened, I asked him, "What is it that you do as an officer at Exeter?"

"I fly."

I froze for a moment. Everyone was mad for the notion of flying, and here I was dancing with a pilot. It was too thrilling. "You fly?"

His cheeks turned a fiery red, visible even in the low ballroom light. "Well, I'm actually a gunner at the moment, even though I'm the 245th qualified aviator in Britain. Soon enough, though, I'll be entering the newly formed Royal Flying Corps." His chest, already quite broad, puffed up a bit at this statement.

"What's it like up there? In the sky?"

For the first time, he unlocked his eyes from mine and glanced up at the frescoed ceiling, as if there, among the artfully depicted faux skyscape with its abundance of cherubs, he might relive the real thing. "Exhilarating and strange to be so near the clouds and to see the world below so small. But quite terrifying too."

I giggled a little. "I cannot even imagine,

though I'd like to try it."

His blue eyes clouded over, and his tone grew more serious. "I haven't chosen flying for the thrill of it, Miss Miller. If there's a war — and I do think there will be one — planes will be vital. I intend to be integral to the war effort, a critical cog in the massive military machine. To help England, of course, but also so I can reap the benefits afterward in my career. When aeroplanes will be an important part of our economy."

His intensity moved me, as did the boldness of his approach. He was quite different from all the men I'd encountered before, whether at home in Devon or abroad in Egypt. I felt quite breathless, and not just from the quick pace of the one-step.

The last notes of "Alexander's Ragtime Band" sounded, and I stopped dancing. I began to untwine myself from him when he reached for my hand. "Stay on the dance floor with me. As you yourself said, you no longer have a dance card. You are free."

I hesitated. More than anything, I wanted to dance with him again, to start to solve the mystery of this unusual man. But I could hear Mummy railing in my head, reprimanding me for the untoward message a girl sent if she danced with a gentleman twice in a row, particularly a girl who was already spoken for. I wanted something in exchange for my trouble.

"On one condition," I said.

"Anything, Miss Miller. Anything at all."

"You tell me your name."

Blushing again, he realized that, for all his valiant gestures with me, he had forgotten the most basic protocol. He bowed deeply and then said, "I am most pleased to make your acquaintance, Miss Miller. My name is Lieutenant Archibald Christie."

CHAPTER FOUR:
DAY ONE AFTER
THE DISAPPEARANCE

Saturday, December 4, 1926
Hurtmore Cottage, Godalming, England, and
* Styles, Sunningdale, England*

"Everything all right?" Sam asks him upon his return to the dining room.

Although he's already crafted an answer to the inevitable question, Archie stammers when called upon to say the actual words. Lying has never come easily to him, even when circumstances as of late have presented him with abundant opportunities to practice. "Oh, it's, um, my mother. She's taken ill, I'm afraid." Before he can explain further, Madge gasps. He holds up his hand and assures her, "Nothing serious, the doctor promises. But she's asked for me, and needs must."

Sam nods his head. "Duty and all that."

"Well, if it's not terribly serious, can you spare Nancy through luncheon?" Madge, recovered from her concern over Archie's mother, asks with a coy glance at her friend. "Sam and I would love to keep her captive for a few hands of whist."

"I don't see why not," Archie says, giving Madge and then Nancy his best approximation of a smile. Nancy, sweet and unchallenging and lovely in her pale-blue frock, deserves a happy, carefree afternoon with her friend.

"Will you be able to return for dinner?" Sam asks, and Archie feels the weight of the Jameses' disappointment. They've been so kind to plan this weekend, and now he's undermined their gesture. One he doubts anyone else would have made.

"I'll ring to let you know whether that will be possible. If not —" Archie breaks off, unsure what to say. He doesn't know what he'll be facing at Styles, doesn't know what the police know, and he cannot plan for the different eventualities. In truth, he hasn't even allowed himself to consider those eventualities.

Sam rescues him. "No need to worry, old chap. We will take Nancy to her home if the evening plans prove impossible."

Gratitude surges through him, and he rounds the table to shake his friend's hand. Just as their fingers touch, a knock sounds at the door.

"Again? That damned maid." Sam grunts in irritation, then yells out, "What is it now?"

"Sir, there is a policeman at the door," the maid says through the crack.

Archie feels sick. He knows, or thinks he knows, why the police wait at the Jameses' front door.

"What?" Sam couldn't have looked more astonished if his maid had informed him that his beloved foxhound had spontaneously turned into a poodle. Police officers were for dealing with scrapes among petty laborers, not for knocking on the front door of country houses.

"Yes, sir, a police officer, sir. He's asking for the colonel."

"Whatever for?"

"He won't say. Just keeps asking for the colonel."

The humiliation of being summoned by a police officer — giving the lie to his concoction about his mother's condition — almost overshadows his concern about the summoning itself. What must Madge and Sam think of him? How will he explain this to them? To Nancy?

As he proceeds down the road, a rock causes his Delage to spin out, and he nearly loses sight of the police car he's meant to be following. The momentary separation from the vehicle plants a seed of reckless- ness in him. What if he just drove off, evad- ing the situation at Styles? Would the police car be able to catch him?

No, he will face his comeuppance like a man. No matter how his actions will be judged, he never wants it said that he's a man who shirks his duties, who runs from his mistakes.

Following the police car, he turns down the familiar lane leading to his home. The dust from the official vehicle blinds his vi- sion for a second, and when his sight clears, the Tudor peaks of Styles materialize, nearly as impressive as the first time he saw them. *How much has changed since that day,* he thinks, forcing that memory from his mind.

Archie knows that he must somehow grasp the upper hand of this situation. Perhaps it will help if he sets the tone by as- suming his rightful role as master of Styles? Accordingly, he does not wait for the police- man to alight from his car. Instead, he marches past the other police cars parked in Styles's governor's drive and heads directly to the slightly ajar front door. When he pushes it wide open, he is surprised to note that not one of the black-uniformed officers gathered in the kitchen like a swarm of deadly bees gathered around their queen takes notice of him. Archie realizes that he has been given a singular chance to assess the situation before he speaks.

He scans the long mahogany table lining the foyer's right wall to see if any calling cards lie on the silver receiving tray. The tray is bare, but he notices something unusual. Peeking out from underneath the tray is the corner of an envelope, his wife's distinctive ivory stationary.

Glancing at the police officers absorbed in the loud yet strangely muffled voice of a man he can't see, undoubtedly their supervisor, Archie slides the envelope out from under the silver tray. Then, keeping his footsteps light, he creeps into his study and quietly closes the door behind him.

Grabbing the ivory-handled letter opener from his desk, he slices open the envelope. The sprawling, spiky handwriting of his wife stares out at him from the notepaper within. Time presses upon him urgently, but he needs little more than several seconds to scan her words. As he finishes, he looks up, feeling as if he's awoken from a deep slumber into a nightmare. When on earth did she have the time — nay, the prescience, the shrewdness, the patient calculation — to write these words? Had he ever really known his wife?

The narrow walls of his study seem to constrict, and he feels like he cannot breathe. But he knows he must take action. The letter has made clear that he's no longer the executor of a plan but merely its subject — one trapped in a labyrinth at that — and he must find a way out. Tossing the letter down on the desk, he begins pacing the room, which grows gloomier by the second with an impending storm. What in the name of god should he do?

He is certain of only one thing. While he is prepared to pay his penance, he doesn't plan on handing over the keys to the jailor. No one can be allowed to see this letter. Walking over to the hearth, he drops the letter and envelope into the flames and watches Agatha's words burn.

CHAPTER FIVE:
THE MANUSCRIPT

October 19, 1912
Ashfield, Torquay, England

I raced across the lane from the Mellors' estate back home to Ashfield. I'd been quite happily playing badminton with my friend Max Mellor when his maid summoned me to the telephone. Mummy, quite cross, was on the line, ordering me home because an unknown young man was there, "waiting endlessly" for me. She'd told him that she expected me within a quarter of an hour, and when I didn't appear within the anticipated time — and when he didn't leave as the minutes passed and I failed to appear — she felt compelled to phone. The poor fellow, whoever he was, obviously hadn't registered any number of cues my mother sent his way that he should take his leave.

Other than Mummy's pressure, I had felt no compulsion to return home, especially since Max and I were having a grand time.

Life in Torquay was chock-full of these lazy days. Impromptu picnics and sailing and sports engagements and riding outings and musical afternoons by day. Carefully orchestrated garden parties and evening dances and house parties by night. Weeks and months floated by in a pleasant, carefree dream — with a girl's only goal being the landing of a husband — and I had no wish to wake up.

I guessed that the caller was the stuffy naval officer from the previous night's dinner party, who'd begged me to read his heavy-handed poems aloud to the other guests. Even so, while I had no desire to resume our stultifying conversation, I didn't wish for him to irritate Mummy for too long a time. While Mummy was patient and sweet-natured, particularly with me, she could become crotchety in the presence of a bore or someone who set her off schedule. Since my father's death nearly ten years ago, I'd become my mother's focus and companion, particularly since my elder siblings Madge and Monty had long since moved on with their own lives, and I relished it. Mummy and I had a lovely relationship — no one in the world understood me as she did — and I felt quite protective of her, even though she was much stronger than she appeared on first glance. The shock of my father's death and the challenge of the financial circumstances in which he left us had knitted us together tightly, the two of us against the world and all that.

My cheeks flushed and warm from hurrying down the lane, I wiggled out of my cardigan and handed it to Jane, our housemaid. Before I walked from the entryway to the drawing room, I glanced at myself in the mirror to make certain I looked presentable. My dun-colored hair, kissed by the sun into a dark, glimmering blond, looked rather fetching despite — or maybe because of — the tendrils that had escaped my braid. I decided not to tuck the loose pieces back into my hairpins, but I did smooth my hair. Even though I didn't care much for the opinion of the fellow I suspected sat in the parlor, I always liked to meet Mummy's expectation that I was a "lovely girl."

I entered the drawing room, where my mother looked over at me from her usual spot in an armchair near the fireplace. Putting aside her embroidery in order to flee the room at the first polite opportunity, she rose, as did the man sitting opposite her. I could only see the back of his head, which was a sandy blond shade quite a bit lighter than I remembered the naval officer's hair being.

I walked toward both of them and bobbed in an abbreviated curtsy. Looking up from the floor into Mummy's face first and then the gentleman caller's, I realized with a start that it was not the naval officer I expected. It was the man from the Chudleigh ball — Archibald Christie.

Astonished, I didn't speak at first. I hadn't heard from him in the seven days since the ball, and I had begun to think I never would. Most gentlemen would have expressed their interest in a girl within one or two days of a ball — never seven.

Mummy cleared her throat and finally said, "Agatha, this young man — Lieutenant Christie, I believe — tells me that you two met at Chudleigh."

Collecting myself, I answered, "Yes, Mummy. This is Lieutenant Christie, who is in the Royal Field Artillery. He is stationed at the garrison at Exeter, and I did indeed meet him at the ball given by the Cliffords at Chudleigh."

She looked him up and down. "You're quite a ways from Exeter, Lieutenant Christie."

"Yes, ma'am. I happened to be driving my motorbike through Torquay, and I remembered that Miss Miller lived here. I inquired of a local I passed on the road, and here I am."

"Here you are." She sighed. "What a coincidence that you should happen to find yourself in Torquay."

No one could miss the sarcasm and disbelief in my mother's voice, and I found it surprising that my gentle, adoring Mummy could be so sharp with a stranger. What had he done to her in the span of a quarter of an hour alone to elicit this unusual reaction? Was it simply that he wasn't Reggie? I glanced over at Lieutenant Christie, whose cheeks shone bright red. I felt badly for him and rushed in to save him.

"I remember you mentioned at the Cliffords' ball that you might have an errand in Torquay, Lieutenant Christie. Of an official nature, that is."

An expression of relief passed over his face, and he grasped at my proffered excuse. "Indeed, Miss Miller. And you had very kindly suggested that I call when in the neighborhood."

This exchange did not fool Mummy, but it did return to Lieutenant Christie a modicum of his dignity. It also provided my mother with license to leave the drawing room. Unlike the continent, it was the custom in England for unmarried men and women to be left alone, as long as chaperones were in the vicinity or the unmarried people were busy dancing. "Well, I must see Mary about the dinner menu. It was a pleasure meeting you, Lieutenant —" She feigned forgetfulness, telegraphing her opinion of this young man.

"Christie, ma'am."

"Lieutenant Christie," she said as she left the room.

I fancied that we simultaneously exhaled when Mummy left the room. Determined to lighten the mood, I said, "Why don't we take a walk in the gardens? The day is cool, but our grounds hold some interest. And I'd love to see your motorbike."

"That would be lovely, Miss Miller."

After the servant helped us on with our coats — a longer walk required more warmth than a cardigan could provide — we trundled outside. Passing by the kitchen garden, I explained to Lieutenant Christie that we would not be stopping behind its high walls because its sole allure was its abundance of seasonal raspberries and apples. I directed him instead to the garden proper.

Watching Lieutenant Christie squirm under my mother's scrutinizing gaze made me bold with him. With a broad smile, I teased, "Can I trust you with the secrets of my garden?"

He did not smile back. Instead, he fixed his bright-blue eyes on mine and said, "I hope you can trust me with *all* your secrets."

His intensity left me a bit flustered, but after showing him the familiar ilex, cedar, and Wellington trees, as well as the two firs previously claimed by Madge and Monty, my nerves calmed. "Here is my particular favorite, the beech tree. It's the largest in the garden, and when I was a girl, I used to gorge myself on its beechnuts." I ran my hand along its trunk, remembering all the girlish days I spent in its branches, days now gone.

"I understand why the garden is special to you. It's lovely," he said, then pointed ahead to a thick copse of trees in the distance. "Are those your woods as well?"

His eyes were bright and full of awe. I supposed he thought we were rich; Ashfield and its grounds *were* impressive, if one squinted to blur out the spots of decay and peeling paint. While we had been wealthy during my early years, financial worries set in when I was about five, and my father — who'd been born the son of a rich American man and never worked a day in his life, expecting that his money would last — struggled to keep the family afloat. Only by renting Ashfield and living on that income abroad, where it was comparatively cheap, did we maintain some semblance of our lifestyle. The unfamiliar stress of these concerns affected his health and led to the decline of my poor, sweet papa, who died ten years ago. Now Mummy and I limped along on the benevolence of our friends and family as well as a small income, recently reduced when the investment firm from which we derived a portion of our meager draw liquidated.

"Yes," I answered as I led him on the path through the ash trees. "But its trees are more common and provided less magic for a young girl. Not to mention the path leads to the tennis and croquet lawns, which I never much enjoyed."

"Why not?"

"I guess I lived more in the world of the imagination as a child than the world of sport," I said, but Lieutenant Christie did not respond as he examined the croquet and tennis lawns with interest and satisfaction. He couldn't know how decidedly unathletic my performance had been there, despite my valiant efforts; only in the realm of simple badminton did I experience a modicum of success. Having witnessed too many heart-breaking attempts, Mummy, ever supportive, directed my enthusiasm toward music, drama, and writing instead. In that realm, I flourished, particularly during my years of schooling in France, although recently I had abandoned hope of undertaking piano or singing professionally on the advice of the esteemed pianist Charles Furster and my London voice coaches. Writing, however, had remained a passion and became my habit, much as my friends might dabble in embroidery or landscape painting. But I always understood that my writing must remain a trifle, something to pass the time only, and that my Fate stemmed from my husband. Whoever he might be. Whenever he might surface.

When Lieutenant Christie continued to study the croquet and tennis lawns without a word, I asked, "Did you have a special place when you were a child?"

His brow furrowed, casting a shadow over his eyes. "I spent my early years in India where my father was a judge in the Indian Civil Service. As soon as my family returned to England, he fell from a horse and died. We stayed with my mother's family in southern Ireland until she remarried William Hemsley, a schoolmaster from Clifton

College, after which I went to Clifton. So you can see, I moved around, never really had any special place as a child — no place to call my own anyway."

"How terribly sad, Lieutenant Christie. Well, if you like, you can share Ashfield's gardens with me. Come and visit them whenever you can get to Torquay."

He turned those blue eyes on me again, as if trying to capture me in them. "If you mean it, Miss Miller, I would be honored."

I wanted to see this unusual man again. The thoughts of my own commitment to Reggie began to creep in, along with a certain amount of guilt, but I held fast. "Lieutenant Christie, I would like nothing more."

CHAPTER SIX:
DAY ONE AFTER THE DISAPPEARANCE

Saturday, December 4, 1926
Styles, Sunningdale, England

As he hurries out of his study, Archie nearly collides with the round-hatted young policeman who'd procured him from Hurtmore Cottage. He gives the man a dismissive glance and storms off to the kitchen where a gaggle of police have assembled. As he stomps off, he prays he's embarking on the right approach by playing the part of the aggrieved, furious husband.

"What is the meaning of this? Why are the lot of you huddled around in my kitchen instead of combing the vicinity?" Archie barks at them, forcing a vitriol he doesn't feel into his tone.

One of the officers, a younger fellow with surprisingly soft features, ignores Archie's scolding and says instead, "Sir, I'm sure this is all very overwhelming. And distressing, of course."

43

"That is an understatement," Archie says, then assumes all of his six feet in the hopes of asserting his dominion. "I want to see the officer in charge."

The young policeman scurries off to fetch a middle-aged man, dressed in an ill-fitting gray suit and a rumpled overcoat, who emerges from the throng of officers. Archie studies this barrel-chested officer, jowly and unkempt with a few crumbs in his sandy-colored mustache, as he approaches with an outstretched hand and a genial half smile. It's the sort of expression that attempts to convey both sympathy and warmth at the same time, one the officer has trotted out on countless other occasions, perhaps in his guise as a country police officer. It seems false, and in the policeman's wary stare, Archie also senses an undercurrent of suspicion and latent intellect. He will have to tread cautiously.

"Mr. Christie, I'd like to introduce you to Deputy Chief Constable Kenward," the junior fellow says, giving a half bow in this Kenward's direction. *How does this man manage such deference from his men with such a disheveled appearance?* Archie wonders, but then the eminent nature of the man's title registers, and it gives him a start. Why has such a senior police detective been

44

assigned to this case?

As Archie scrambles to assemble his thoughts and adjust his approach, Kenward says, "Good to meet you, Mr. Christie. The Surrey County Police Headquarters has referred the case to me for oversight, you see, and I'll do all I can to help." He does not react to Archie's little tirade.

Archie shakes Kenward's rather damp hand and, reassessing his approach, finally responds. "Apologies for the outburst, Deputy Chief Constable Kenward. As you can imagine, it's a very upsetting time. I appreciate your assistance, and I'm sorry to be making your acquaintance in such trying circumstances."

"Of course, sir, we understand that emotions run high in such times. But I'll do my best by your wife, I can promise you that. That way, you won't feel the need for such a flare-up in the future, I hope." The rebuke is implicit — Archie will be allowed this one eruption only — and the nattering of Kenward's underlings ceases as he delivers it. The room grows uncomfortably silent, a stillness brimming with unspoken judgments.

"Thank you for understanding," Archie says, and police officers begin their chatter again.

"I assure you that we are doing all we can to locate your missing wife," Kenward repeats.

My missing wife, Archie thinks to himself. Those three words spoken aloud by a senior police official make the unthinkable very possible, and he finds himself unable to speak.

Kenward fills the void. "I have a few questions for you, Colonel, of an ordinary sort. Might we retire to your study to discuss them?"

Archie suddenly realizes that he does not want to be interrogated amid these officers, that he craves the privacy of his study if personal demons are to be aired. He also recognizes that he needs the brief walk to gather himself and his answers.

With a nod, Archie pivots and leads Kenward back into his study. Suddenly uncomfortable having the lawman so close to the hearth — he can't risk the constable ferreting out a wayward scrap of the singed letter amid the ashes — he directs him to the chair farthest from the fireplace. Then Archie selects a chair for himself such that Kenward must face away from the flames.

Pulling out a leather-bound notebook and a fountain pen from the inner pocket of his overcoat, the constable begins. "All routine questions, sir, I assure you. We are trying to establish a timeline. When did you last see your wife?"

"On Friday morning, around nine o'clock. Just before I left for work."

The scratch of pen on paper fills the air, and a wave of recollection washes over Archie. That distinctive sound belongs to his wife and usually permeates Styles. It is the sound of his wife's thoughts.

"Do you recall the exchange you had that morning?" Kenward asks, shaking Archie loose from his reverie.

With a start, Archie wonders about the staff. Have the police interviewed them already? He'll have to be cautious.

Willing himself not to stammer, he answers. "Not with any degree of precision. I imagine that we had the usual morning discussion. Schedules, news, little stories about our seven-year-old daughter, Rosalind, things like that."

"Did you discuss your weekend plans?"

Was the policeman laying a trap? What did he know?

Archie gives a vague response. "I don't recall exactly. We may have."

"What were your respective weekend plans, sir?"

"My wife had plans to visit Yorkshire for

47

the weekend. As you know, I spent the weekend with my friends Mr. and Mrs. James of Hurtmore Cottage. One of your men fetched me from there."

"Do you and your wife often spend the weekends separately?" Kenward asks, keeping his eyes fixed on his journal.

Tread carefully, Archie tells himself. Every question might bring him one step closer to a snare.

"When the occasion demands."

"That doesn't answer my question, sir."

"You have my answer, Deputy Chief Constable." As soon as the sharp words leave his mouth, Archie regrets it. He knows that a man worried about his wife — desperate to find her — would not lash out at a policeman for asking routine questions. He would answer any and every question willingly. What must this policeman think of him? Kenward is cannier than his rumpled appearance suggests, Archie suspects.

Kenward's eyes narrow, and his mouth opens, forming a circular shape around the words of his next questions. But before those words meet air, the study door opens with a thud. A young policeman scurries to the officer's side, whispering in his ear.

The constable leaps to his feet with a surprising spryness. "Excuse me for a moment, Colonel. There's been a development."

Archie's stomach flips. What in the name of God have they found so soon? He follows the policeman out into the foyer. "What is it? What's happened?"

Kenward calls back to him over his shoulder. "I'll let you know as soon as I've had a chance to investigate personally. In the meantime, please remain here."

Archie allows his step to slow, and in the absence of movement, panic sets in. He turns around, intending to return to the sanctuary of his study to regain control of himself, but before he reaches it, he encounters Charlotte in the hallway. The dark-haired governess and secretary, her hair cut in a fashionable but unflattering bob, is carrying a tea tray with scraps of an uneaten breakfast undoubtedly belonging to his daughter. "Miss Rosalind has been asking after you, sir," she mentions in an apologetic tone.

"Does she know anything about the situation?"

"No, sir. Although even a child can see that something's wrong, what with the police crawling about the house."

"Let's keep it that way for now, Charlotte. I'll visit her in the nursery presently."

Charlotte's voice, usually brisk and efficient, catches. "Did — did you see the letter, sir?"

"What letter?" Archie feigns an air of innocence, all the while praying he misunderstood the servant. That she meant a different letter than the one from his wife.

"The one from the mistress on the foyer table. I saw it there yesterday evening when I returned from London but left it for you."

"Oh yes, that one," he says, as if he's just remembered. Feigning casualness, he asks, "You didn't mention that letter to the police, did you? It didn't have anything to do with" — he gestures around the house — "all this."

"N-no," she answers.

Without thinking, he reaches for her arm, squeezing it a little tighter than planned. "Good." Charlotte gives a quiet yelp, and he releases her arm. "I'm sorry. I'm just so worried," he says.

"Of course you are, sir." She absolves him, rubbing her arm a bit. "Honestly, now that I think about it, I can't quite remember if I mentioned it or not. The morning's been quite the blur, what with the police to contend with and Miss Rosalind missing her mum today. Should I be keeping the letter private?"

While he does not want to leave Charlotte with a wrong impression, one she might inadvertently convey to others, he cannot risk her disclosure. He could only guess at what the police would glean from a letter left by a missing wife for her husband and then subsequently burned by that husband. Only one conclusion seems likely.

But how best to broach this topic with Charlotte to get the desired result? If he insists on her silence, would she take that demand to the police? He could only imagine the repercussions of that. Perhaps the demand could be framed as a request? A choice?

"I don't want to tell you what to do on this score, Charlotte, but I do think it would be best to allow the constable to focus on the more important matter of locating the mistress, don't you?"

Charlotte glances down at the tea tray she's still carrying and concurs without enthusiasm. "As you like, sir."

He could almost weep with relief but instead keeps his face placid. "Good girl. Anyway, the letter concerns a private matter between my wife and myself that predates the events of yesterday. As such, it can shed no light on her whereabouts."

CHAPTER SEVEN:
THE MANUSCRIPT

November 19, 1912
Ashfield, Torquay, England

"You can run off into the garden now, Jack," Madge announced as we finished tea. I found it hard to believe that Madge's son, James, who everyone referred to as Jack, was no longer a little boy but a growing lad of nine. As soon as Jack received his release from the prison of Ashfield's tea table, he leapt up and ran for the outdoors, undoubtedly hoping to get the last hour of daylight before he was incarcerated within the house's walls again.

"Am I to be excused as well?" Madge's good-natured husband Jimmy asked.

"You know me all too well, darling," Madge said with a smile. "How did you know that we girls would like to have a feminine chat?"

"I do know you a bit after all these years, my dear. Plus, I do have a sister, who's usually in league with you and Agatha in these little talks," Jimmy answered with a reference to his sister, Nan Watts, as he trailed out of the room. He nibbled on a final scone in hand, getting crumbs in his reddish mustache. "Don't forget we've got to head out in an hour," he called over his shoulder when he reached the hallway.

I glanced over at my self-assured sister, her chestnut hair curled expertly around her ear, a triple strand of pearls draped around her neck and bosom, a crimson cashmere cardigan draped over her shoulders and her floral silk dress. Her face was not classically pretty, but the manner in which she carried herself drew people to her almost magnetically. I tried to meet her gaze — to assess why she wanted to have this private chat — but she was staring at Mummy, who nodded in response. What were they planning, and was this "chat" the reason for their unexpected visit to Ashfield? I suddenly felt quite caged.

"Mummy tells me you have a new beau," Madge said as she pulled a cigarette from her silver monogrammed case. I thought she looked the picture of sophistication as she tapped it on the table, lit a match, and then took a long drag, but I knew Mummy disapproved. She found this new smoking fad to be extremely unladylike. "Even though you're still engaged to Reggie Lucy."

Our family had known the Lucys for ages, and Reggie and I were kindred spirits, having been raised in the same lovely, lazy Devon lifestyle. He hadn't much money either, but he had solid enough prospects as a major in the Gunners. Before he left for a two-year stint in Hong Kong, the beautifully shy young man, with lovely dark eyes and hair, quietly proposed, not a formal engagement, mind, but a loose sort of understanding between our families. But the evening of his departure, he told me to see other people — other boys — at dances and parties before we settled down. I had taken Reggie at his word and went about my normal social activities, including formal balls where dancing was de rigueur. I hadn't felt a lick of guilt until Archie appeared and everything seemed to shift.

My cheeks burned hot. I admired Madge and sought her approval, so I found it especially loathsome when she treated me like a child. Or worse, when beloved Mummy sided with her against me. In such moments, I felt the eleven-year age difference between Madge and me like a chasm. Thank God Monty was such an absentee sibling, or it might have been three against one.

My spine stiffened, and my shoulders went rigid. "I don't know what you're talking about, Madge. Reggie didn't want me to stay at home moping. He specifically instructed me to go out to socialize and even see other chaps. After all, he is going to be in Hong Kong for two years." My voice sounded strident and defensive, which I hated.

"I don't think he meant seeing other fellows exclusively, Agatha. The way I understand you are seeing this Lieutenant Christie." She shot Mummy an indiscernible look. They'd obviously been discussing me and Archie behind my back. I'd sensed for some time that Mummy didn't care for Archie — although I couldn't see that he'd given her any particular reason to dislike him other than the fact that he wasn't Reggie Lucy — but this confirmed it. I guessed that Mummy had put Madge up to this conversation.

"It's hardly as if Lieutenant Christie and I have an understanding between us, Madge. He's simply become part of my set, that's all."

Even as I said the words, I knew they weren't true. Over the past several weeks,

Lieutenant Christie had taken me at my word to visit as often as he could. He came frequently and sometimes unexpectedly to Torquay, no longer pretending that an official errand brought him to Ashfield as he had on that first visit. In fact, he'd confessed to the embarrassment he suffered in prying my address out of Arthur Griffiths. Despite his many visits, he remained mostly a stranger to me, but I found his differentness — his intensity and determination — strangely intriguing.

"As *your* fellow, it seems. At *your* invitation. It's not as if he's bosom chums with the others." Madge's voice rose, and then my voice rose accordingly. Perhaps because I knew Madge was right.

"You don't know what you are talking about, Madge. He is not my beau," I yelled.

"So you keep saying, even though the evidence suggests otherwise." She paused, then launched into an assault from a different angle. "We don't know his people, Agatha. Not like we know the Lucys. And if you plan on moving forward with this relationship, you best know that you marry not only a man but his entire clan. I should know," she said with a dramatic sigh. Her complaints about her in-laws were the stuff of legend.

We stood from our tea table chairs and faced each other.

"Girls," Mummy called out. "That is enough." This conversation was escalating into a full-scale argument, and no matter Mummy's feelings toward Archie, she simply couldn't tolerate that level of division between her daughters.

Madge and I settled back into our seats, and she reached for another cigarette. Mummy busied herself with her embroidery as if nothing untoward had just occurred. Madge spoke first. "I hear you've been putting my old Empire typewriter to good use in your spare time."

It seemed that Mummy spared no details in describing my life to Madge. Was there no privacy from my older, bossy sister? I'd hesitated using the typewriter at first, as Madge had created her award-winning essays for *Vanity Fair* on the device and thought she might still claim it. Mummy assured me otherwise.

"Among other things," I answered, still smarting from her sermon about Archie and Reggie.

"Been doing any reading?" she asked, sensing my coldness and trying to warm me with a familiar, shared topic.

Madge and I were great readers, and in

fact, she had initiated me into the world of detective novels. On cold winter evenings at Ashfield, when I was about seven or eight years old, she began the ritual of reading aloud to me before my bedtime from Sir Arthur Conan Doyle's stories. This practice continued until she became Mrs. James Watts, when I took up the reins myself. The book that lassoed me to the genre was *The Leavenworth Case,* written by Anna Katharine Green a full ten years before Sir Arthur Conan Doyle published his first Sherlock Holmes. A true conundrum, the book focused on a wealthy merchant who was murdered in his mansion on Fifth Avenue in New York City in a locked room by a pistol that was locked in another room altogether during the time of the murder.

"Yes," I answered, my tone still chilly. "I just finished the new book by Gaston Leroux, *The Mystery of the Yellow Room.*"

Her eyes brightened, and she moved forward in her chair, closer to me. "I did too. I thought it was quite good. What did you think?"

Our disagreement forgotten, we launched into an animated discussion of the book's merits and flaws. I marveled at the complicated crime in which the perpetrator apparently escaped from a locked room, and

Madge adored the addition of the floor plans that illustrated the crime scene. But while we both enjoyed the intellectual puzzle the book provided to its readers, we agreed that it was no Sherlock Holmes, who remained our favorite.

"I'd like to try writing a detective story with your old Empire typewriter." I spoke aloud the thought that had been running through my mind for some time.

Eyebrows raised, Madge assumed her typical expression and exhaled a long stream of smoke. She finally said, "I don't think you can do it, Agatha. They are very difficult to master. I've even thought about taking a stab at one myself, but it's too tricky."

Implicit in her statement was, of course, that if *she* couldn't manage a detective novel, there was no possible way that her baby sister could do so. I wasn't going to let her dictate my actions — not with Archie and not with writing.

"Nevertheless, I should like to try." I stood firm.

"You are capable of undertaking whatever you set your mind to, Agatha," Mummy chimed in offhandedly as she stitched away. It was a familiar refrain, but the frequency of its repetition didn't diminish Mummy's intent.

"Well, I'll bet you couldn't do it properly," Madge scoffed and then permitted herself a deep laugh. "I mean, how could *you* write an unsolvable mystery, the very core of a detective novel? You are positively transparent."

Oh, I couldn't write a detective story, could I? I thought to myself. I seethed at Madge's patronizing words and condescension, but I also took them as a challenge. While Madge hadn't technically laid down a bet — according to Miller family betting rules, terms must be set — I took it as a firm wager regardless. In that moment, Madge ignited a spark in me, and I vowed to keep it alive until I could fan it into a flame. The bet was on.

CHAPTER EIGHT:
DAY ONE AFTER
THE DISAPPEARANCE

Saturday, December 4, 1926
Styles, Sunningdale, England

Archie closes the door of his study behind him. Leaning against its sturdy four-panel door, he inhales slowly and deeply in an effort to moderate his breathing. He must remain calm. He cannot allow his nerves and latent anger to seep through his exterior of concern.

A soft knock interrupts his efforts. It doesn't bear the authoritative rap of a policeman, but still, who else could it be? He smooths his hair and his suit jacket and pulls opens the notoriously creaky door.

He stares out into the hallway, ready to receive whichever policeman wants to pummel him with more questions. But the hallway is empty. At least so he thinks until Charlotte comes into view.

"Sorry, sir, she insisted," she apologizes, wrapping her arm around her small charge and proffering her to him.

It's little Rosalind. Archie glances down at his seven-year-old daughter. Beneath her heavy dark bangs, her bright-blue eyes, so like his own, stare up at him.

Incomprehensible to him now was his previously held sentiment that he did not want a child. When Agatha became pregnant, he had no suitable employment and did not want to share his wife's affections with a baby. But when Rosalind came into the world and he saw himself in his daughter's face and stolid temperament, he could not imagine a world without her.

He escorts his daughter into his study, leaving Charlotte in the hallway, and closes the door behind them. Rosalind settles into the armchair near the fireplace, her feet dangling above the oak floor and crimson-hued Turkish rug. She appears tiny and vulnerable, and a typical child of seven years of age would cry in this situation, but not his daughter. Instead, she faces the turmoil outside the study door with placid curiosity, and he loves her all the more for it.

Archie takes the armchair across from her, and for a moment, he relives his interview with the police officer. Shaking off the lingering despair from that exchange, he turns to his dark-haired daughter, her usually pale cheeks flushed with color, whether from the warmth of the fire or the trouble brewing in Styles, he can't say for certain.

"You wanted to talk, Rosalind?" he asks.

"Yes, Papa," she answers in an even voice.

"Do you have a question?"

"Yes." Her brow furrows, and suddenly she looks much older than seven. "The house is full of police, and I'm wondering what's happening."

"Has Charlotte said anything to you about it?" he asks, trying to keep his tone as even as hers. Although he'd cautioned the secretary and governess to keep Rosalind in the dark, he knows the child is perceptive and has likely made her own assessment, perhaps even made insistent inquiries of Charlotte. Still, he doesn't want to contradict outright any account Charlotte has offered.

"No, not a word. And, Papa, I've asked."

If the situation weren't so dire, he'd chuckle at the thought of his persistent daughter.

"Well, Rosalind, the police are here to help with your mother," he answers with the most benign response he can fashion.

Her eyebrows raise quizzically as she processes this unusual, rather vague explanation. "To help with Mama?"

"Yes, my dear."

"Is she ill?"

"No. Not that we know, anyway."

Rosalind's nose scrunches up as she contemplates another possibility. "Well then, is she in some sort of trouble? Is that why the police are here?"

"No, not at all. They are looking for your mother."

"Why on earth would the police do that? Has she gone missing?" The smallest hint of worry surfaces in her tone, and Archie wants to make sure the escalation stops at this level.

How to phrase this without causing alarm? Archie settles on a harmless description that adheres somewhat to the facts. "It seems as though Mama decided not to go to Yorkshire this weekend, where she was expected. And while I'm *certain* she simply changed her plans at the last moment and forgot to tell us, the police want to make sure. They are very thorough fellows. Undoubtedly, she's traipsed off somewhere to do her writing. As she has done frequently in the past."

"Ah," she says, the furrow in her brow softening. This was an explanation that made sense. Agatha had felt the compulsion to escape Styles to write before, leaving Rosalind in Charlotte's excellent care and, to a lesser extent, his. "That's all?"

64

"That's all, Rosalind," he answers with a nod.

"Good," she pronounces, a satisfied set to her features. As she rises, smoothing the folds of the pressed navy pinafore in which Charlotte had thoughtfully dressed her, Archie feels an almost physical pang of emotion, reminding him that he will never, ever let his child go.

CHAPTER NINE:
THE MANUSCRIPT

December 31, 1912
Ashfield, Torquay, England

"Must this Lieutenant Christie accompany you and your friends tonight?" Mummy asked as I took my leave. "After all, New Year's Eve is for close friends and family, not for new acquaintances. If" — she paused — "he is in fact only a new social acquaintance, as you've maintained."

Was Mummy testing me? As I'd suspected from my conversation with Madge, Mummy wasn't keen on this burgeoning connection, and our November discussion had opened the floodgates. At first, I chalked it up to the fact that "the young man" or "this Lieutenant Christie," as she called him, was nearly as impoverished as myself. But then she began making barbs about his callow nature, his underdeveloped sensitivity, and his overly handsome face; I couldn't understand the source of these remarks, aside

66

from his obvious attractiveness, of course. I knew she wanted me to stay the course with the gentle, kind Reggie, whom she believed would make me very happy indeed, but did that desire really justify the negative remarks?

"Mummy, he's already been invited. In fact, he'll be meeting us at the ballroom. It's far too late for any changes in plans," I said as I slipped into my coat.

"He didn't even have the courtesy of fetching you for the party," she tsked, her voice quiet but audible enough for me to hear her disappointment. "It's hardly gentlemanly behavior."

"Mummy, the party is much closer to his barracks than to Ashfield. He wanted to come and get me, but I insisted that I meet him there," I said, apologizing for him. No matter what happened in the future, I didn't want her disliking Archie any more than she already did. And nothing had more significance to Mummy than a man acting like a gentleman and a woman acting her part as a lady in turn.

As we exchanged embraces and farewells, wishing each other an early happy new year, I thought about how different Madge and I were. Unlike my sister, who'd been very strategic in her marriage, I intended to marry for love, and I wasn't certain that I loved Reggie. My clever older sister, with her claim to authorship fame and her strong, captivating manner, had an abundance of suitors when it came time for her to choose. She had selected the reserved James Watts, who was, unsurprisingly, wealthier than all her other beaus as well as the heir to Abney Hall. While I sensed she admired and rather liked Jimmy, who was a fine fellow and quite kind to me, I often wondered if she felt the deep grip of passionate love for him that I believed necessary for marriage. It was that sort of love I was determined to find. I had noticed that since I met Archie, I'd been putting Reggie's letters away in a drawer, always intending to read them at a less busy time but never retrieving them, instead of racing to my bedroom to read them alone as I had before. This behavior didn't seem a hallmark of love. By contrast, I found myself thinking about Archie almost constantly, and I had been daydreaming about ringing in the new year with him for weeks.

The grandfather clock on the far side of the ballroom showed fifteen minutes to midnight. We should have been ebullient, getting ready to cheer in the first chimes of 1913 at the New Year Ball. Instead, while my friends did the one-step to "Scott Joplin's New Rag" on the dance floor, Archie and I sat silently on a bench.

I was frustrated. Sullen since the evening began, Archie had become almost morose as the clock ticked closer to midnight. Whenever I ventured a topic of conversation, even something as welcoming to him as sport, his responses were random, as if I'd asked him an entirely different question. Even when Nan ventured a discussion with Archie, he answered in monosyllables. In the two and a half months that I'd known him, I'd become accustomed to his occasional bouts of quiet introspection, but this behavior was entirely new. Had I done something wrong? Was he not the man I'd believed him to be?

"That Whistling Rag" started to play. When Archie didn't invite me to dance, I took the bold liberty of asking, "Shall we?"

"I don't think so," he answered without even meeting my eye.

I had reached the limit of my patience. "Whatever is wrong, Archie? You have not been yourself tonight." Mummy would be humiliated by my whining tone, as it went quite against her admonitions to remain constant and cheerful in the company of a gentleman.

His eyes registered surprise at my unlady-like outburst, but he answered calmly enough. "I got my orders from the Royal Flying Corps today."

I was confused. Why wouldn't this news have made him elated? He'd been waiting to become a member of the flying corps for months.

When I did not respond, he said, "I have to leave for Salisbury Plain in two days' time."

I finally understood; his departure was looming rather faster than he'd hoped. Was his sadness at his separation from me? My heart fluttered at the thought of making someone pine.

"I'll be sorry to see you go, Archie," I said.

"Will you?" He met my eyes for the first time that evening, searching for something inside them. My statement had sparked him into life, it seemed.

"Of course. I've enjoyed our time together these past few months," I answered, feeling my cheeks burn. This was rather an under-statement, but as Mummy had instructed me, a girl could only say so much without going too far.

He took my hands in his and blurted out, "You've got to marry me, Agatha. You simply must."

My mouth dropped open in shock. Admittedly, I felt something for Archie — something almost indescribable — that I hadn't felt for Reggie or Wilfred Pirie or Bolton Fletcher, other serious suitors before Reggie who were, of course, family friends. But in my world, monumental decisions were not based upon such short acquaintances but on long family history, as Madge had made abundantly clear in our little chat, a sentiment with which Mummy clearly agreed.

He continued, his vivid blue eyes staring into mine. "I have known since I first saw you at the ball at Chudleigh that I must have you."

An unfamiliar sensation, almost like longing, surged through me. It was time for the truth. But how could I tell him about Reggie *now*? I'd been musing over the topic for several weeks as our visits grew more frequent and very nearly had crossed the breach, only to lose my courage at the last second. I worried that if he knew about Reggie, Archie would accuse me of stringing him along when there was no future in our relationship. But that simply wasn't the case. Reggie had given me leave to see other fellows, although he couldn't have foreseen the arrival of someone like Archie. Nor could I.

"Oh, Archie, that's simply impossible. You see . . ." I inhaled deeply, then took the plunge. "You see, I'm engaged to someone else."

I explained about Reggie and our families and our loose engagement, assuming that Archie would be furious. Or at the very least hurt. Instead, he waved his hand dismissively. "You will just have to break it off. After all, you didn't know what would happen between us when you agreed to the engagement. If that's even what you can call it."

"I couldn't possibly do that." An image of Reggie's kind face alongside his equally benevolent sisters flashed through my mind, and I felt sick. I would be disappointing not only Reggie but the network of Torquay families to which we belonged. Not to mention Mummy.

"Of course you can. If I had been engaged to someone when I met you, I would have broken it off immediately," he said flippantly.

"I can't. Our families are old, dear friends. The Lucys are lovely people —"

"No." He cut off my excuses, and I realized he'd never belonged to a community — maybe not even to a family — the way that I did. But then he drew me close, and

72

all thoughts of anything but him vanished. "If you truly loved this Reggie, wouldn't you have married him straightaway? The way that I want to marry you."

Breathless from my proximity to him and my heart pounding in my chest, I gave him the explanation we gave everyone else. "We thought it best to wait until he returned, when our situations would be more stable."

"I wouldn't have waited, Agatha. I feel too strongly to wait for you." His voice sounded thick with longing. To be wanted so desperately made me want him even more. Was this that passionate love for which I'd been waiting? Was this the surge of desire I'd only read about in books?

Archie's words struck a chord in me. Had I ever had these feelings for Reggie? I recalled one spring evening when he and I broke away from the group to stroll on the lawn after a large dinner party of neighborhood friends. We'd been chatting about the boats being readied for the upcoming sailing regatta — nothing really, just the stuff of usual Torquay life — when a shiver overtook me, even though the night wasn't particularly cold. Without missing a step or a beat in our conversation, Reggie removed his jacket and placed it upon my shoulders with a touch surprisingly gentle for his large hands. For a long moment, our gazes met, and I experienced a sensation of complete comfort, as if I knew I'd be safe and well cared for in his arms. But I felt nothing more.

In truth, I had known for some time that I didn't care for Reggie with the proper emotion a wife should have for her husband. Instead, I felt a contentment and peacefulness with Reggie that one feels with another very like oneself. It was almost as if, together, Reggie and I were too alike, too right, and honestly, too boring. I felt none of the things with Reggie that I felt with Archie. Archie felt like *the one.* He must be *my Fate.* The one we girls were meant to be waiting for.

I laughed. "You're mad."

He smiled for the first time that evening. "I am mad. For you."

Even though it went against ballroom protocol, he pulled me even closer to him. I could feel his warm breath on my cheek and on my lips as he asked, "Agatha Miller, will you marry me? Right away?"

Without warning, Madge's cautionary face flashed into my mind alongside Reggie's kindly smile, but I dismissed it. Then, in spite of Madge's admonition — or perhaps because of it — I answered him from the core of my longing and my feelings.

"Yes, Archibald Christie. I will marry you."

CHAPTER TEN:
DAY ONE AFTER
THE DISAPPEARANCE

Saturday, December 4, 1926
Styles, Sunningdale, England
What the devil is that noise? Archie wonders. It's one thing to have the constant murmur of police officers and the slam of doors as they trudge in and out of the house, but this booming voice, tinged with authority, echoing through the hallways of Styles is an entirely different matter. He covers his ears with his hands, and yet the voice worms its way down the corridor to his study, where a constant stream of police have been overwhelming him with questions all day. It's too much. He can't think.

Even though Archie knows his decision carries some risk, he must shush this unnerving voice. He's the distressed husband of a missing wife, isn't he? *Doesn't that warrant a bit of peace?* he nearly says aloud and then catches himself. He rises, thinking that he'll approach whoever is speaking so bloody loudly to request a modicum of quiet, when the door to his study opens without the courtesy of a knock.

It is Detective Chief Constable Kenward, and Archie realizes that it is the detective's voice he heard reverberating down the hallways of Styles. This knowledge silences Archie's ability to complain; he must suffer the noise.

"I know you were barraged with questions earlier, but I have a few more if you can tolerate it?" Kenward asks, though it's not really a question. He pulls out a small tablet and a pencil from his voluminous trench coat.

"Anything if it will help find my wife," Archie says but does not mean.

The men settle into the armchairs facing one another across the hearth, and Kenward asks, "Do you mind running through the details of yesterday morning again, Mr. Christie?"

This again, Archie thinks but doesn't dare say. Instead, he says, "Of course. Happy to do so. As I told you and the other officers before, I awoke, readied for work, and had my breakfast, all at the usual time —"

"What would that be, sir?"

"Nine o'clock in the morning."

"You are certain?"

"Oh yes, I always follow the same routine each morning at the same time."

"Man of habit, are you?"

"Oh yes," Archie answers, squaring his shoulders. He's quite proud of the regularity of his schedule, but then he stops short, wondering whether this is the correct response. Might his orderly ways have some downside in the deputy chief constable's view?

"After you engaged in your usual morning routine, did you see Mrs. Christie?"

"Yes, she came down to breakfast right as I was finishing up."

"What did you two discuss?" he asks, scribbling notes on his pad.

Kenward's lack of eye contact makes it easier for Archie to answer with the pat response he's been giving all day. "The usual morning chatter about work, schedules, and our daughter, Rosalind."

"Did you see your wife after this usual morning chatter?"

Did he hear skepticism in Kenward's voice when he repeated the phrase "usual morning chatter," Archie wonders. Or had he imagined it?

"No, I did not see her after I left for work that day," Archie answers.

"You had no contact with her throughout

that day."

"No."

"Do you have any sense of her where-abouts during the day?"

"No."

"But you talked about schedules in the morning, didn't you say that?"

"Just schedules in general."

"Did that general conversation include upcoming plans for the weekend?"

"I suppose, in part." Archie tries to adopt an offhand air.

"Remind me. What were your respective weekend plans, Mr. Christie?"

"My wife was planning on going to Beverly in Yorkshire. And I had committed to stay with the Jameses at Hurtmore Cottage, closer by. As you know." *This is old ground,* he thinks. He'd even gone over this with Kenward before, not to mention the other officers. There must be some other purpose, some trap being laid.

"Did you often spend your weekends apart?"

"When the occasion demanded," Archie answers with a deliberately vague response. He knows that it isn't commonly done for couples to make separate weekend plans.

"And the occasion demanded here?"

"Yes."

79

"Was that because your wife was not invited to the Jameses'?" Kenward asks, his voice all innocence and his gaze averted. *This is what Kenward has been building toward,* Archie thinks, and the rage begins to mount within him. It is no bloody business of the police who the Jameses invite to their home.

With this sudden understanding, Archie scrambles to recover, trying hard to keep the anger from his voice, trying to make it seem perfectly plausible and normal that his wife wouldn't be included at the Jameses'. "Of course she was invited. But the Jameses are golfing friends, and my wife didn't — doesn't — golf. So when she had the opportunity to go to Yorkshire, she chose that instead."

"It wasn't the other way around, sir?"

What in the devil has this man heard? And from whom? Treading cautiously, Archie says, "I don't quite catch your meaning, Deputy Chief Constable Kenward." He is irritated at having to say "deputy chief constable" each time he refers to the policeman. Why doesn't Kenward offer a shortened form of his title?

"I mean, weren't you invited to Yorkshire with your wife but chose Hurtmore Cottage instead?"

80

Archie freezes. To whom has Kenward been speaking? Where in the bloody hell is he hearing things? "I don't know what you're on about. We made separate plans according to our separate interests this particular weekend." He maintains his position, running through the dictates of the letter in his mind and assuring himself that he is following its instructions as he answers — while at the same time protecting his other interests.

Paper and pencil in hand, Kenward plows forward as though they hadn't just waded through some murky waters. "Who was in attendance at the Jameses' residence at Hurtmore Cottage this weekend?"

"Ah, let's see, Mr. and Mrs. James, of course," Archie answers, hoping to leave it at that.

"Of course. Anyone else?" Kenward asks, although Archie suspects that he already knows the answer.

"A Miss Neele." At the mention of Nancy's name, Kenward arches his eyebrow. Panic takes hold of Archie, and he blurts out, "She was to serve as the fourth."

Kenward's expression changes from curious to confused. "The fourth?"

"For our golf foursome. It was a golfing weekend. We needed four to play."

"Ah. Miss Neele was a friend of Mrs. James, I take it?"

Archie seizes the opportunity Kenward inadvertently provides with his question. "Yes, yes indeed. She is a friend of Mrs. James. They used to work together in the city from what I understand. Thick as thieves then and now."

Opening his mouth as he forms another inquiry, Kenward clamps it shut when a policeman barges into his study. Anger surges within Archie at this second unbidden entry into his sanctum, but before he can protest, the policeman leans down to whisper into Kenward's ear.

Turning his attention back to Archie, Kenward says, "Remember when you offered to help with anything if it will help find your wife?"

"Of course," Archie answers irritably. "That was only moments ago."

"Well, sir, it looks like you might just get your chance to do anything."

"What do you mean?"

"An abandoned car of your wife's make — a Morris Cowley — has been discovered near Newlands Corner. We will need your help."

CHAPTER ELEVEN:
THE MANUSCRIPT

January 1913 to November 1914
Torquay, England

Marriage did not come with the speed or welcome that Archie wished. Mummy first expressed her displeasure privately on the morning of New Year's Day, when I shared my news. She lamented the loss of Reggie as a husband and son-in-law, and she despaired at the unknowability of this stranger I'd chosen. Her dismay didn't soften by afternoon when Archie arrived to ask Mummy for my hand in marriage. With an unusually frank approach, she laid bare some of her concerns about Archie as a husband — to him.

"What money do you have to get married on?" she asked straightaway as he twisted his hat in his hand so forcefully I felt certain he'd ruin it.

"My subaltern's salary," he said, his eyes not meeting Mummy's. For once, she had laid aside her needlework to focus on the conversation. "And a small allowance that my mother sends."

"I hope you are not operating under the illusion that Agatha comes with a dowry or significant income," she said bluntly, and it took all my willpower not to screech aloud. Such matters were meant to be discussed obliquely, over tea. *Surely, she will stop at that,* I thought. But to my dismay, she went on. "She has only one hundred pounds a year under her grandfather's will. And that's all she'll ever have."

His eyebrows lifted in surprise, but he did not waver. "We will find a way to make ends meet," he said, to which Mummy only shook her head. She knew all too well how debilitating the struggle over finances could be; it had killed my father. When Papa's inheritance began to ebb away due to poor investments and economic trends outside his control, his joie de vivre ebbed away as well. And when he was forced to try to find work — for the first time, as a man well into his fifties — not only did his zest for life disappear but illness took its place, filling the void. Bit by bit, sickness took him over, body and spirit, until he gave in.

In the days that followed, we sifted through the possibilities, trying desperately to overcome the Flying Corps' overt discouragement of its young pilots to marry, and of course, we informed Archie's family. I was nervous when he told me he would be sharing the news, even when he chose to make his announcement to them privately, because I understood his mother to be old-fashioned in her stolid Irish ways. It seemed that her years in India with Archie's father hadn't mellowed her in her second life as wife to an English head of school but in fact had made her cling all the more to her Victorian ways. So when Archie updated me on Peg Hemsley's reaction, I wasn't surprised that she made clear, undoubtedly in her thick Irish lilt, that her precious son needn't race into marriage with a girl who wore the Peter Pan collar. This newly fashionable feature on dresses, adopted by all my friends, allowed us to abandon the old high collars with their uncomfortable boning for a turned-down collar inspired by the main character in Barrie's play. How I loved Peter Pan, but I supposed that the old-fashioned Peg found the practice of showing four inches of neck below the chin to be unimaginably racy for a prospective daughter-in-law. While she was always lovely to me in person, I knew she sang a very different sort of Irish ballad behind the scenes.

While our families provided the brakes upon our haste, we busied ourselves preparing for a war I felt sure would never come: Archie with training with the Flying Corps on Salisbury Plain, and me with first aid and home nursing classes. When we managed to cobble breaks from Archie's training, we huddled together, plotting a pathway to marriage. This heightened the drama and romance of our fleeting time together and made me ever more certain that I must marry this enigmatic, passionate man. Only the sad reply letter I received from Reggie when I broke off our engagement gave me any pause.

After all the waiting and preparing, the war came in a rush, just as Archie had predicted. For the many months of our engagement, I had maintained that the assassination of some archduke in Serbia had nothing to do with us, that surely, such a faraway incident could not pull England into war. But on August 4, Great Britain could no longer forestall its entrance into the melee.

The Royal Flying Corps was immediately mobilized, and Archie's unit was among the first to go active. Since the German Air Force had a fearsome reputation, the early Flying Corps boys were certain they would be killed. I tried to stay stoic when Archie made such pronouncements in a shockingly calm manner, but privately, even thinking of them set me off on a crying jag once he left. Soon, however, I had no time to harbor such maudlin thoughts.

Women were called upon to help in the war effort alongside the men, although the work itself was, of course, different. I opted to pursue service as a wartime nurse, feeling that I might make the most impact tending to the injured soldiers than in knitting scarves and mittens for them on the front. I was assigned to a detachment near Torquay, and at first, we passed the time furiously making bandages and swabs and setting up the wards in the makeshift hospital we'd converted from the town hall. Once the wounded soldiers began pouring through the doors, thinking itself became a luxury. As I wheeled the bloodied boys through the halls, I heard mention of their battles — Marne, Antwerp, among others — but my days passed by in a blur of cleaning bedpans and urinals, scrubbing vomit, preparing hygienic towels for doctors as they passed from patient to patient, and changing dressings on suppurating wounds — the mainstay of most informally trained wartime nurse aides.

I surprised myself with my stoicism over the blood and guts and gore that routinely appeared in the ward. The other nurse aides, mostly well-bred girls like myself, couldn't tolerate the state of the wounded, and more often than not, I had to assist them when they'd become nauseated from the sight of the soldiers' injuries. The experienced, professionally trained nurses who actually ran the hospital took note of me, and I soon became a regular in the surgeries and amputations and the requested caretaker of the more seriously injured.

Mummy, to my astonishment, did not object to this unsavory work, although she found curious the stride in which I took this nursing. "For goodness' sake, Agatha," she exclaimed with a shudder one evening over tea. "You treat these horrors matter-of-factly." I guessed that she tolerated my work because she hoped I'd stumble across a more suitable young man in the hospital who would distract me from Archie. But she had no understanding of the reality of the wards and the state of the soldiers — the unlikelihood that the boys I tended could think about anything but survival — or the omnipresence of death.

In fact, spending my days in the presence

of injured soldiers and watching the more seriously harmed only knitted me more tightly to Archie. The boys reminded me how tenuous one's thread to life really was. For each wound I cleaned and each amputated limb I dressed, I said a silent prayer that Archie stayed safe as he soared and swooped in the European skies.

Days turned into weeks, and those weeks built into three months before Archie had a leave. As I packed for our chaperoned meeting, I thought about how those three months might as well have been three years for all that I'd experienced. I felt utterly changed by what I'd seen and done. But if the war had altered me from the sidelines, I could not imagine how it had transformed Archie, who lived amid terror, bloodshed, combat, and death every day. Would I recognize the man with whom I'd fallen in love?

CHAPTER TWELVE:
DAY ONE AFTER
THE DISAPPEARANCE

Saturday, December 4, 1926
The Silent Pool, Surrey, England

The cluster of police blocks the view of the Silent Pool. But Archie doesn't need to see the stagnant body of brackish water to know that it lies down the hill just beyond the men, past where he's been told the Morris Cowley sits near the rim of a chalk pit next to Water Lane. Archie has been there often enough to know its precise location.

His wife had found the dark, unreflective pool — a small, spring-fed lake about three hundred yards from a picturesque plateau called Newlands Corner — oddly inspiring. Its gloomy aspect, ringed so thickly with trees that sunlight could scarcely penetrate, had provided fodder for her writing, she'd claimed, as had the legends surrounding the Silent Pool. Local lore had linked the site to the legendary King John, who'd allegedly abducted a beautiful woodcutter's daughter.

It was said that King John's unwelcome amorous advances had forced the girl into the pool's deceptively deep water, where she drowned. But the drowning hadn't silenced the girl, local folks claimed; if one was unlucky enough to be in the pool's vicinity at midnight, one could witness her rise from its depths. It was nonsense, of course, and he'd told Agatha so.

In their early days living at Styles, Archie had begrudgingly accompanied her for walks around the pool. She'd wanted him to understand its allure. But in recent years, he'd refused to join her in those strolls, preferring the order, tradition, and wide spaces of the golf course and his companions there. Now, in recent months, Agatha had taken to visiting the Silent Pool alone.

"Colonel Christie, over here," Kenward calls to him.

He doesn't want to see what the police have found, but a man desperate to find his missing wife would rush toward any sign of her whereabouts. The letter has made him constantly cognizant of how he must act and in fact specifically instructed him to join in any searches that might arise. Consequently, he races to Kenward's side.

The uniformed men part to allow him entrance into their ghastly circle. There, at its center, is a gray, bottle-nosed Morris Cowley. The vehicle sits halfway down a grassy slope leading toward the Silent Pool. Thick bushes conceal the hood and keep it from sliding headlong down the steep hill toward the chalk pit.

"Can you confirm that this is your wife's car, Colonel?" Kenward asks.

"It certainly is the make and model of her vehicle. Whether it is hers, I cannot say." His voice quivers, and his legs feel unexpectedly spongy. He hasn't anticipated that the sight of his wife's car would cause him to shake. She'd purchased the Morris Cowley with the proceeds of the first of her three published novels, and she adored prowling about the countryside behind its wheel. He himself has only recently purchased a car — the sportier French Delage, albeit a secondhand one — which isn't as well suited for rural drives. But then, he doesn't really use the Delage for that purpose, does he? He travels back and forth to his job in London and back and forth to the golf course.

"A pricey one, that Morris Cowley," one of Kenward's right-hand men remarks.

The deputy chief constable shoots a displeased look at the man. "There seems to be very little damage to the car, Colonel. The glass windscreen is unbroken, and the folding canvas roof is unpunctured. The only part that seems to have been impacted is the hood. From the skid marks leading up to the car, it appears as though some unusual circumstance led to the car careening off the road, if you can call that dirt path back there a road. And the only thing that stopped the car from plunging into that chalk pit was those bushes."

Kenward calls over to his men. "Let's have a look at the glove box to make certain about the ownership." He directs two men to search the front seats and glove box.

As Archie watches the police officers rummage through the car, he asks a question that had been niggling at the back of his mind. "How did you ever find her car in this remote spot, Detective Chief Constable Kenward? And so soon after we discovered her disappearance?"

"The headlights of the car must have been left running when your wife dis—" He stutters a bit as he realizes he must choose his words carefully. "When your wife left the vehicle. They were still running at seven o'clock this morning when a local fellow on his way to work noticed them shining out from the wooded area surrounding the Silent Pool. The sighting was called in, and while we'd planned on checking on it later today, we got caught up with your wife's disappearance, only now connecting the two events."

Archie nods, still watching the police search the car. At Kenward's instruction, the officers poke about in the back seat of the car while Archie and the deputy chief constable stand by. The men find nothing of interest at first, but soon one of them calls out, "Chief, there's a bag underneath the back seat. And a fur coat."

Archie feels as though he cannot get a proper breath, watching these strangers pawing around his wife's Morris Cowley, but he knows he must maintain his composure. The officers eventually crawl out of the car, each carrying a parcel carefully wrapped in some sort of plain, official fabric.

"Let's have a look." Kenward motions for the officers to spread the objects on the ground before them.

The officers peel back the rough fabric in which they'd wrapped the items, revealing a dressing case and a fur coat. Under Kenwood's watchful eye and very specific directions, the men methodically open the case and discover within a few ladies' garments and some toiletries.

"It's packed as if she'd planned that Yorkshire weekend after all, isn't it, Chief?" one of the men asks Kenward. "Those plans got derailed by the look of it."

"Assuming it's her car, that is. And these items, hers," Kenward answers briskly. He clearly disapproves of his officers positing theories within earshot of Archie and redirects their focus to the coat. The men pat down the long fur, finding nothing but a plain linen handkerchief in the pocket.

"Odd that," Kenward mutters, almost to himself. "It was a brisk night to begin with, and then the temperature dropped from forty-one degrees at six o'clock last evening to thirty-six degrees at midnight. Wouldn't a warm fur coat like that have been welcome if you'd had the choice to wear it? The chance to put it on?"

Archie glances over at him. For a police officer who actively discourages his men from conjecturing in the presence of interested parties, the speculative statement is strange. Is he trying to bait Archie by suggesting that something untoward happened to Agatha because she didn't have time to put on a warm coat before leaving the car? He will not take the bait. In fact, the letter forbids it.

"Sir," one of the men yells, waving a small rectangular piece of paper. "It's the driving license. It was buried in the bottom of the dressing case."

"Does it bear the name —" Kenward asks. The excited young policeman interjects, "Yes, sir, it belongs to the wife."

Visibly irritated at the interruption, Kenward takes the document from the eager officer, reviews it for a moment, and then says, "Well, Colonel, I'm afraid there's no other possible course at the moment. We must proceed with this investigation with suspicion of foul play."

CHAPTER THIRTEEN: THE MANUSCRIPT

December 23–24, 1914
Clifton, England

A faint tap sounded at the bedroom door. The soft noise roused me from the light sleep into which I had just drifted. I sat up and glanced around the unfamiliar bedroom. *Oh right,* I realized. I was in Clifton, at Archie's parents' home to celebrate Christmas. When Archie suddenly got leave three days prior, we met in London, and after a few awkward days with my mother in tow as chaperone, we took the train to Clifton alone where the mood lifted considerably after we shared a bottle of wine.

The war had altered us both, in ways we were still discovering. On his prior leave — he'd had only two since deploying — we greeted each other with a desperate, loving embrace, but within minutes, we were interacting like strangers, unsure of which topics to discuss and what tone to take.

Archie had been strangely casual about the war and his experiences, almost dismissive, in a way that disturbed me. How could he be so glib about such horrific destruction? It wasn't as if I was unaccustomed to the reality of war and he needed to protect me from it; I tended to it daily in the wards, and he knew it. I was perhaps more emotional and less carefree than the girl he'd known, and it took us days to connect with each other again. Even then, something had been lost in translation between us, something we hadn't rediscovered on this leave either. Not yet, anyway.

Reaching for my robe, I wrapped it tightly around myself before opening the door. I'd overheard Archie's mother make another snide remark about the Peter Pan collars on my dresses, and I wanted to ensure I did nothing else to scandalize her, should she be standing behind the door. But it wasn't Peg. It was Archie.

Walking into the bedroom, he quietly closed the door behind him. He slipped his arms around my waist and kissed me deeply. The feel of his lips on mine and the scent of his cologne made me light-headed. We kissed and caressed each other until shivers ran through me. I felt us moving backward toward the bed, and while I longed to acquiesce, the thought of his mother — and propriety — stopped me.

"You shouldn't be in here. Imagine what your mother would say," I whispered, pushing him away gently.

He pulled me toward him but made no motion toward the bed. "We've got to get married, Agatha. At once. Let's marry tomorrow." He was breathing heavily.

"But you said —" Earlier, on the train, he'd declared that getting married during wartime was selfish and wrong, never mind the scores of young people hurrying to the altar and his sense of urgency about our engagement. It was greedy, he said, to rush into marriage, only to leave behind a widow and perhaps a child. Yet the conversation about marriage continued to bind us together.

Archie interrupted me. "I was wrong. Marriage is the only sensible thing to do in the circumstances. And I simply cannot wait to make you mine."

"I am yours, Archie," I reassured him.

"Fully mine," he whispered into my ear as he drew me even closer to him. "Just think, we have two days together before I go back. We will get married tomorrow morning, and after a Christmas lunch here with my parents, we will take the train to Torquay to share the news with your family, and we'll still have time to honeymoon at the Grand Hotel."

"Can we manage it so quickly?"

"We will check with the vicar in the morning." Burrowing his face in the curve of my neck, he said, "Then, once we've done our familial duty, I have no intention of letting you out of our Grand Hotel room until I have to report for duty."

The morning brought neither the swift trip to the altar for which Archie had hoped nor parental blessings. Peg was beside herself at our hurry; she collapsed into hysterical tears at the very thought of our "race" to marriage, although — in the privacy of my thoughts — I thought it hardly deserved to be called a race, given its many years in the making. But I understood her point and felt hesitant myself, even though Archie and I had known each other for over two years by now. Archie's lovely stepfather, William Hemsley, took control of the situation, calming Peg and encouraging us onward, and with his blessing, we scurried around Clifton, trying to secure the necessary paperwork, and any misgivings I had about our haste and disregard for protocol were swept away by Archie's ebullience.

In an effort to expedite matters, we approached an ecclesiastical headmaster at the school where Archie's stepfather worked to see if he had the authority to marry us, to no avail. A visit to the registry office to assess whether they could perform the legal marriage ceremony yielded a demoralizing spurning, as we didn't have the requisite fourteen days of notice. Dejected, we stood on the steps of the registry office, lamenting our luck, when a registrar stepped out and saw us, all desperation and melancholy over our predicament.

A spark of recognition shone in his eyes as he spotted Archie. "My dear boy, you live here in Clifton, don't you?"

"Yes, I do."

"With your mother and stepfather, the Hemsleys, if I'm not mistaken?"

"Yes, that's right, sir."

"Well, as long as you keep some belongings here at their house in Clifton, you can call Clifton home. In that case, you don't need a fortnight's notice to get married here. You can purchase what's called an ordinary license and get married at your parish church today."

Archie whooped in delight, thanked the thoughtful registrar profusely, and swung me around in the air. We ran around following his instructions and borrowing the necessary eight pounds from Archie's stepfather. License in hand, we tracked down the vicar at his friend's home where he was enjoying tea, and he agreed to perform the ceremony that afternoon.

Yet even as we mounted the steps to Archie's parish church, we weren't certain the marriage would proceed. We'd noticed that the license required a second witness to the ceremony, and Peg refused to leave her bed, where she'd collapsed in despair at our announcement. Archie's stepfather had agreed to serve as a witness, but we still needed one more.

Perhaps our inability to proceed with the ceremony right now is for the best, I thought to myself. After all, Mummy would be extremely disappointed to miss the event, not to mention Madge and my grandmother, who we called Auntie-Grannie. My sister's wedding had been a grand affair with nearly a dozen in the wedding party and festivities that lasted for days with all our relatives and family friends in attendance, and while no one anticipated a similar fete during wartime, Madge, Mummy, and Auntie-Grannie, at the very least, would want to be included in whatever celebration took place for our wedding.

But when I broached this idea, Archie disagreed and insisted on proceeding. "The decision has been made," he pronounced, "and how would it look if we changed our plans at the eleventh hour?" He pulled me onto the street outside the church to see if we might approach a complete stranger and request their service as a second witness. It was then that I heard my name being called. Turning around, I was astonished to see Yvonne Bush, an old friend with whom I'd stayed in Clifton several years earlier, before I'd even met Archie.

Archie grasped my hand and exclaimed, "We've been saved!" Turning toward me, he added, "I told you our marriage was meant to be. Go ask your friend if she'll serve as our marriage witness."

I raced to her side, and before I even greeted her properly, I made the request. Yvonne gamely stepped into the impromptu bridesmaid role, and with her by my side and William Hemsley standing for Archie, the vicar performed the marriage ceremony. Surrendering to the inevitably of this hurried affair, I almost laughed at the bride I made in my everyday dress and coat, my only adornment a small purple hat. But I knew it didn't matter.

Because I was no longer Agatha Miller. I was Agatha Christie.

CHAPTER FOURTEEN:
DAY TWO AFTER
THE DISAPPEARANCE

Sunday, December 5, 1926
The Silent Pool, Surrey, England

Although Archie knows how quickly news spreads in the Surrey countryside, he's astonished at how rapidly word of his wife's disappearance overtakes Shere, Guildford, and Newlands Corner. By Sunday morning, not only does the entire population of these villages know that his wife is missing but many have volunteered their services to search for her. Confronted with their expectant faces — not to mention the police officers' assumptions and the letter's strictures — Archie has no choice but to mobilize alongside them.

The volunteers march out into the thicket and the tangle of the woods and brush surrounding the Silent Pool like a ragtag army unit. Under the supervision of the police, they are fanned out in every direction around him, linking hands in organized lines to thoroughly comb through the high grass and brush. After all, the undergrowth is nearly waist-high in places, deep enough for a woman to lie hidden. They blanket the southeast, including Newlands Corner, Shere, and the wilderness encompassing the Silent Pool, and the northwest, including an area known as the Roughs. Archie walks alone, of course. It wouldn't be seemly for him to link hands with these regular folks, not in his current predicament.

Even though the Morris Cowley is some distance from the Silent Pool, the searchers are drawn to the environs around the dank body of water almost as though it has a macabre, magnetic lure. Archie considers what attracts the locals to the stagnant pool. The old violent legends? Are they hoping to find his wife's body floating in its murky depths? He assumes that's the explanation, as no evidence has emerged linking the car to the waters.

Yesterday afternoon, after they discovered the car, Archie followed along with the preliminary search undertaken by the police and the special constables, Surrey men who are registered with the constabulary to assist in the event of an emergency. Kenward thought it advisable to pursue the possibility that his wife was flung from the vehicle into the thick underbrush and is either wandering around, lost and possibly injured, or is unconscious within the thicket. But that initial inspection hasn't unearthed a single clue, and they are back at the hunt today, casting a wider net with the motley crew of volunteers. Although, as the hours pass, Kenward's theory is becoming less and less likely.

Archie hasn't wanted to rejoin the investigation. He would have preferred to stay behind at Styles, but Kenward's reaction to that suggestion has made clear the manner in which this decision might be perceived. Not to mention the words from that damn letter his wife has left behind are haunting him: *Follow my instructions closely if you wish the safety of the first path.*

So he's back at it today, listlessly poking his walking stick into bushes and peering underneath them, while terrifying thoughts plague him. What will happen if Charlotte lets the proverbial cat out of the bag? He knows the police questioned her and the rest of the staff yesterday, but she's held up so far. Perhaps he should invite that blasted sister of hers — Mary, the one she's always going on about and hinting at permission to host as a houseguest — to keep her occupied and out of the police's hair. *That's the ticket,* he thinks. And it will have the added advantage of keeping poor Rosalind distracted.

Heartened a bit at this plan, he returns to his task of tromping through the trees and brush and around streams and their rivulets, making a show of poking through every branch, and listening to the volunteers talk. From their chatter, these folks seem to be enjoying this, almost as if it's a mad, morbid caper. What would make these people break from their regular Sunday routines to search for a woman they don't even know? He certainly wouldn't do it. In fact, he wouldn't have joined in the search today but for the specter of the alternative.

Even though Archie cannot see the volunteers and he's hidden from their sight, he can hear them jabber away. They've been blathering about their daily lives and village gossip, but then he hears the voice of a young man say, "Hurtmore Cottage," and his heart starts beating wildly. Archie has been assuming that his whereabouts on Friday night and Saturday morning would remain secret, but how idiotic of him. Why has he assumed that the policemen would have more discretion than the villagers? He's been a damn fool. After all, the police officers are little more than villagers themselves.

He freezes, straining to hear what the man and his companions say next. Other than the word *James,* he cannot make out anything else, and he begins to relax, reframing their speculations in his mind. *What of it?* he thinks. *Why can't a man spend a golf weekend at a friend's home without his wife?* As far as anyone knows, that was the precise nature of his plans.

By God, though, Archie hopes that he can keep the Jameses, Hurtmore Cottage, and Nancy out of this mess. What must she be thinking today as more details have emerged? He phoned Sam and Nancy last evening when the police were busy holding a logistics meeting in the kitchen. After he explained the situation to each of them — which they'd already heard from the local gossips — they decided there should be no communication until the situation is resolved. But now he wishes that they hadn't made that agreement. He'd welcome their familiar voices.

Instead, he plows forward with his sham of a search, suffering through the bitterly cold hours of the afternoon. Only when the daylight begins to wane does Kenward finally call it off and seek him out. Branches crack and leaves crunch under the weight of the detective chief constable as he makes his way toward Archie.

Panting at the exertion, Kenward says, "I hate to say it, Colonel, but I think the likelihood that your wife suffered some sort of minor accident and either collapsed somewhere in the thicket or wandered off in confusion is diminishing."

Kenward stares at him, assessing his reaction. What in the name of God does he expect Archie to say? The futility of this search is apparent to even the simplest villager. Still, Archie says, "I'm very sorry to hear that, Detective Chief Constable Kenward."

"Detective Chief Constable! Detective Chief Constable!" One of Kenward's men calls to him, and two police officers race toward Archie and Kenward. Archie notes that the detective doesn't even offer his men a shorter version of his title to use; he must want to have his lofty designation bandied about, reminding everyone who is in charge.

"Yes, man, spit it out," Kenward barks at the panting man.

"There's a report from Albury." The policeman references the small village nearby as if that explains the urgency and his haste.

"And?"

"A woman who works at the Albury hotel saw a woman fitting the description of the colonel's wife. We have a sighting."

CHAPTER FIFTEEN:
THE MANUSCRIPT

October 14, 1916
Ashfield, Torquay, England

I wandered up the hill and veered left onto the lane leading to Ashfield. As I ambled, I passed houses that had practically brimmed with life in my childhood. Croquet at the MacGregors, dances at the Browns, idyllic summer picnics and badminton at the Lucys — nearly every home along the way contained memories of laughter and Torquay folks spilling out onto the lanes. Now those villas and houses and lanes were dark and silent; the war had shuttered them, in one way or another. I wondered if my perspective would be different if I'd married Reggie instead of Archie, an event that occurred an incredible two years ago. At once yesterday and a lifetime ago.

Once I crested the hill upon which Ashfield sat, I glanced out at the commanding views of the sea, thinking not about sailboat escapades of my youth but the naval fleet now battling the Germans. I'd seen too many of those sailors while nursing, horribly wounded after their skirmishes, and now, staring out at the whitecaps of the stormy ocean, I couldn't help consider the poor souls who lay at the sea's sandy bottom. While I worried constantly about Archie soaring the European skies as he fought the aerial war, the sailor's lonely death was one fear I hadn't contemplated until now.

When I opened the front door of Ashfield and finally entered the embrace of its fragrant parlor, it was like stepping back in time. Every object, every surface, every rug, every floorboard returned me to my youth, and I felt twelve years old again. I ran my finger along a dog figurine Papa had particularly adored, realizing how different the china dog — and my hand — looked now with my ring finger caressing it than it had when my unadorned, twelve-year-old finger touched it nightly. I was staring at the hand of a woman waiting for her real life to begin.

"Agatha, is that you?" The familiar voice rang out through Ashfield's halls.

"It is, Mummy," I called back and walked toward the back of the house.

"How was your day, darling?" Her voice

113

grew louder as I neared the solarium where my mother and grandmother spent most of the day sitting side by side in cushioned chairs, two near invalids each pretending to be the other's caretaker. The room could be drafty with all the windows, but the pair always selected this room above all others, seeking out every ray of light like a pair of tropical birds.

I peeked my head around the corner, and there they were, just as I'd pictured. "Yes, dear, do tell us," my grandmother added in her quivering voice, turning her wrinkled face in my direction. Her cataracts rendered her nearly blind, so she leaned toward the sound of my voice.

I wanted to nestle a chair in between theirs and curl up like a kitten. Or a young girl. Instead, I sat across from them and asked, "Shall I tell you about the poisons I distributed today?"

Auntie-Grannie tittered at my dramatic inquiry, and even Mummy giggled a little. It was a safe bit of danger to hear about my handling of hazardous liquids and powders in the Torquay dispensary — although the actual peril was quite small — and it gave them a thrill without the actual fear that accompanied discussions of the war. After all, although he spent a long stint running through other people's money on boat schemes in England and Africa and living well beyond his means, my brother, Monty, was back in the army, and his safety was never far from any of our minds.

They gazed at me expectantly, and I was struck by how much they resembled one another. *Was it a trick of the light?* I wondered. After all, they weren't mother and daughter biologically, only legally, although they were bound by blood as well. Auntie-Grannie had adopted Mummy when she was a little girl, when her biological mother — Auntie-Grannie's younger sister, who we called Granny B — had fallen on hard times. Her husband, a sea captain, had died and left her five children but not much in the way of pension. Auntie-Grannie, who'd married a wealthy, older widower with children but never had offspring of her own, offered to adopt one child, and Granny B had selected Mummy, her only daughter. My mother had never fully recovered from the sense that she'd been surrendered. Somehow, it didn't appease her feelings of abandonment that she'd had a more afflu- ent life than her brothers because she'd married Auntie-Grannie's stepson, my papa.

Wide-eyed, my mother and grandmother waited for the details of my day. I'd left nursing and taken on the position at the dispensary after a bad bout of flu last year forced me out of the hospital and into my Ashfield bed as a temporary invalid. When I recovered, I learned that my old friend Eileen Morris was running the dispensary, and she wanted me on staff, at a higher salary and with fewer, more favorably timed hours that would allow me to help out more at home, which was important once Auntie-Grannie moved into Ashfield over a year ago. But what began as a job chosen for convenience turned out to be a position with unique benefits. I adored the science — and the latent danger — of the dispensary.

"The morning began with a request for Donovan's solution, which a doctor needed to treat a soldier who also suffered from diabetes. Now, this medicine contains a reasonable amount of arsenic, which, you know, is —"

Mummy interjected, "Highly poisonous. Now I do hope you were careful, Agatha."

"Always," I assured her and patted her hand. "But just as I finished mixing the solution, I noticed that our pharmacist, who was mixing the solution for a tray of suppositories, had gotten the decimal point wrong in the key ingredient. It would have made the suppositories quite toxic."

Auntie-Grannie gasped, and Mummy asked, "What did you do?"

"Well, if I'd mentioned the error to our pharmacist directly, he'd have denied it and distributed a batch of very dangerous suppositories. So I pretended to stumble, and I knocked the entire tray to the ground."

"Brilliant, darling," Mummy said with a little clap, and I enjoyed the private fanfare. Most of the day at the dispensary passed quite slowly, as the work was monotonous; incidents like these and my own imagination were the only things that staved off the boredom of the hours where we waited for orders. But I knew better than to complain about the tedium of wartime, when most people faced unimaginable dangers.

Auntie-Grannie clapped too. "What is that little pharmacist like, anyway?" she asked.

"You've stumbled upon quite the right word for him — little. He's a tiny man with a tiny man's ego and defensiveness. But he has an unorthodox, slightly thrill-seeking side, which is a bit disturbing in a pharmacist."

"Whatever do you mean, Agatha?" Mummy asked impatiently.

"Well, within a week of meeting him, he told me that he kept a cube of curare in his

117

pocket, in a lethal dose. He confessed that he stored it there because it made him feel powerful."

My mother visibly shuddered, and my grandmother tsked, saying, "I don't think I'll get my prescriptions filled by him any longer."

I reveled in my newly acquired — and hard-won — knowledge of medicines and poisons, one of the intriguing benefits of the position. In order to serve in the dispensary, I'd studied for, taken, and passed the challenging assistants' examination at Apothecaries' Hall. For months, I'd spent weekends under the tutelage of commercial chemists, not to mention shadowing pharmacists to learn preparation techniques and memorizing medical tomes and various measurement systems. I'd never be so bold as to liken my experience to a pharmaceutical degree, but I certainly knew enough to be dangerous.

These women supported and championed me unconditionally, so why was I reluctant to discuss with them what else I worked on in the dispensary during the long hours when we had little to do as we awaited instructions from doctors and hospitals? What made me so hesitant to tell them that I'd written a novel? Not just any novel —

I'd attempted a few over the years and completed one, as they both knew and had encouraged all along — but finally a detective story.

Did my reluctance stem from the origin of this book? I liked to think the inspiration came solely from the rows of poisons on the apothecary shelves and my knowledge about how one might wield them dangerously and secretly, but in truth, the genesis stemmed from Madge's challenge. I was determined to prove my self-assured sister wrong, that I *could* write an unsolvable mystery. The elegant bottles of poisons on the shelves — so deceptively seductive with the sinuous shape of the glass and the vivid colors within — only fanned that spark into a blaze; I had at my disposal, literally and figuratively, the weapons to meet her challenge. Perhaps that is why I shied away from telling Mummy, because I didn't want her to know that it was sibling rivalry that motivated me. Having never had a sister of her own, she desperately wanted Madge and I to have a supportive, loving bond.

"Shouldn't you be packing, Agatha?" Mummy interrupted my thoughts. "Don't you need to be ready to meet Archie tomorrow morning at the New Forest? Please don't tell me his leave has been changed again."

Archie's last leave had been cancelled the night before we were supposed to meet, and even though part of me had been desperately disappointed not to see my husband, part of me had been the slightest bit relieved. His letters leading up to the planned leave had been increasingly depressive, even angry, and while I certainly understood the toll that the dangers of flying took upon his nerves and his body — not to mention watching so many of his fellow pilots die — I worried about his stability. I vacillated between wanting to race to his side so I could nurse him back to health and protecting myself from his mounting anger.

"No, Mummy, it's still on. I suppose I should start packing." I pushed myself off my chair, but before I left the solarium, I gave each of these elderly women a thorough assessment. Of course, I couldn't wait to see my husband, but I still had lingering concerns about his state of mind, and Mummy and Auntie-Grannie looked especially frail. I was afraid to leave them alone. We'd had a rotating series of maids after Lucy replaced our stalwart Jane. Girl after girl left to join the Women's Volunteer Reserve, and how could we complain? They were doing their wartime duties, just as I was doing mine. Finally, two elderly maids stepped in to help care for Mummy and Auntie-Grannie, and I now worried about the maids, too, both called Mary, funnily enough, nearly as much as my mother and grandmother. "Are you certain that you can manage without me for a few days? I do worry."

"Don't be silly, Agatha. We manage while you're at work, don't we?"

"Yes, but that's only a few hours. And I'm just down the road if there's an emergency."

My mother stood and glared at me. She could be strangely formidable for such a kindly woman. "Agatha, how many times must I tell you? You must go to your husband. A gentleman cannot be left alone for too long."

CHAPTER SIXTEEN:
DAY TWO AFTER
THE DISAPPEARANCE

Sunday, December 5, 1926
Styles, Sunningdale, England

Archie paces his study. Back and forth over the crimson Turkish carpet, he cuts a path across its intricate design, almost as if he's slicing it in two. He knows he shouldn't be acting out, but the policeman's announcement has riled him up.

Kenward stares at him. On the surface, the constable's expression appears concerned and serious — all business — but Archie senses the smug delight that must lurk beneath that facade. The glee the detective must feel at exerting power over his superior in class and the irritation with Archie when he tries to reclaim some control.

"I believe I asked you a question, Detective Chief Constable Kenward," Archie repeats, while rubbing his right temple. His head is pounding. "Why on earth are you sending my wife's image to police stations and newspapers across the country? I fear you are turning a private matter into a public spectacle."

"I thought I'd let you calm down before answering, Colonel." Now Archie is certain he sees glee on the policeman's face as he holds fast to a course of action Archie detests. All Kenward's pretense of concern vanishes.

"This is as calm as I'm likely to be," Archie seethes, feeling that familiar heightening of emotion that he used to experience with his wife. It would begin with slight irritation at her constant chatter over plots and characters that would boil over into fury and a throbbing headache as she continued with her flights of fancy and indecent discussions of feelings when all he wanted was the peace of a quiet dinner, the serenity of an orderly house and the evening newspaper, and the weekend spent on his club's tidy eighteen-hole golf course with a pleasant woman nearby. But as soon as the words slip out, he knows they are a mistake. He cannot allow the police officers to see the mounting rage; a furious demeanor is not in keeping with the image he's been instructed to maintain — that of concerned husband — or else.

"Well then, Colonel, I'll speak plainly and explain we can no longer treat this as a private matter. We've combed a wide vicinity around her car and uncovered nothing. We've checked the rail stations and nearby towns and found no sign of her. We've tracked down the alleged sighting of her in Albury, which proved false. We have to extend our reach in the event, however unlikely, that she walked away from her car and traveled elsewhere."

He forces himself not to allow his fear to assume its full voice, even though the emotions are very near the surface. If the police cast their net widely, the very facts he's trying to hide will undoubtedly be revealed. But he'll tip his hand regardless unless he gets a handle on his emotions.

Taking a deep breath, he says, "I'm sorry that I sounded ruffled, Detective Chief Constable Kenward; I guess that I am mostly confused. Why are you spreading her image and the news of her disappearance all around the country if you think it won't yield anything?"

"I don't think that's what I said, Colonel." Kenward's voice is cold. He's no longer keeping up pretenses either. "It is standard police procedure and may well yield important clues to your wife's whereabouts. Why are you so reluctant to spread the information widely?"

It is Archie's turn to ignore a question. "Are there additional avenues we can pursue?" he asks instead.

"Only interviews with your staff." Kenward pauses and then says, "We are almost all the way through the list — barring one part-time person who's been tricky to track down — and they are proving illuminating."

His rage disappears, only to be replaced with a surge of fear. What has the staff told the police? Archie doesn't dare answer and doesn't dare fight back against Kenward again.

"Shall I share our findings with you?" Kenward says. "I know you want to do anything to help locate your missing wife."

Archie still says nothing. What does Kenward know? The terror has frozen him.

"I'll take your silence as a yes, Colonel," Kenward says with a self-satisfied smile. "We will put aside the breakfast you shared with your wife on Friday morning for a few moments while we discuss what she did with her day after you left. According to the housemaid, Lilly, your cook, the gardener, and the family secretary and nanny, Miss Charlotte Fisher —"

"Charlotte?" The word escapes from

Archie's mouth before he can stop himself. He's assumed the woman who serves as Rosalind's nanny and his wife's secretary would remain silent in the face of police inquiry. She's been such a loyal employee, and he's assumed her sister Mary's presence at Styles would distract her. What on earth has she said to make Kenward so gleeful?

"Yes, Charlotte Fisher. She is a member of the staff here at Styles, is she not?"

"Yes."

"After interviewing the members of your staff, we were able to put together a timeline of your wife's movements on Friday in the hopes that it will help shed some light on her whereabouts now. It seems that after you and your wife spoke at breakfast —" Kenward reaches for his notes, and Archie wonders whether he's imagining that the policeman used the word *spoke* with an ironic tone.

Holding his notes up, Kenward continues. "Here we go. After breakfast, she played with your daughter for a while before Miss Fisher took Rosalind to school, as per their usual routine. She then left the house in her Morris Cowley for a bit, presumably to run an errand, but returned for lunch. Afterward, she and Rosalind drove to Dorking

126

for afternoon tea with your mother, whom Agatha told she was going to Beverly for the weekend. They left your mother's around five o'clock to make the drive back to Styles. There, she played with Rosalind some more, did a bit of work, and then sat down to dinner. Alone. Then she received a call sometime after dinner, perhaps around nine or ten o'clock. The maid wasn't sure of the precise time."

"That all seems very normal. I'm not certain how that tells us what happened to her later Friday night."

"I think it gives us a sense of her frame of mind, which in turn can help us understand what happened Friday night." Kenward breathes in deeply, expanding his already wide chest. He does not bother to mask his pleasure at sharing the next bit of news. "Of course, the argument between you and your wife on Friday morning may have set the stage for everything that followed."

Archie thought about denying the fact of the fight but knew it was fruitless. Presumably several members of the staff had heard the raised voices and would corroborate one another. But he could put a tourniquet on the wound to prevent it from being fatal. "What are you getting at, Detective Chief Constable Kenward?" he asks, as calmly as possible.

"I think you know what I'm getting at, Colonel Christie. You and your wife had a heated argument over breakfast on Friday morning about where you would choose to spend your weekend."

"You have the details of our disagreement all wrong. I don't know who told you that was the nature of our discord."

"Every single member of your staff told us that. They all recounted the same facts: your wife wanted you to accompany her to Yorkshire, and you wanted to stay with your friends the Jameses at Hurtmore Cottage for a golf weekend. The staff was aware of this row because you and your wife were screaming at one another. Your voices could be heard all over Styles."

I was right to not deny the fight, Archie thinks. But at least that's the extent of what Kenward knows. "Married couples do have arguments, you know."

"According to your staff, this was the worst quarrel between you two they'd ever heard." He consults his notes. "In addition to the raised voices — 'yelling' was the word used by your housemaid, Lilly — everyone heard the shattering of glass and china. When that same housemaid stood at the threshold of the dining room to clean up, you were gone, and she found your wife sitting on the floor of the dining room, crying with lacerations on her legs and hands from the broken china and glass. She summoned Miss Fisher before entering, believing that — given the close relationship between Miss Fisher and your wife — Mrs. Christie would prefer Miss Fisher to assist her. Lilly then reentered the room as Miss Fisher was helping Mrs. Christie up so that she could clean up the china."

Archie's body goes rigid, hearing Friday morning recounted. It is as if Kenward is speaking about something that happened to someone else. This cannot be his life. Yet if he bristles or resists Kenward's description in any way, he runs up against the boundaries set forth in the letter, the commands that he play the part of distressed husband.

Archie wants to say nothing, to run from this room and this nightmare and escape into Nancy's arms. Only there can he find solace. But he knows he cannot. If he seeks her out, as he desperately wants to do, he will only lead the police directly to her and heighten their interest in her.

But he cannot allow the depiction of Friday morning to stay completely uncommented upon. Even a desperate, worried husband would defend himself to some extent. So he says, "The staff is prone to exaggeration, Deputy Chief Constable Kenward. I would not give them much credence on the details of my exchange with my wife. In any event, that morning and my wife's disappearance are unconnected, and it sounds as though you may need to consult with your superior before you go too far down the wrong path."

"You won't have to worry about any lack of consultation on my part, Colonel Christie. You see, given that Styles sits on the border between Berkshire and Surrey counties, this case will be overseen not just by me but also by Superintendent Charles Goddard, who is head of the Berkshire Constabulary. As a result, two police forces — and two police chiefs — will be investigating your wife's disappearance. There will be plenty of consultations before we go too far down any path."

Chapter Seventeen:
The Manuscript

October 18, 1916
New Forest, Hampshire, England

Archie pulled me back into the bed. The inn's mattress was lumpy and uncomfortable, but we didn't care. We didn't really use the mattress for sleeping anyway.

With his arms wrapped around me under the warmth of the cotton coverlet, I felt safe. Nearly as protected as in those summer days of my childhood at Ashfield, where everyone I loved had gathered safely under one lovely roof. Feeling foolish to have ever doubted my husband's state of mind, I surrendered into his embrace and indulged in the fantasy of this security, knowing it was only temporary and would vanish the moment Archie returned to the dangers of war. His survival thus far was nearly miraculous, and I feared that the odds were no longer in our favor.

"I have something to tell you," he whispered into that vulnerable crook in my neck and then kept his face nestled there. His words sent a shiver down my spine. After the awkward, disjointed reunion on his last leave and the strange rages of his recent letters, we'd found one place where we understood each other perfectly — in bed.

"Something delightful I hope," I whispered back.

He pulled away ever so slightly, enough to convey that this disclosure wasn't the romantic sort, and I saw trepidation in his expression. What was he anxious to tell me? "You know how I've been struggling with my sinuses while flying?" he asked, burying his face back in my neck.

From the beginning of his aviation training, Archie suffered terribly in his sinuses — his ears never seemed to equalize, and the pressure was often unbearable in the air and on the ground — but he insisted on persevering. I'd found his bravery and fortitude in these circumstances awfully attractive, but I knew it made flying extra taxing for him. "Of course. You've been so strong to suffer through all that pain for the good of England."

"I've been grounded. For good."

I understood now that he'd hidden his face in my neck because he couldn't meet my eyes. He was devastated that his wartime contributions would be cut short and fearful that I'd think less of him. But he was thinking of the innocent young girl I'd been and how she'd been dazzled by the young pilot he'd been. Did he not realize that I was no longer her exactly, that I'd seen suffering and death, that all I cared about was his safety? Had this announcement been brewing while he wrote me that spate of disturbing letters?

I knew what I had to say, and I meant the words. "Thank God," I cried.

Pushing himself up on his elbow, he looked down at me. "Do you mean it?"

"Of course. You'll be safe. It's the answer to my prayers."

"You won't be disappointed that I'm not serving as a pilot in this war?" His voice quivered.

"How could you think that, Archie? You've served as a pilot for two long years and survived, and I'm blessed in that. Our country is blessed with your service. But no more. This grounding is a gift. Your life means everything to me."

"You are everything to me too," he said. Leaning down, he kissed me long and hard, an indistinguishable blend of passion and relief. I allowed myself to be engulfed by him.

Later, we roused ourselves from the comfort — and delights — of the bed and decided to take a stroll in the New Forest, a royal forest since 1079 and a place Archie had reveled in exploring since his youth. Stepping into its woods felt like stepping back into the forest primeval. A wondrous mix of pasture lands, woodlands, and heath, alight with autumnal color, we proceeded hand in hand in rare, companionable silence, focusing on neither future or past but relishing our present.

After an hour or so, we stumbled upon a post hand-painted with the sign *To No-Man's-Land.* Archie turned to me with a wide smile. "I've always wanted to follow that path."

I smiled back. "Let's follow it. Now."

He looked hesitant. "Are you sure?"

"Positive."

He grabbed me close and said, "God, I love your spontaneity and sense of adventure. Let's go."

We ambled down the dirt trail to the enigmatically named No-Man's-Land. Eventually, the wild tangle of the landscape grew orderly, and we realized that No-Man's-Land was actually a poorly tended apple orchard. The crimson apples gleamed, and we were tempted to pull a few off the trees. I urged Archie to wait for permission, and soon enough, we spotted a woman in the orchard.

"Good morning, ma'am. Can we buy a few of your apples?" he asked.

The woman, ruddy-cheeked from a life spent outdoors, could have been thirty or fifty. She smiled at us and, taking note of Archie's uniform, said, "No need for payment. I see from your uniform that you are air force, as was my son. He was killed —"

Archie turned ashen, and I couldn't stop from interjecting, "Oh, I'm so sorry, ma'am."

She put up a hand to stop my flow of condolences. "He was doing his part for our country, just like your man here. Eat your fill and take as many as you can carry. It's the least we can do," she said and turned away.

We took her at her word, although her disclosure had turned the permission bittersweet, and Archie couldn't start picking apples until he'd smoked a cigarette, a new habit he'd developed since his last leave. An hour later, bellies full and pockets stuffed with apples, we sat down on a stump, beyond satiated. We chatted about nothing

— certainly not my work as a nurse or in the dispensary and definitely not his pilot service — until I decided to make my own disclosure to him. Without his personal confession about flying, I don't think I would have had the courage.

"I have something to tell you," I said.

"You do?" he asked, appearing simultaneously curious and alarmed.

"I've written a book." I forced myself to say the words I hadn't even said to my mother.

Archie glanced over at me as if he hadn't heard me correctly. "A book? You've written a book?" His voice wasn't judgmental, merely perplexed. He knew that I'd dabbled in writing in the past — I'd explained that after my aspirations in music faltered, writing filled the void nicely, with its ebb and flow not unlike performing music — but I hadn't mentioned it for some time. It seemed silly and inconsequential in light of the war.

I gave him a small, slightly bashful smile. "Well, you told me to stay busy while you were gone."

He laughed. A big, boisterous laugh, the sort I'd never heard from him before. "Did you bring it for me to read?" he asked.

"I did," I admitted. "It's back in the hotel

room, in my suitcase." I didn't mention that I'd buried the manuscript in the bottom of my suitcase, uncertain as to whether I'd have the nerve to show it to Archie.

"What sort of story is it?" he asked.

"A murder mystery."

"You?" He laughed again. "My sweet wife? You wrote a murder mystery?"

"Yes, it's a story about a rich elderly woman who's been poisoned at her home, a manor house, while several possible culprits are staying with her as guests. One of the houseguests, a soldier by the name of Arthur Hastings recovering from the war, enlists the help of his friend, a Belgian refugee by the name of Hercule Poirot." I explained to him how the story and characters unfolded for me during the slow hours at the apothecary, in particular how my detective evolved from my experience helping the group of Belgian refugees who'd settled in the parish of Tor after a harrowing escape from the Germans. But, I explained, once I'd conceived of Hercule Poirot, he'd grown on the page of his own accord, as if he were a real person.

"Sounds very timely and ingenious, no doubt." Shaking his head, he said, "Still, I can't believe you wrote a murder mystery."

I laughed along with him. "I'm sure it

sounds far-fetched, but Madge bet me that I couldn't create a mystery that a reader couldn't solve —"

He finished my sentence, having grown to understand the nature of my relationship with my sister. "And you certainly wouldn't lose a bet to Madge."

I thought about the wagers Madge and I had made over the years, each one furiously fought and each one fixed with set terms. The backgammon games that went long into the night. The increasingly high horse jumps that required us to defy gravity. The book challenges that led to teetering stacks all over Ashfield. In retrospect, it seemed as if Madge, eleven years my senior, was trying to strengthen my courage and resolve, because Mummy was determined solely to cosset and baby me. I supposed I should thank her for her efforts, but that would spoil our ongoing game and give her an edge I wasn't willing to yield.

"Certainly not." I smiled but then hesitated. "Would you read it? To see if you like it? To see if you can solve it? I know it will take away from our time together, but —"

"I'd love to," he said, then asked, "What's it called?"

"The Mysterious Affair at Styles."

CHAPTER EIGHTEEN:
DAY THREE AFTER
THE DISAPPEARANCE

Monday, December 6, 1926
Styles, Sunningdale, England

Archie settles at the breakfast table after a sleepless night. The usual order of the table — the silver and crystal arranged just so, his coffee poured and steaming, and his eggs waiting under the silver dome, which the housemaid lifts as soon as he enters the dining room — calms him. Until he reaches for the morning newspaper. There, emblazoned in enormous script, is the headline he has feared, the one that kept him tossing and turning all night: *Mystery of Woman Novelist Disappearing in Strange Circumstances.* The article sets out Agatha's authorial accomplishments — her three novels and the magazine serial stories that made her a modest success, if not exactly a household name — followed by a blow-by-blow of her vanishing.

Nausea wells up inside him, and he has to

turn away from his breakfast — those damnable runny eggs — in order to gather himself. How on earth did the reporters grab hold of this story so quickly? When Kenward told him that he'd circulated his wife's pictures yesterday, he'd assumed that he had a few days to gain control of the situation before news leaked out, that the information would remain in the hands of various police precincts. The speed with which the press has seized upon the story and begun its own investigation is unprecedented.

What to do, what to do, he begins to worry, *to avoid the inevitable. Stop,* he tells himself. *This is all down to Kenward's obvious dislike of him, nothing more.* He cannot let the dramatic headline of one newspaper rattle him.

Despite his efforts, the specific, familiar pain takes hold. Reaching like the nimble arms of an octopus, it penetrates his temples, his brow, and then finally, his sinus cavity. With the gripping, paralytic pain comes the past. Suddenly, the quiet sounds of Rosalind and Charlotte and the chatter of the police officers in the kitchen disappears, and the roar of a plane engine drowns out all other noise. He sees not the heavy silk curtains and patterned wallpaper of his dining room but the vast expanse of sky and cloud through the impeded view of his aviator's goggles. The rat-a-tat of gunfire begins to sound until a loud *thud* interrupts his fully immersive memory. Glancing up, he sees not the edge of his pilot's goggles but Lilly with a fresh pot of tea. And he returns to the present moment, although the headache lingers.

Hands trembling, he reaches for a cigarette and folds the newspaper so that he cannot see his wife's face peering up at him. Instead, he begins reading an article on the forty-third council session of the League of Nations that is set to begin today in Geneva, anything to push this ordeal from his thoughts. He's considering the focal point of the meeting — Germany's request that the league abandon a military commission left over from the Great War — when he hears the phone jangling in the distance. He pays it no mind, as the phone has rung almost constantly since Saturday morning, and he knows that Charlotte will summon him if it's necessary. In less than a minute, he knows it's necessary. It is his mother.

"Archie, have you seen the headlines?" she asks by way of greeting. He'd spoken to his mother extensively over the weekend about the disappearance and subsequent search.

His mother, no great admirer of his wife, had her own theories about the matter, but Archie refused to engage with her on the subject.

"Yes, Mother, I read the *Times* every morning." She has an unnerving way of making him feel ten years old again. When she uses a particular tone of voice, he's transported back to his first day at Hillside Preparatory School in Godalming, arriving in the very strange world of England after spending his whole childhood in India. When his father died during his service as a barrister in the Indian Civil Service, Archie, his brother Campbell, and his mother had been forced to return to England and begin anew, after a stint in his mother's native Ireland. And he never felt like he belonged. Until recently.

"I don't just mean the *Times*. I mean the *Gazette* and the *Telegraph* and the *Post*. Honestly, Archie, I could go on and on, but I won't. The articles are small in some papers and front and center in others, but every newspaper is reporting your wife's disappearance."

"How do you know?"

"When we received our regular paper this morning with that dreadful headline, I sent your stepfather out to the newsstand. He picked up an edition of the other papers, and they all had some version of that same headline about your wife."

"My god." He now understands that Deputy Chief Constable Kenward sent the reporters more than just a photograph of his missing wife. In order to garner this sort of coverage, Kenward must have insinuated that an unseemly act lurks at the center of this. And that Archie sits at that center. The damn man is responsible for the story of Agatha's disappearance blanketing the newspapers.

"It's terrible, Archie. All this public airing of your private life." She pauses and then whispers, "Who knows what might be revealed?"

"Yes, Mother, I understand that better than anyone," Archie says, desperately wishing that today's newspaper coverage was the end while at the same time fully understanding that it is only the beginning. He cannot afford having these awful rags prying more deeply into his and Agatha's private life; they could find out about his relationship with Nancy. This cannot happen.

After he replaces the phone in its cradle, he passes through the entryway, nearly knocking into Charlotte and Rosalind. They'd left while he was on the phone with his mother, hurrying Rosalind off to her day school. Why were they back? He had far too much on his mind to worry about his daughter's attendance record. That was Charlotte's province and, to a lesser extent, his wife's.

He tries to scurry across the entryway without encountering Charlotte and Rosalind, without success. "Colonel Christie, Colonel Christie," Charlotte calls out to him, although he's only a few yards away.

"I'm right here, Charlotte." He tries not to sound irritated. Much relies on Charlotte's discretion, and it seems his hosting of her sister Mary at Styles will only go so far.

"Sir, it's a circus out there. It's not safe to take Rosalind to school."

As Charlotte helps his daughter out of her coat, he notices for the first time that her hair is disheveled under her cloche hat. And the secretary governess is always impeccable. "Whatever do you mean?"

"Colonel, there must be fifteen or —"

"Twenty, Papa," Rosalind interjects. "I counted twenty reporters on the front lawn. Some with notepads, many with cameras. The flashing was so bright it hurt my eyes."

He squats down next to his daughter, who is more composed than Charlotte. Incredible, given the circumstances. Pushing aside a delicate brown curl that's fallen into her eyes, he stifles the brewing fury that his daughter should have to deal with this onslaught. She cannot witness his upset; he must remain the essence of calm in her presence. "Are you all right, darling?"

"Yes, Papa. They were very silly men. Quite stupid, actually. They kept asking where Mama was. But don't they know she's at Ashfield writing?"

"I guess they don't, darling."

"I almost told them, but Charlotte said I shouldn't speak to the men."

"She's quite right, darling. The men are strangers, and as you said yourself, they're silly." He stands up. "In any event, I'm about to tell them to push off, so you won't have to trouble yourself about them anymore."

"Papa!" Rosalind squeals at Archie's rough language. "Push off" is a definite no-no for his daughter.

He squeezes her small hand, then passes her into Charlotte's care. Squaring his shoulders, he opens the front door, ready to order the press from his land with an authoritative roar. He will drive them from his home, no matter the impossible position in which he has found himself, hamstrung between the implicit accusations from the police as they investigate a disappearance that increasingly points toward him and the explicit instructions left to him in the letter upon which his future depends. But when he swings the door open wide and squints into the flashing lights, Archie comprehends the magnitude of the public eye and realizes nothing will ever be the same.

CHAPTER NINETEEN: THE MANUSCRIPT

February 2, 1919
London, England

I'd expected that the Archie who returned from the war would be the same Archie who had left for it. Or at the very least the same Archie as in his magical last leave over two years ago. But the Archie who came back to me was a very different man.

The dashing, enigmatic figure became simultaneously restless and sedentary, unreadable in his unhappiness but not romantically intriguing as he'd once been. Each one of life's daily stresses seemed to further darken his mood, and sometimes, the slightest noise set off his headaches and his rage. Nothing seemed to satisfy him, certainly not the endless stream of cigarettes he smoked when his mood turned black and certainly not his job. On his return from the war, he took a position with the Royal Air Force but maintained that there was no long-term future for him there, although I questioned the truth in this statement. In the privacy of my own thoughts, I believed that from the moment his sinuses robbed him of the ability to pilot, Archie had been robbed of his zest for flight, and it pained him to be around pilots and planes. I didn't like to think that he might be suffering from one of the depressive states I occasionally saw when I nursed wounded soldiers in the Great War. But I could not fathom what passion might substitute for his previous love of flying. It certainly didn't seem to be me.

Mummy's marital advice ran through my thoughts day and night: a husband required attention and management. I began to think that if only I tended to Archie in precisely the right way, I might return him to his earlier state. If only I could serve him the perfect meals, clean the flat until it shone, provide the most interesting dinner conversation, become the ideal lover, then he'd be content. It was my duty, I believed, to restore him to that state, and that goal became the focus of my post-war days. It was the least I could do for my husband, one of the few who'd returned home at all.

I marched up the stairs to our flat in Northwick Terrace, the shopping basket draped over my forearm. I tried to keep my step light as I climbed the three flights, as I did not want to attract the attention of Mrs. Woods. While I generally appreciated the domestic advice and kindnesses of our building's caretaker, she was strangely critical of my skills at selecting produce and meats at the local market. Never did she find the postwar scarcity of many foods to be an excuse for my choices. Apparently, though, my footsteps hadn't been light enough.

"Mrs. Christie." Her voice rang out up the two flights of stairs I'd already climbed. It would be rude to ignore her, so I walked down the steps I'd already mounted.

"Good afternoon, Mrs. Woods," I greeted her, trying to mask my annoyance.

"I'm so glad I caught you, Mrs. Christie. When I was at the market earlier today, there was a veritable abundance of new carrots, and I took the liberty of picking up a bunch for you and your husband."

"How kind." I reached in my purse. "Let me repay you."

She wagged her finger at me. "No, no, not at all. It's my treat." Peering into my basket, she added, "And it's a good thing too, as your vegetables have seen better days."

I thanked her again as I trudged back up

the stairs to our two-room flat. Initially, I'd been grateful for her instruction in all arts domestic; Mummy never thought to guide me in anything but the management of staff, which I no longer had. As of late, however, Mrs. Woods's counsel had become unbearably intrusive.

I placed the pork, vegetables, and potatoes in the sink, rinsed them, and began preparing them for our dinner, following the recipe to the letter. Once I slid the dish into the oven, I looked around the flat for another chore. Mummy's primary domestic lesson about the care of one's husband was at the forefront of my mind, but I wondered how I was meant to tend to my husband if he was at work and all the household duties were completed. For hours, I was left to my own devices, with the understanding that all my efforts should be directed to his care. It was a conundrum.

When I stumbled upon an ad for cookery classes, I thought I'd found my focus. The lessons gave me something to do after the tidying and shopping had been finished for the day, and Archie wasn't due home until evening. But they didn't completely fill the time, and without a social calendar, as all my friends lived in Devon save Nan Watts, and she hailed from such a different economic class, I couldn't possibly entertain her, I had hours free. Even a course in book-keeping and shorthand that I'd stumbled upon and decided to pursue filled only a fraction of my spare hours. Although I was supposed to be grateful for my husband and his safety, I couldn't help but miss the camaraderie of the hospital and dispensary, the familiar community of Torquay, and especially the companionship of Mummy and even Auntie-Grannie, who remained on at Ashfield with additional staff.

From time to time, when I'd finished making dinner and I waited for Archie's return, my thoughts would turn to *The Mysterious Affair at Styles.* Archie had declared the novel "quite good" upon reading it, even "unsolvable," much to my delight, with its ingenious use of poisons to stump the readers, and suggested I submit it for publication.

"Does it not seem a bit frivolous in wartime?" I'd asked him.

He'd squeezed my hand for support. "Agatha, people *need* distraction — even frivolity — in wartime. Your puzzle should keep people distracted for quite a while."

At his prompting, I'd sent the manuscript out to several publishers, including Methuen and Hodder & Stoughton, and they all sent me rejection letters. I hadn't expected success; after all, I was just a housewife, without any formal training in writing. But the rebuffs had smarted, and I hadn't attempted another novel even when ideas preoccupied me, leaving me with too many unoccupied hours with which to ponder my husband.

Consequently, when I wasn't cleaning for Archie or shopping for him or sewing for him or cooking for him, I was thinking about him. My thoughts swirled around one central core: he had changed. In my darker moments, I wondered whether this was always the real Archie, that I'd only grown to actually know him.

I banished any troublesome thought from my mind, because tonight, everything would change. His mood, our marriage, our future.

"How's the pork?" I asked, painting a bright smile on my face. A grimace had briefly passed across Archie's face after he'd taken the first few bites, and I could never be certain if it was my cooking or my husband's surprisingly sensitive stomach. The Millers of Torquay were known for their hearty appetites and steel stomachs, so this delicacy was a new experience for me.

"Surprisingly, it tastes quite good, but we will see how it settles in," he said with a rub of his belly.

The dinner table became quiet again. Archie seemed comfortable with silence, even over evening meals, which had always been a source of connection and laughter at Ashfield. I shouldn't have been surprised; tea at Archie's mother's home was always a stilted affair.

"How was your d—" I stopped myself before I could finish the question. This was meant to be a memorable evening, full of wonder and delight. A conversation about his work at the Royal Flying Corps would deaden the mood completely. Perhaps a complete change of tactics was the thing. Instead of waiting until the end of the meal to make my announcement, I decided to plunge in even though a full hour of practice hadn't yielded the precise wording.

I took a deep breath and blurted out the news. "Archie, I'm going to have a baby." An irrepressible grin took over my face.

"A baby?" His tone puzzled me, and I wondered if I'd misread it. He didn't sound excited as I fully expected. In fact, he sounded angry.

When he spoke again, I realized I hadn't misconstrued his reaction at all. "You're having a baby?" he asked in that same vexed tone.

I was stunned. How could he possibly be angry at the thought of having a baby? And here I thought that my husband would leap to his feet and twirl me in the air when he heard that I was expecting. For the first time, Archie had rendered me speechless.

He stood up so abruptly that his chair clattered to the floor behind him. As he paced around the dining room, my usually quiet husband spoke a steady stream of harsh sentiments, most of which I hoped to never hear again.

"You do realize that this will change everything between us, Agatha. A baby always does," he practically seethed at me.

While I knew he didn't mean that the changes would be positive, I tried to cast a rosy light upon his statements. "Yes, Archie. Of course, there will be changes. But they'll be wondrous changes."

"No, they won't," he yelled. "Your focus will be on the baby and not me. I will be forgotten."

I suddenly realized that rather than uniting us and bringing my restless husband a modicum of joy, this baby could bring us to the brink. I would never, ever allow that to happen. After all, it was my job to tend to him and his happiness.

Standing, I walked to Archie's side and

placed a consoling hand on his shoulder. "I promise you that you will forever be my focus. You and no one else. Not even this baby."

placed a consoling hand on his shoulder. "I promise you that you will forever be my focus. No one and no one else 'til even his

CHAPTER TWENTY:
DAY THREE AFTER
THE DISAPPEARANCE

Monday, December 6, 1926
New Scotland Yard, London, England

Archie stops midstep as he passes through the iron gate into the bowels of Scotland Yard. Is he acting the fool by placing himself directly into the hands of the reigning authorities? He didn't think so when he left Styles in a rage over the throngs of press camped out on his front lawn. He only wanted to remove himself and this blasted investigation from the torrid glare of the public spotlight — where that damnable letter dictates how he can behave and what he can say — and have a higher authority take over the police inquiry from the clearly prejudiced Kenward, who seemed hell-bent on including the press every step of the way. At least then he could shield Nancy.

Even as he completed the hour-and-a-half drive and pulled up to the curb on the Victoria Embankment in his Delage to glance up at the Scotland Yard headquarters — a fortress-like building striped in red and white stone, not unlike a prisoner's uniform, and bordered on one side by the River Thames — he believed in this decision. But now, standing within the penitentiary-like building amid the clusters of animated round-hatted police officers ready with wooden truncheons to subdue any suspects and handcuffs to immobilize them, he wonders if he's made a fatal blunder.

"Is there a problem, Colonel Christie?" William Perkins, his solicitor, turns and asks. He must have heard the slowing of Archie's footsteps.

"No, not at all. Just, just —" He bungles his words, then says, "Studying the structure." *Stupid answer,* he thinks. But better than the truth.

"There's no mistaking the purpose of this building, is there?" the solicitor asks in the closest thing to a joke he's ever heard the man tell. The mask of impassivity takes hold again, and Perkins says, "We best keep our pace. Don't want to be late for our appointment with Commander Reynolds. He's a known stickler for punctuality."

Archie lengthens his stride, walking alongside his solicitor. Perkins hadn't reacted at all when Archie called him this morning, demanding he arrange a meeting with Scotland Yard to take this matter away from Kenward and the press. But then Perkins is recalcitrant to a fault. Archie supposes this quality is excellent for his business; he never disappoints if he never overpromises or over-reacts.

The scent in the air changes as they enter the labyrinthine building. The unpleasant stench of decaying fish and waste from the River Thames dissipates and is replaced by the expected smell of unwashed police, cigarette smoke, and something less defin-able. But what? Archie doesn't want to spec-ulate.

They pass by uniformed officers and detectives in everyday suits, all purposefully undertaking the important work of the Metropolitan Police. He spies a sign for the Fingerprint Bureau, which uses a new-fangled method of identifying criminals, and when he peeks inside, he sees it is crammed with men in suits and uniforms alike. Does he imagine that the eyes of these men linger on him? Are they judging him?

Archie and his solicitor are guided to a sizable corner office on the second floor of the building. The office is dark, even though the hour hasn't passed two o'clock. There, sitting behind his desk, in the cavernous shadows of his office, sits Commander Reynolds.

As soon as Archie looks into the commander's eyes, he knows he has made a mistake coming here. This man will see right through him if he isn't cautious. It's his job to read people's souls, isn't it? To decide if they are guilty or innocent? Archie feels as if he can hardly breathe, and yet he must proceed.

"I'm sorry to hear about the disappearance of your wife, Colonel Christie."

"Thank you, Commander Reynolds. I appreciate you taking the time to see me today." Archie hopes his voice doesn't quiver.

"What can I help you with?" Although the commander's expression is pleasant, his tone reveals a certain impatience. Clearly, he'd like to dispense with their visit quickly.

"It's about the investigation."

"Yes?"

"I worry that your more" — he hesitates — "your more rural police forces don't have the skills of the Scotland Yard officers, skills that may be necessary to locate my wife. As a result, the detectives have taken to baiting the press to get broad coverage." After he says this, Archie thinks that a concerned husband might want that broad coverage

159

and realizes he must shift the focus. "I'm worried that their lack of experience in more complicated police matters might not yield the desired result."

"I see." The commander's hands form a triangle, and he glances down at them as though deep in thought. He then abruptly looks up and says, "But Deputy Chief Constable Kenward did lead the investigation into the Frenchman Jean-Pierre Vaquier — the Byfleet murderer — to a successful conclusion, did he not?"

Archie has no idea who this Byfleet murderer was or what role Kenward played, but he knows what he's meant to say. "I suppose. But it seems that they could do with a bit of oversight. A pulling at the reins if you will."

"Ah, I *do* see."

Reynolds stands, walks around to their side of the desk, and leans against it as he talks to them. "Colonel Christie, I do not doubt that you are" — he forms his hands into the triangle again and considers them before continuing — "troubled by the disappearance of your wife and the rather overwhelming media coverage. But Scotland Yard cannot intervene in the investigation unless the Surrey or Berkshire constabularies who are in charge of the investigation request assistance. That is the law."

Perkins has intimated that Scotland Yard might not stick its nose in the investigation, but he has never mentioned it was actually against the law. Archie was assuming Scotland Yard's policy of noninvolvement was an unspoken rule, so he plowed ahead with the meeting. But now he sees that this is a waste of time. And a potentially dangerous one at that. Why would his own damn solicitor not explain everything to him?

The commander must take Archie's silence as disappointment, because he offers, "Scotland Yard could place an ad for your wife in the *Police Gazette* alerting all the police stations across the country to her disappearance if you like?"

"Your offer is much appreciated, Commander Reynolds, but I feel like the newspapers have already alerted all the police stations, along with the regular populace."

"And perhaps that was the intention of Deputy Chief Constable Kenward and his colleague Superintendent Charles Goddard?"

"Perhaps," Archie answers.

"Is there a reason why you wouldn't want broad newspaper coverage of your wife's disappearance?" Reynolds's arms cross and his brows arch, and Archie knows with complete certainty that he has placed himself in the line of fire by coming here. As soon as they leave Scotland Yard, he will have Perkins's bloody head for not preventing him from calling this meeting.

Archie cannot ignore the question this time with this man; there will be no side-stepping it as he had with Kenward. He says the only thing he can. "I do have a young daughter, sir. And she's been finding the constant press presence and the chatter about her mother most disturbing."

"It seems to me that she'd find the absence of her mother even more disturbing, Mr. Christie." His intimation is clear, and with that, the matter is closed.

With a birdlike quickness, Reynolds turns toward Perkins. "I believe your client is in capable hands with Deputy Chief Constable Kenward. I have every confidence that he will solve this mystery." Reynolds then stares Archie up and down, locking eyes with him, and says, "I will do you the courtesy of keeping your visit here today confidential and not informing Deputy Chief Constable Kenward and Superintendent Charles Goddard. I do not think it would bode well for your treatment in this investigation."

CHAPTER TWENTY-ONE:
THE MANUSCRIPT

August 1919 to January 1920
London, England

Although my pregnancy was riddled with nausea and fear, a wave of relief washed over me when I made plans to stay at Ashfield for my final month and the planned delivery. *Mummy would take care of everything,* I told myself as Archie and I traveled home. My hopes became reality when Mummy swept me into her arms and the care of the nurse she'd arranged for the delivery and the baby afterward, the efficient and pleasant Nurse Pemberton. The two women fussed over me while Auntie-Grannie clucked happily in the background, and my fear turned to anticipation.

Rosalind arrived with the pain and terror that I'd heard described by Madge and my friends. When the nurse placed my daughter in my arms for the first time, I cooed in delight at her tiny fingers and toes and her sweet rosebud lips, but I reminded myself that she could not become my focus. I could not allow her to dislodge my husband as my polestar. So I returned her to the care of Nurse Pemberton and allowed Mummy to coddle me.

As I drifted off to sleep, exhausted from the labor, Mummy sat in the armchair next to my childhood bed, holding my hand. "Mummy, don't go away," I begged. "What if I should need you in the night?"

"Of course not, darling. I'll stay right here by your side."

And indeed she did. For the weeks of my convalescence, it was as if Mummy and I formed a cocoon around ourselves, not unlike that of my childhood, and Rosalind was an occasional visitor. On those nights when I longed to hold my baby in my arms, even sleep with her in my bed, I told myself that this distance was necessary practice. How else could I ensure that Archie maintained his position at the center of my affections? How would he take it if Rosalind got used to sleeping with me in my bed? In time, it became easier and easier, and I felt more like a daughter myself than a mother to a daughter.

I kept my promise to Archie. Rosalind changed nothing. Nothing, as far as Archie was concerned.

On our return to London, my first order of business was interviewing nurses, after finding a suitable flat for our small family, of course. I would only be able to maintain the balance I'd struck at Ashfield with live-in help for Rosalind and a maid to help with the house. After securing a flat — no mean feat in the postwar rush — and meeting and rejecting several nurse applicants, I finally found Jessie Swannell, and I set about creating the sort of life I thought Archie wanted. I located, rented, and decorated a four-bedroom flat for us so that Rosalind and Jessie would have ample space separate and apart from Archie and myself. I cooked him recipes I knew he'd adore, and we dined alone, focusing exclusively on his day in his new position with a financier in the City. Occasionally, we accepted or extended social invitations, even though Archie disliked mingling, but generally, it was just us two. I toned down my natural exuberance and chatter, because Archie found it cloying and more than a little twee. From the outside looking in, I'd fashioned a perfect life, one that Mummy, with her warnings and advice, would applaud. A perfect life for Archie anyway, and one that he seemed to slip right into as if nothing in our existence had changed.

"There's an official-looking letter for you on the table in the front hall, ma'am," Jessie called out as I walked into the flat with my dark-haired, dark-eyed Rosalind. It was the sole weekday afternoon when I took the baby out for a walk in her pram instead of the nanny, because Jessie needed the day for the laundry.

The brisk walk through Kensington with Rosalind in her heavy pram had been cold and exhausting, and I deposited her with the nanny as I went to retrieve the mail. At the top of the pile of letters for Archie's attention sat an envelope for me with the return address of the Bodley Head Publishers.

The Bodley Head? Hadn't I submitted *The Mysterious Affair at Styles* to the publisher a lifetime ago? Why were they writing to me after nearly two years?

My hands shook as I sliced open the envelope with my opener. Out spilled a letter from the Bodley Head publisher John Lane. Lifting the letter up to the rather dim gaslit lamp, I read, "We invite you to arrange a time to visit our offices to discuss your novel, *The Mysterious Affair at Styles.*"

The Bodley Head wanted to see *me* about my book? The news was unexpected and nearly unbelievable. I wanted to dance around the apartment, but the respectable, orderly Mrs. Archibald Christie no longer engaged in the fanciful behavior of Miss Agatha Miller. Instead, I strode to my desk and wrote a reply to Mr. John Lane, informing him that I would visit his offices tomorrow afternoon.

By the time I announced myself to the Bodley Head receptionist the next day, all the excitement and confidence I'd felt the night before had disappeared; in truth, it began to ebb away as I tried on every suit I owned and found only one still fit after Rosalind's birth, confirming Archie's rather constant declarations that I still hadn't lost the weight I'd gained with my pregnancy. My exuberance had been replaced with dread. Who did I think I was, telling Mr. Lane that I'd be stopping by his office at precisely one o'clock, as if he had nothing else to do than meet with a housewife? I'd utterly forgotten myself and my status when I wrote that letter, and now I'd have to reap what I'd sown. *The only saving grace was that I hadn't told Archie about the letter or my appointment,* I thought, *and would be spared the humiliation of my rejection here this afternoon.* This thought made me momentarily sad, as I would have adored telling the old

167

Archie about this promising, unexpected development and wouldn't have hidden it away for my protection and his comfort. But this was a different Archie.

Perched on the edge of the reception area chair, pondering my escape, I nearly jumped when a man called out, "Mrs. Christie?"

"Yes?"

An older gentleman with a trim gray beard and vivid blue eyes walked toward me with his hand outstretched. "I'm Mr. John Lane. Delighted to make your acquaintance," he said.

After we shook hands, he guided me into his office, a rather stark affair that was decorated with gloomy old masters paintings and dimly lit except for the pool of light on the surface of his desk thoughtfully provided by a green-shaded lamp. I supposed he needed the illumination to review manuscripts. I settled into the seat across from his desk and waited.

"Well, Mrs. Christie. Apologies for the about-face on your manuscript." He picked up a sheaf of papers, which I recognized as my own. "I'd initially declined the work, because the first few pages didn't really lure me in. But then, last week, when I had the chance to read further, I began to believe that your book might — I only say *might* —

have possibility."

"You, you do?" I blurted out, chastising myself immediately afterward. I should sound confident about my work, not surprised by the compliment.

"Yes, I do. There would have to be some significant editing — as one example, you'd have to eliminate the courtroom scene with that detective fellow Poirot at the end — but it has real promise. With the right modifications, I think we might just publish it, likely as a serial. Your use of poison as the murder weapon showed ingenuity, that's certain."

I couldn't quite catch my breath, so when I answered him, I sounded strangely breathless. "That's wonderful news, Mr. Lane."

"Even the edits?" he asked.

Recovering the strength of my voice, I responded, "Those edits would be no problem at all, Mr. Lane. To tell the truth, for some time now, I've been thinking that the court scene should be removed." I'd been thinking no such thing.

Mr. Lane sat back in his chair and clapped his hands once. "Excellent, Mrs. Christie, excellent." He fiddled with some papers on his desk and assembled a small pile. He then retrieved a fountain pen and handed me the lot.

"I have confidence that we'll be able to make good use of *The Mysterious Affair at Styles,*" he said with a nod toward the pile of papers on my lap.

"And these are?"

"Your contract with the Bodley Head, of course. It's all industry standard. Ten percent on any English sale more than two thousand copies. The right to have the first look at your upcoming five novels."

My contract? Had he just said my contract with the Bodley Head? My heart raced, and I wondered if I should wait to consult with Archie. But what if Mr. Lane changed his mind in the meantime? Anyway, hadn't Archie implicitly consented to this contract when he suggested that I submit my book for publication? I couldn't stop thinking about what we could do with the extra funds. With Archie's salary and my small income from a family trust, we were doing fine financially on a day-to-day basis, but if we ever wanted to own a home of our own, we'd need more. And this might just provide those funds.

I pretended to skim the contract pages, but in truth, my head was swimming, and the words swam across the page along with it. I signed where indicated and then handed the stack of papers and the pen back to Mr. Lane.

"Welcome to the Bodley Head family. You know" — he paused, looking at the ceiling for a moment — "we've had considerable interest in serials lately. You seem to have a sense of the genre."

Squaring my shoulders a little — I had a contract with the Bodley Head now, after all — I said, "I like to think so."

"Well, then, we just might make quite the writer out of you yet, Mrs. Christie."

CHAPTER TWENTY-TWO:
DAY THREE AFTER
THE DISAPPEARANCE

Monday, December 6, 1926
Styles, Sunningdale, England
How long has Kenward been waiting? Archie wonders as he spies the constable through the window, pacing the front hall of Styles. As he pulls the Delage alongside the drive, past the reporters camped out on the lawn, he considers whether the constable received word of his attempt to go over his head to Scotland Yard, despite Reynolds's promise to the contrary. Girding himself with his litany of righteous defenses and ignoring the reporters calling out his name, he opens the door to Styles and steps into his entryway.

"Colonel Christie," Kenward greets him with an odd smile. There is another man, outfitted in a black policeman's uniform but of a different design than Kenward's men, standing to the left.

"Yes, Deputy Chief Constable?"

172

"There has been an interesting development. But before we discuss it, I'd like to introduce you to my counterpart from the Berkshire Constabulary, Superintendent Charles Goddard. I mentioned to you earlier that he'd be sharing leadership of this operation." He gestures toward the other man. Not quite dismissively but not quite respectfully either. It is clear that Kenward believes himself to be in charge.

As Archie shakes hands with the new officer, his mind is on this "interesting development" Kenward mentioned. What is it? Has Kenward discovered more about his relationship with Nancy through his incessant baiting of the press?

Archie notices that this Goddard is meticulously dressed, finding his neatly pressed uniform, with its knife-edge crease along the pants, a welcome break from Kenward's slapdash attire. When Goddard removes his hat, Archie notices that the constable's near-black hair is as tidily tended to as his uniform. This similarity to his own grooming habits calms him and gives him hope that this policeman might be more inclined toward him than Kenward. More inclined to believe him innocent, that is.

"So what's this development?" he asks both men, trying not to sound overly concerned though possibly eager for news about his wife's whereabouts.

Ignoring Goddard altogether, Kenward says, "Seems your brother has received a letter from your wife."

How peculiar, Archie thinks. The two have always had a pleasant relationship, but surely he must have misheard Kenward. "My brother?"

Kenward consults his ever-present notepad. "Captain Campbell Christie, instructor at the Royal Military Academy at Woolwich. He is your brother, is he not?"

"Yes, he is," Archie answers guardedly.

"You don't seem particularly happy about this communique," Kenward observes.

"It's, it's just that —" Archie searches for an explanation. "I'm surprised. That's all."

"Was your wife not in the habit of writing letters to your brother? Is that why you're surprised?" Kenward launches into questions before Archie can even ask about the letter's content.

"She did not have a regular habit of corresponding with him that I'm aware of. Except perhaps the odd invitation to dinner or something along those lines."

"Would she address her letters to his place of work or home?"

"I cannot say, given that she had no such

habit to contact him at all. But if I had to venture a guess, I assume that she would address correspondence to his home."

"So this letter from your wife to your brother — if such a letter in fact existed — would be doubly strange, not only in the fact of its writing but in that Captain Christie told us that the letter was delivered to his office. Triply strange, actually, if you think about the fact that she wrote a letter to your brother, not you, her husband."

Kenward's words send a momentary sense of relief through Archie; he still hasn't heard about the letter Agatha left him. This realization preoccupies his thoughts until Goddard clears his throat, presumably at the inappropriate comment from Kenward. Or perhaps Goddard objects to Kenward's tone? The deputy chief constable seems oblivious to Goddard's signals, because he rambles on.

"Apparently Captain Christie was unaware of your wife's disappearance, so when he received a letter from her at his place of work yesterday, he did not think much of it. But when he saw the newspapers today, he reached out to your mother, Mrs. Hemsley, and told her. Curious . . ." he says.

Archie is irritated that his mother chose to discuss his personal business with his brother, and he is troubled by this peculiar letter from Agatha to Campbell. Why would she write to him? It's not as if they were particularly close. And upon what did this strange letter focus?

Flustered at this turn of events, Archie instinctively asks, "What's curious?"

"That your brother didn't reach out to you directly to inform you about the letter," Kenward answers, delighted that Archie took his little bait.

Archie could smack himself for walking directly into Kenward's trap on that question. "My brother and I are not in any usual habit of communication, but he does speak with my mother regularly. I presume that he wanted to speak with her first about it. There's nothing curious about that." Archie redirects the conversation, asking, "How did you find all this out? I spoke with my mother early this morning, and she didn't mention it."

"Mrs. Hemsley rang my office late this morning when she could not reach you. I gather you were out?" he asks with a single raised eyebrow.

He knows about Scotland Yard, Archie thinks. Kenward's gesture telegraphs his feelings about Archie's visit to London, but what does this more inscrutable Goddard think? Will Archie be somehow punished for trying to go around the local authorities to Scotland Yard?

"What did the letter say?" Archie asks the expected question.

"Your brother said your wife made some reference to visiting a spa for ill health. But it's strange," Kenward comments and then pauses for a long moment. Archie will not be lured into inquiring again, so Kenward is forced to continue. "He threw out the letter, so we don't know what she actually wrote. We only have his word for it — and his recollection."

"I suppose it makes sense that he wouldn't keep it, as he didn't know she was missing."

"True enough. Although he did make a point to keep the envelope in which the letter was posted. It's all very peculiar." He stares at Archie. "Perhaps your Friday morning argument is the reason for her feeling ill?"

Archie chooses to treat this as a rhetorical question. "What did the postmark show?"

"That the letter was postmarked at 9:45 a.m. on Saturday morning in the SW1 area of London, which means that it had been posted sometime in the early hours of Saturday. It suggests that she was alive and well on Saturday morning."

Archie tries to tamp down his annoyance at his brother's interference, likely prompted by his mother. The word *stalwart* from that damn letter his wife left him comes into his mind, and he tries to follow its directive: *You will have to be stalwart, even when the road is rocky.* In an effort to react as a worried husband might and yet still draw Kenward's attention away from his thought about the existence of other letters, he says, "But it's wonderful news, isn't it? It shows that my wife is fine somewhere, perhaps even London. And we can stop this terrible search through the fields and forests." He thinks but does not say that perhaps it will deter the reporters as well. Without the possibility of a gory body to find in the fields, maybe the story of Agatha's disappearance will be less intriguing to them.

Kenward opens his mouth in protest, but Goddard inserts himself into the conversation. Finally. "You're right, Colonel, this is a positive development, and it must be a massive relief to you. But we haven't seen the letter, and we cannot be certain whether your wife wrote and posted it or someone did so on her behalf." Goddard turns to Archie and says, "I don't mean to upset you, sir, but we've got to think it through. Isn't it possible that the letter was posted much earlier and postmarked later? And isn't it also possible that Mrs. Christie entrusted someone else to post the letter? I was happy to see that this letter has come to light, but I'm not certain it's dispositive on the timeline or on her whereabouts. Until we ascertain these facts — and actually locate her — we will have to continue with the search. It's standard protocol."

Even though this Goddard delivers the unpleasant news that the search will not cease — with all the attendant press coverage it generates — he shares it with a softer touch than Kenward. As if he thinks there might be a chance Agatha is still alive. As if, unlike Kenward, he hasn't already decided that Archie murdered his wife.

CHAPTER TWENTY-THREE:
THE MANUSCRIPT

December 18, 1921
Ashfield, Torquay, England

"How lovely that Archie doesn't mind you writing," Mummy said. Sipping her steaming hot cup of tea, she sighed in satisfaction. Over the tea or my writing, I couldn't be certain.

Mummy, Madge, and I were gathered around the worn, nicked tea table at Ashfield, a site shot through with memories. Madge had pushed for us to spend Christmas at her Dickensian manor, and in the past, the notion of retreating to Abney Hall, with its vast halls, endless nooks, and unexpected staircases and its decor of burnished woodwork and dusty tapestries, would have enticed. After all, Mummy and I had spent many wondrous holidays there with the Watts family after Papa died. But Archie felt uncomfortable at Abney, even though Madge's husband and the entirety

180

of the Watts family offered him nothing but an open-armed welcome, especially my dear friend Nan with whom I'd reconnected. Archie's own background contrasted starkly with that of the Wattses' heritage, and he perceived slights around every corner, even though I felt certain they were imaginary. This made an Abney Hall holiday difficult for me, so I'd entreated Mummy to host instead, and Madge and I had arrived at Ashfield early to help her with the holiday organizing and planning.

Madge exhaled cigarette smoke as she reclined on the sofa even further, ever assuming the pose of the confident older sister and first daughter. "Yes, I mean, imagine. Archie — of all people — allowing his wife to work."

I knew better than to think Madge's comment was a compliment; her barb about Archie's lack of sophistication was hidden in plain sight. For the first time, I wondered if Archie's sense of being mocked wasn't paranoia after all. "Why ever should Archie mind if I write? It's not as if it affects his daily existence in any way. I still arrange for his meals and dine with him every evening. The house and his wardrobe are well cleaned, and Rosalind is tended to beautifully. My writing is an invisible part of the fabric of our lives."

I forced a confident smile upon my face, hoping to end this topic, as I knew it would devolve into a quarrel if the exchange went much further. Jealousy was motivating Madge's thinly disguised critique. She was the one who'd shown the early promise in writing, getting her short stories published in *Vanity Fair,* and it irked her that I was now enjoying a modicum of writerly success. How apt were the title of those early short stories — *Vain Tales* — I thought to myself, and part of me was tempted to brag about the fifty pounds I was going to receive for the serialization of *The Mysterious Affair at Styles* from the *Weekly Times.* Shouldn't I be able to share my small successes with my family in any event? But I swallowed the words, knowing that they would just exacerbate the situation.

"Oh, I can see that Archie is getting everything he needs," Madge answered, not bothering to hide her snide smirk behind her cigarette.

I'd been willing to put aside her remarks the first time but not twice. Twice, she had to be called out and answer for herself. "What are you getting at, Madge?"

"Archie gets what he needs, but aren't you stretched a little thin?" She took a long drag of her cigarette. "I'm just looking out for you, Little Sister."

Madge's attempt to hide her critique in the guise of protection of me was laughable. And insulting. "Your husband has allowed you to work when opportunity knocked," I said. Then, because I couldn't resist it, I added, "And if you had a book contract, I'm sure he would again."

Her eyes narrowed as she understood my meaning. An angry spark ignited within those eyes, and she launched right back out into the battlefield. This time, using her financial superiority as a weapon, she said, "Agatha, that's completely different. I have a full staff."

Sensing the sibling discord, Mummy interjected, "What matters is that Archie believes that he is the most important thing in your life, that he's always made to feel first. Madge, it sounds like Agatha is doing exactly that" — she paused for a smile at her youngest daughter — "all the while managing a successful career. The serialization of *The Mysterious Affair at Styles* in the *Weekly Times* was quite a coup, Agatha, and I'm guessing a financially beneficial one as well, and I'm sure *The Secret Adversary* is the same. I only wish Auntie-Grannie had lived to see it." Mummy's eyes glistened with tears at the thought of her mother's death, only a short while after Rosalind had been born. I was surprised to see this wellspring of emotion, because I'd always found their relationship to be cordial but not warm.

"At least she got to see Rosalind," I offered, relieved that Mummy had taken the conversation by the helm and steered it to safer, more placid waters.

"Yes, that is something, isn't it?" she replied.

Mummy's efforts notwithstanding, Madge wasn't going to let me win this little skirmish. "But we are ignoring the toll it must take on Agatha to perform this sleight of hand on a daily basis. To run the house, organize the meals, entertain the husband, oversee the child, while secretly writing books. On such a reduced staff."

Enough, I thought to myself. *Why can't Madge let me have this one triumph? Can't I enjoy the minor popularity of my two novels and magazine serials?* Wasn't it enough that she'd married into great wealth and had social standing I'd never attain as Mrs. Christie? Rage threatened to take hold as Madge clung on to her pretense of concern for my well-being, and I finally said, "It's not a secret, Madge. I have Archie's full support. And anyway, why are you speaking for me? I'm a grown woman, and if I tell you that I've reached a happy balance, then I have." I hoped I sounded utterly self-assured, because in truth, some days, the so-called balance I'd struck overwhelmed me. Not that I'd ever let on to Archie, of course. Or Madge. I might be asked to stop writing, and I couldn't do that, couldn't let my family down.

"I think I know better than —" Madge continued.

"Girls, girls, that's enough of your bickering," Mummy interrupted with a rising tone. This was a familiar pattern. Madge ignited a heated discussion, and once I'd added fuel to the fire with my remarks, Mummy dampened the flames. She couldn't tolerate dissension between her daughters.

Once we quieted, she reached out and squeezed each of our hands. "I am proud of both of my girls, and I'm tickled that you're here at Ashfield with me for the holidays. This house has been empty of merriment for far too long." She clapped her hands and practically squealed, "I know. Let's play a game. We have an hour or so before Archie should arrive from the train — and then Rosalind and her nanny will undoubtedly be on the scene." She wagged her finger at me. "Careful you don't spoil the child, Agatha. You know a little neglect goes a long way."

Ignoring Mummy — I'd heard her views about the importance of hands-off child-rearing often enough, which confusingly contradicted my own upbringing — I asked, "What shall we play?"

"Oh, I know," Madge exclaimed. "Let's play confessions."

Mummy clapped with delight. "What a wonderful idea, Madge! It's been an age since we played confessions."

As we gathered the paper and pencils necessary to play the game, I was assigned scribe, and Mummy and Madge began calling out the categories in which we'd have to confess our truths. Favorite virtue, preferred color, beloved heroine, worst lie, present state of mind, perversion, chief characteristic, idea of happiness — the list went on and on. We laughed as we concocted our list and conjured up past remembrances playing with Father and Monty, who was due to return next year from whatever schemes he'd been up to in Africa. With all his absences, my brother was hardly part of my life, aside from whatever worries he caused Mummy with his gambling and dubious business deals.

Just as we settled down to play the game, one of the two remaining maids at Ashfield — the Marys — knocked on the door. "Mrs. Christie," she called out through the crack in the door she'd just opened a sliver. "Mr. Christie rang. Work has detained him, and he will be arriving on the morning train instead of the one this evening."

"Thank you, Mary," I called back. I was disappointed, but what could I do?

Mummy eyed me and said, "Careful not to let him be alone too long, Agatha. He needs to be looked after."

These last four words I repeated along with her. I'd heard them so much in my youth and my adulthood that I knew them by heart. "It's not as if I'm in control of his work hours and obligations, Mummy. You know I tend to him whenever I'm given the chance."

"I hope so," she said. "And I hope you orchestrate chances so you can tend to him when he doesn't present you with opportunities."

Although she hadn't joined us in this exchange, Madge now interjected. "Why don't you ever say that to me, Mummy? That Jimmy needs to be looked after? That I shouldn't leave him alone for too long? In fact, you encourage me to come visit you at

Ashfield for long stretches even when you know Jimmy cannot join me."

"Isn't it obvious, Madge? You don't need to follow my advice. Your husband isn't uncommonly sensitive or uncommonly handsome."

Chapter Twenty-Four:
Day Four after
the Disappearance

Tuesday, December 7, 1926
Styles, Sunningdale, England

The dawn of a new day does nothing to diminish the search for his wife or the press's relentless pursuit of information. As Archie studies the pile of local and national newspapers over breakfast, he sees that the thirst for details about his wife and her disappearance has only grown. It seems as though the search has become an end unto itself for these reporters rather than one step toward resolution.

He shakes his head at the speed with which the press gathers and disseminates material, thinking, not for the first time, that only inside access could yield some of the more intimate details. Although he has no proof — and doesn't understand why — Archie suspects that Kenward has been predisposed against him from the start and has been feeding the press salient particulars, perhaps in the hope of smoking out a reaction from him. But Archie knows that it's more than one reporter's simple desire to beat a rival reporter to the latest tidbit about Agatha's zippered purse or the color of her fur coat that is causing the frenzy. The idea that his missing wife — now mythologized into the beautiful novelist happily married to the handsome war hero — has turned into the victim in one of her own mystery books is an irresistible tale to reporters and their readers alike.

What in the name of God is he going to do? How will he maintain the facade of the concerned, loving husband for much longer? How can he ensure that his relationship with Nancy stays secret? Styles is at the center ring of a very public circus, and everyone is looking to him as if he's the ringmaster. And a caring ringmaster at that.

He rubs his pounding temples, searching for relief from his stress and the noise, when the dining room door opens with a slam, sending a stabbing pain across his brow. Who dare burst past the guards Kenward installed to protect Archie and Rosalind from the aggressive throngs of reporters staked outside Styles? Kenward explained that the guards were for their protection, but Archie suspects that the constable assigned the guards primarily to keep an eye on him.

It's Kenward, of course. He brushes past the housemaid, Lilly, who has admitted him, and strides directly to face Archie. Goddard glides into the room in Kenward's wake, an apologetic half smile on his face for the interruption.

"Will you be coming to the dredging? We've got to get started, you know. We have men and equipment lined up, so we can't lollygag, Colonel," Kenward barks, which elicits a wince from Goddard. "We've been standing around waiting for you."

"The dredging?" Archie is confused. What is Kenward on about now? "I'm not certain I understand."

"I know I told you. How could you forget?" Kenward says with a roll of the eye. "We are slated to drag nets through the Silent Pond and the Albury Mill Pond today. Just in case Mrs. Christie fell into one of the ponds after wandering around once her car broke down." Either Kenward doesn't comprehend the horrific scene he is painting for Archie, or planting that image in his thoughts is precisely Kenward's goal.

Whatever his intention, even Goddard seems repelled. "Deputy Chief Constable Kenward, I think that might be a bit much.

Perhaps Colonel Christie could sit this one out. We are talking about his wife, after all."

Kenward looks over at Goddard as if he's just realized he's in the room. "But Colonel Christie could help identify the bo—" Goddard shoots him a scathing glance, and Kenward changes course. "Ah, yes. I see. I suppose it might be a good idea to stay behind."

"Here's an idea, Deputy Chief Constable Kenward. What if Colonel Christie spent that time with me? You have the dredging well in hand, and Mr. Christie and I haven't had much of a chance to talk one-on-one about the investigation and the events leading up to the disappearance." Goddard turns to him. "Is that agreeable to you, Colonel?"

If I have to spend the morning with another policeman, it's more palatable, he thinks as he nods in agreement, *to spend it with one who hasn't already decided I'm a murderer.*

Once Kenward and his men leave and Lilly pours fresh, steaming tea into the china teacups, Archie settles into his study chair and submits to another round of questioning. He assumes that it will resemble all the others — a barrage of inquiries focused on his whereabouts and those of his wife on the day she disappeared in a vain attempt to catalogue and comprehend each of their movements of the fateful Friday night. The police seem to believe that only then will they learn what's happened to his wife. But Goddard doesn't seem to be like the other officers.

"How would you describe your wife, Colonel Christie?"

"Her hair has a reddish hue but is streaked with gray —"

Goddard interrupts, "My apologies for being vague, Colonel. How would you describe your wife's personality?"

"Hmm." Archie is surprised at the query; it's one he hasn't been asked yet. "I suppose she's like any wife and mother in some ways."

"But in others?"

"She has an artistic temperament, I guess. Creative interests. She's a writer, you know."

"I do, and I wondered whether she has that fiery temper we always hear about with artists." Goddard says this with a smile, as if it's a grand joke.

"I wouldn't say she has a temper. But she is highly strung and prone to share her emotions and thoughts, sometimes with great feeling. As you hinted at, artists aren't known for their restraint."

Goddard leans toward Archie as if they are sharing an important secret. "The more witnesses I interview, I find that they share your description of Mrs. Christie's disposition. In my years of police work, in which I've encountered many who share your wife's high-strung character, I've seen that if those people become overwrought — for whatever reason — then they may take flight."

Archie holds his breath. Is this policeman actually offering a hypothesis for his wife's whereabouts? One that doesn't involve his malfeasance, as Kenward clearly believes?

"This is all hypothetically speaking, of course," Goddard adds.

Archie knows he has a very fine line to walk. Venturing a hopeful expression, he says, "You know, Superintendent Goddard, I do believe that you are the first policeman on this case holding that view. I think —"

The study door vibrates with a steady knock. "Colonel Christie, sir, there are two policemen here who say they must speak with Superintendent Goddard," Lilly calls out.

"Let them in," Archie calls back.

Two of Goddard's men, distinctive by their uniforms, enter the room. "It's a deluge, sir," the older-looking one reports.

"A weather report justifies the interruption of my meeting with Colonel Christie?"

Goddard asks, his anger barely contained. It is a different side to the amenable superintendent than he's presented thus far.

"Apologies for being vague, sir, but it's not that sort of deluge. Jim Barnes of *Daily News* has been covering Mrs. Christie's disappearance, and he's just offered one hundred pounds for information leading to the location of the colonel's wife."

"I see."

"In the two hours since the announcement was made, we've had nearly a dozen reports of sightings." The policeman checks his notepad and says, "We've got Ralph Brown of Battersea claiming to have seen Mrs. Christie on Albury Heath on Saturday morning walking about distracted. There's Mrs. Kitchings of Little London — that's near Newlands Corner — reporting that she saw a woman matching the newspaper photos of Mrs. Christie walking in a lane near her house around noon on Saturday. A railway porter named Mr. Fuett maintains that he was approached on Sunday at Milford station by a woman fitting Mrs. Christie's description. The list goes on, sir."

"It looks like we've got some claims to investigate in order to locate your wife, Colonel Christie. I apologize for having to end our discussion," Superintendent Goddard says as he rises. He then places his hand briefly on Archie's shoulder, saying, "I am certain we will find her."

CHAPTER TWENTY-FIVE:
THE MANUSCRIPT

February 15, 1922
Mount Nelson Hotel, Cape Town, South
  Africa

"Oh, you do shuffle the cards well, Mrs. Christie. Will you please sit with us and deal our hands?" Mrs. Hiam asked. What sounded like a request was actually more like a command, and she knew I had no choice but to obey. But now that Archie was sick in the hotel room again for an indeterminate period with who knows what ailment — likely his stomach — I had no choice. At least one Christie had to perform his or her designated duty lest we risk sanctioning by our mercurial leader, Major Belcher.

I had wanted to take advantage of this brief break in our itinerary to finish up my short story. Despite the overwhelming demands of the Empire Tour schedule — which traversed from South Africa to Australia to New Zealand to Hawaii and finally to Canada before returning home — I'd managed to meet my deadlines for the *Sketch* magazine. But my next due date was fast approaching and much work remained. My editor at the publication had commissioned twelve stories with Hercule Poirot at the center, and I enjoyed fleshing out this peculiar little detective, who'd sprung fully formed from my imagination like the goddess Athena who'd sprung from Zeus's skull grown and battle ready. Well, mystery ready anyway.

My book outline called to me as well. Our journey on the RMS *Kildonan Castle* from England to South Africa, where we kicked off the Empire Tour, had prompted an outpouring of notes on a setting for a new novel, as had the magnificent sites we'd seen since docking in South Africa. Still, nothing provided more inspiration than the tour's leader, Major Belcher. What he lacked in leadership and organizational abilities, he more than made up for in quirky qualities, which I could use for character material.

I was bursting to write. While traveling, I felt like a different person, in a different life. Shed of the daily responsibilities of normal existence — paying bills, doing chores, writing letters, managing a nurse and a maid, which was the bare minimum of staff, shopping at the market, mending clothes, and, most importantly, tending to Rosalind — I felt light and brimming with energy for creative endeavors. Entire scenes appeared in my mind fully formed, pulling me toward my hotel room and my typewriter, and I longed to deny Mrs. Hiam's request.

But that wasn't what I did. It wasn't what I said. Instead, as always, I did and said what duty demanded. Even if I had duties of my own from my profession, I knew those would not be considered equal to the duties emanating from my husband and his position. Suppressing any irritation I might feel at this disparity, I turned toward the ladies with a smile.

"Of course, Mrs. Hiam. It would be my pleasure to assist you ladies," I said. I wasn't certain I could withstand another steaming hot afternoon in the company of these dull, self-important ladies who spent most of their time complaining instead of admiring the views. Mrs. Hiam's favorite topics were — in no particular order — the oppressiveness of the heat, the overabundance of dust, the constant threat of malaria and sleeping sickness, the unpleasantly Dutch appearance of the South African houses, the unpalatability of the food, and the ceaseless buzz of mosquitos. She circled back to those subjects every day, much as she probably discussed the rain and tuberculosis at home, and I wondered why she'd bothered to travel so far from home if she desperately longed for England.

As I cut the deck and shuffled the cards, I made idle chatter with Mrs. Hiam, two other ladies staying at the hotel whose names escaped me, and Mrs. Belcher, who was my boss for all intents and purposes. Her husband, Major Belcher, was the assistant general manager of the 1924 Empire Exhibition, and this grand tour upon which we'd embarked was meant to promote the exhibition to the political leaders and key businessmen in the dominions of the English empire. When Archie came home from work last December with the news that his old Clifton instructor Major Belcher had invited him to join the Empire Tour as financial advisor, I was euphoric. Once I learned that I'd been invited and that the one-thousand-pound stipend Archie would earn for the trip would cover my expenses, that was. I dreamed that the trip might restore Archie's spirits — which constantly hovered between dejected and depressed over his prospects at his new firm, Goldstein's, and the propriety of some of the work undertaken by it — and that we'd finally be able to rekindle the passion of our earlier days. Perhaps, I thought, there might even be time and mental space left over for my creative endeavors to flourish. What I didn't understand then was that our main task on the Empire Tour would be to babysit the capricious, often explosive Major Belcher and to smooth over the ruffled feathers he left in his wake. I was often left wondering at what cost we paid for the privilege of this trip.

At the thought of the tour's cost, I was reminded of Rosalind. She'd looked so much tinier than two years old when I waved goodbye to her from the deck of the RMS *Kildonan Castle* on that frigid January morning, and I'd experienced an almost overwhelming pang of regret as she reached for me from the dock. But then Archie wrapped his arms around me, an implicit reminder of his admonition to make him my priority, and I knew I'd made the right decision. I could almost hear Mummy's voice in my head when I asked her advice — even more strident than usual — about the trip: *A wife's duty is to be with her husband, because her husband must come first, even before her children. If a wife leaves her husband alone for too long, she will lose*

201

him. But even though I knew Madge and Mummy would take good care of Rosalind, I constantly wondered whether I'd done the wrong thing by agreeing to leave my baby behind for a year.

"Mrs. Christie?"

I heard my name as if from a distance as I shuffled and reshuffled the cards, lost in my thoughts about the tour.

"Mrs. Christie," Mrs. Hiam said again, practically yelling this time. She felt comfortable taking extensive liberties in her treatment of me because she was Mrs. Belcher's closest friend and felt that she was my boss by proxy. "I believe the deck is thoroughly shuffled. You may stop and deal."

"My apologies, ladies," I said with a broad smile. "My thoughts had wandered to the intriguing exhibit we saw this afternoon at the Cape Town Museum. Wasn't the lecture about cave paintings and the evolution of early skulls simply fascinating?" I'd been captivated by the museum's collection of early skulls, from *Pithecanthropus* and beyond, with all the variations over time, particularly in the jaw and jaw angle, and I'd been dismayed to learn that early excavations had lost critical parts of the skulls in their haste to loosen the relics from the earth. It had been one of the most illuminat-

202

ing afternoons I'd ever experienced, making clear that mankind's evolution was very circuitous and not the linear path we'd once assumed. Perhaps this was mankind's fate — to learn that none of our paths were as straight as we believed they would be.

I received a chorus of "oh yeses," but my attempt to lead the ladies into a conversation revolving around culture petered out. It wasn't that the ladies on the tour were completely immune to the lure of ancient artifacts or unique cultural practices, but the moment they returned to the familiarity of the hotel or the ship, they also returned to the conversations and behaviors of home. In some ways, it was as if they never left their England.

I feigned interest for the tenth time that afternoon alone, even though I could practically faint from the heat and the exhaustion. The day's itinerary had been grueling in and of itself; after I'd spent a late night nursing Belcher's septic foot back to some semblance of mobility, a task assigned to me because of my work as a war nurse, we'd started the morning with a tour of a fruit farm after an early breakfast, then lunched with a local official, followed by the tour of the museum and a hike around nearby gardens. We now had this brief respite before a garden party at the archbishop's residence. The exuberance that Archie had begun to beg me to tamp down he now relied upon to maneuver both of us through these events. But it wasn't the schedule that exhausted me; it was the unrelenting banality of the people. It was the same reason I kept to myself and wrote stories instead of mingling with the other mothers and wives in my London neighborhood.

My eyes felt heavy, and I was in danger of drifting off when I spotted Archie walking into the lobby. My spirits lifted as I watched my handsome husband lope in my direction. He lifted his hand in a half wave, and I wondered if we might slip off for a bit of surfing.

We had just discovered the sport of surf bathing with planks and were hooked on it. Archie and I began surfing at Muizenberg, a picturesque bay bordered by mountains that plummeted directly into the sea, which was easily accessible from the tour hotel by a short train ride. When I first held the surfboard in my hands, the thin wood seemed flimsy, and I wondered how on earth it would support me in a lying position on the rocking waves, let alone standing. But over time and after I scraped my arms and legs several times upon the sandy shore, I got the hang of it, even more quickly than Archie in fact. By the end of our first afternoon surfing, I was riding the waves into the shore with relative ease. I remember grinning over at Archie, water dripping off my face, hair, and bathing costume, feeling alive and blissfully happy with the sport, and him returning my smile. The connection for which I'd longed seemed possible in that golden moment.

Keeping Archie's gaze, I mimed surfing and then gave him a quizzical expression. His face lit up, and he nodded at me. Making my excuses to the ladies, I began to rise from the card table when I spotted Belcher making a beeline for my husband. I held my breath as the changeable major — as wont to have a temper tantrum as to bestow an elaborate compliment — gesticulated wildly to Archie. My husband struggled to maintain his usually placid expression, and I thought that I might be able to rescue him from Belcher if I intervened immediately.

As I took my leave from the ladies and turned away from the card table, I heard my name. It was Mrs. Hiam again.

"Oh, Mrs. Christie, my ivory evening dress will certainly need a press before tonight's dinner. Oh, how the heat wilts my silks!" she announced, then glanced around the table to ensure she received the tittering she sought. "You will help me with that, won't you?"

Glancing across the room at Archie, I saw that he was helpless as well; Belcher had conscripted him for some task. We gave each other a feeble smile, and I knew we'd find time to head to Muizenberg again. I knew that duty would call us again and again on the Empire Tour, but I felt confident that we'd string these brilliant times together so we'd return home stronger than before.

CHAPTER TWENTY-SIX:
DAY FIVE AFTER
THE DISAPPEARANCE

Wednesday, December 8, 1926
Styles, Sunningdale, England, and the Rio
Tinto Company Building, London, England

Tuesday night is not kind to Archie. The evening started with private police reports and public newspaper articles on the slew of purported sightings. Although the reward certainly incentivized most of the reports — the spurious and the earnest claims alike — the revelation that some reporters actually paid some citizens to file fake claims so they'd have fresh sensational articles has astonished even the crime-hardened police. The night continued with the newspapers releasing details about his wife's letter to his brother, homing in on Agatha's reference to feeling ill: what, the reporters had posited, or who could have caused Mrs. Christie to be so ill that she'd flee? Archie worries that this inquiry will lead them back to him.

His apprehension becomes reality. Reporters and readers cast about for a source of Agatha's illness, and by Wednesday morning, their eyes land on Archie. He's certain that suggestions and innuendos Kenward has been feeding to the press — or so he believes — have fanned these flames. Overnight, he is transformed from handsome war hero in an idyllic marriage to suspicious catalyst for his wife's flight.

Kenward and Goddard are overwhelmed with the sighting accounts, and their collective forces are tasked with interviewing the involved citizens. As a result, the official search is halted for the day, even though civilians still prowl the fields and woods for clues. Despite experiencing relief at the shift in focus, Archie feels aimless after Charlotte and the police escort take Rosalind to school. He decides on a dose of normalcy and heads to his office in the Delage.

As he drives toward London, he's tempted to swerve off course to see Sam James or Nancy; to bolster their spirits, he rationalizes to himself. But then he realizes the true reason he wants to see them is to quell his own nerves as well as his fears about what they might have said to the authorities. Even though they'd all agreed to temporarily halt communication with one another, he finds himself veering toward the exit to Hurtmore

Cottage first and then to the home Nancy shares with her parents. Each time, just as he's about to make the turn, he stops himself.

Archie congratulates himself for having made the correct decision a few minutes later when he notices a plain gray Morris following his route into the city. Has the car been there the entire time but he too enmeshed in his own thoughts to notice? Or has he become paranoid? Taking an earlier exit to London than usual, he watches to see if the automobile mimics his quick turn. It does. As he weaves in and out of traffic and traverses down side streets to reach his office building, the Morris never loses sight of him. He begins to feel irritated at Kenward, who undoubtedly ordered this surveillance, but he tells himself not to worry, that protocol must demand it regardless of how the constable perceives him.

Instead of focusing on Kenward's perception of him, he allows London to envelop him, with its bustle of cars and trucks and busy people. The hubbub heartens him. The entirety of London is not focused upon the disappearance of his wife. Life proceeds in the capital. He wants to slide into its bustling masses and become anonymous.

Almost feeling like himself, he parks the

car alongside Broad Street. Walking to the Rio Tinto Company building, where his office is located, he notices that the men in the car tailing him have exited their vehicle and walk in his wake. It seems that the trilby-wearing detectives plan on keeping an eye on him while he works. *Well, let them,* he thinks. *They can stand outside in the cold while I take my time in the office.* There will be nothing to see but the daily doings of work.

He strolls into the lobby as if it is any other day. As he waits for the elevator, he imagines a productive day ahead in his office at Austral Limited, where he serves on the board of directors. He nearly bristles with excitement at the prospect of routine paperwork and office meetings. Orderly, ordinary life.

The elevator announces its arrival with a ding. Archie reaches out to slide open the cage to the interior when he realizes another man is behind him. Entering, he presses the sixth floor button and then moves to the back of the elevator to allow the man access. Only when the man faces him does he realize that it is Sebastian Earl, who sits in the office next to his.

"Morning, Sebastian," he says by way of the usual greeting.

"Morning, Archie." Sebastian pauses, and as he visibly hesitates, the elevator is filled with an awkward silence. "I'm so sorry about . . . Well, you know."

How should Archie respond? He hasn't really prepared himself for dealing with Agatha at work. But it isn't as if his wife's *death* has been reported, so why is he receiving condolences already? Still, he's sure that Sebastian means well, so he settles on a simple thanks.

Sebastian continues, "I must say, I am surprised to see you."

Archie is a little taken aback. He didn't expect anyone to directly address his wife's disappearance and his role in the search for her. He anticipated oblique stares and some whispering, of course, but nothing quite so head-on. "I see," he says, unsure what else to utter.

"I mean, your wife is missing. I assumed you'd be out scouting for her alongside the police and all those volunteers I saw in the paper. That's all." Sebastian scrambles to avoid any offense from his statements.

Archie stares up at the slow-moving metal hand indicating the floor reached by the elevator; the sixth floor cannot arrive quickly enough. This questioning is intolerable, and he feels he cannot get a full breath in this minuscule elevator. "I did spend my weekend doing exactly that."

"But she hasn't been found yet. Surely, your Austral work can wait? No one would hold it against you."

Why is Sebastian continuing on with this line of questioning? All Archie wants is a normal day at the office, away from the search and speculation about Agatha's disappearance, and the letter guiding his behavior did not prohibit it. Anger and fear surge through him in equal measure, and he blurts out, "I don't think the police really want me at the search."

"Why ever not?" Sebastian asks, all innocence, although Archie suspects this entire line of questioning stems from his morning review of the very suspicious *Mail* and *Express*.

"They think I murdered my wife." Archie rushes to add, "Which I obviously did not."

"Obviously," Sebastian is quick to reply.

Finally, the elevator stops at the sixth floor, and Archie lunges for the door, slides it open, and steps out without another word to his coworker. Any momentary elation he'd experienced in the lobby has disappeared, and he strides down the hallway to his office, hoping that he does not encounter a single person en route. When he finally arrives at his office door, he rushes in, closing it behind him. Safe for a brief moment.

But how long can that last?

"Have you seen this?" asks Clive Baillieu, his friend and boss, after he's spent three largely uninterrupted, glorious hours doing his regular work. Who would have thought paperwork could be so satisfying? Clive tosses a paper across Archie's desk.

"No," Archie answers, grabbing the afternoon edition of the *Daily Mail* before it slides off his desk. Clive is the only person in the Austral offices with whom Archie has talked today, and sensing his need for normalcy, Clive hasn't mentioned his wife, instead focusing on Austral business. "What is it?"

Glancing down at the headlines, he has his answer: *Missing Novelist's Husband on Golf Weekend at Hurtmore Cottage on Fateful Night.* By God, the information he has prayed would stay quiet has become public. His fears have become real. Some of them anyway.

How much more do the reporters know? Scanning the article, he sees reference to the Jameses in the first paragraph, followed by a quote from Sam. Good chap that Sam is, he defends Archie vigorously and describes their "innocent" golf foursome. But when Archie reads the paragraph closely, he notices that the quote was given today — which means that the reporters have already descended upon Hurtmore Cottage. Thank God he didn't stop by their house on the way to work; he could imagine the press reaction. Oh, the debt he owes the Jameses.

It isn't until two paragraphs later that he sees Nancy mentioned. He freezes at the sight of her name. He almost cannot continue but forces himself: *The mysterious fourth for the golf weekend was Miss Nancy Neele. The clerk for the Imperial Continental Gas Association hails from Rickmansworth in Hertfordshire where she lives with her parents. She could not be reached for comment.* Archie rereads the sentences, finding them to be less damning than he'd anticipated. But then he catches the last sentence of the article, one that references his wife's mysterious letter to Campbell: *Is Miss Neele the "illness" that caused Mrs. Christie to flee — or worse?*

Archie stands up so abruptly that his desk chair clatters to the floor. Oh my God, what is he going to do? One of his greatest dreads has come to pass.

"Sorry, Archie, I thought you'd rather hear about it from me than some bloke on the street," Clive says apologetically. "And I

214

hate to add salt in the wound and all that, but I think it's best to stay home until this all blows over. We can't have the police and reporters gathering outside the office doors, can we?"

Archie nods, only half hearing Clive's instruction. The banishment from his office might have stung in another set of circumstances, but at the moment, it hardly matters. If the police and the public continue to believe that he is guilty of his wife's disappearance, his entire reputation and livelihood are at stake. Not to mention that of Nancy.

Wordlessly, he begins packing his bag, prompting Clive to ask, "Are you all right, old fellow? I hope you're not sore. Duty and all that."

"No hard feelings. I understand," Archie tells Clive as he walks out of his office, and he means it. He would have done the same thing.

Now he must undertake an odious task for a private man. Archie must face the public and tell his story or forsake his reputation forever. But if he strays beyond the limitations of the letter, the same outcome awaits him. Any misstep will lead him down the same damnable path.

CHAPTER TWENTY-SEVEN:
THE MANUSCRIPT

May 20, 1923
London, England

"Rosalind, come to Mama," I called out to my daughter as I stepped out of my study and into the garden.

The day was bright, the sky a vivid, almost unreal blue. It was as if the weather had tired of being English and was trying on Italian citizenship for size, or perhaps Australian. I squinted into the sunlight; I'd spent the past few hours much as I had the past few months, behind my typewriter, my mind slipping in and out of the world of my new book, *The Man in the Brown Suit.* The Empire Tour had inspired the setting and characters for this mystery, and I'd itched to write the story that had grown in my mind since we boarded the ship to South Africa. As I dove into the narrative, I'd enjoyed fashioning a puzzle that drew on many of my recent experiences — the long voyage from England to South Africa, including my seasickness and the deck games once that subsided, the landscape and culture of South Africa, the sight of Table Mountain in Cape Town once we'd made land, the personality of Major Belcher and his secretary, Mr. Bates, which I'd fictionalized in the characters of Sir Eustace Pedler and his secretary, Guy Pagett, even the name of the ship on which the characters traveled, the *Kilmorden Castle,* was a play on our ship, the *Kildonan Castle.* Most of all, perhaps, I'd adored losing myself in the main character, the intrepid Anne Beddingfeld, the sort of young woman I might have been, naturally plucky and adventuresome but who, in the end, turned out more like myself, a woman who makes sacrifices for the man she loves.

Finally, my eyes adjusted, and I made sense of the tiny green space that constituted the garden behind our London flat. Rosalind sat on the lawn, rolling a red ball around with her new nurse, whom we called Cuckoo. Mummy had been forced to hire this vastly inferior nurse while we were away when she had a falling out with Rosalind's prior governess, the indomitable Jessie Swannell. Even though I'd heard Mummy's tale a hundred times, I still couldn't imagine what Jessie could have done to infuriate her; I chalked up the entire affair to the fraying of her nerves from Monty's troubling behavior. On his return to England, he'd plunged right back into his old tricks of scheming and overspending.

The sunlight caught Rosalind's hair, and although it was usually dark and flat, the strands began to glimmer in the unexpected afternoon sunlight as she played. *If only there were a photographer here, what a picture she would make,* I thought to myself. I was drawn to my daughter, but instead of walking to her side, I called to her again. I needed to see what she would do.

Rosalind didn't move. Cuckoo looked up at me and whispered something inaudible into my daughter's ear. As I watched the back of her small head shake from side to side, I understood that Rosalind had emphatically declined Cuckoo's suggestion. And without being told, I knew precisely what that suggestion was: "Go to your mama."

It had been six months since we returned from the Empire Tour, and my daughter still hadn't forgiven me.

Tears began to well up in my eyes, and I turned away from Rosalind and Cuckoo. As irritating as Cuckoo could be — with her infuriating habit of standing outside my study door and, in full voice, saying aloud to Rosalind things she didn't have the nerve to say to me directly — I appreciated her efforts at reestablishing the bond between me and my daughter. But I couldn't risk losing my authority with her by allowing her to see me cry.

As I stepped back into the flat, I heard the clatter of footsteps in the front hall. Quickly, I wiped away the single tear that had trickled down my face, pinched my cheeks and bit my lips to give them color, and painted on a bright smile to greet Archie.

A squeal broke out behind me, and before I could reach the front hall, Rosalind raced past me toward her father. "Papa, Papa," she cried out.

I froze. Why had he been forgiven our long absence but not me?

I listened as father and daughter greeted each other, delighted with their small reunion. How strange, it struck me, that Archie hadn't wanted this child, and yet their bond was the stronger one. So interested were they in each other that they were oblivious to my presence. I was an outsider in my own home, and no one was waiting in the wings to invite me in.

But I couldn't dwell upon this exclusion,

and in fact, I understood that I must insert myself into their conversation, invited or not. "Darling, how was your day?" I greeted my husband with a warm embrace, as if nothing upsetting had just transpired. Today was a day to focus on Archie's triumph — his new job.

Rosalind wiggled her fingers away from his hand, and the beaming expression faded from Archie's handsome face. His brows knitted together, casting a shadow over his eyes. He sighed instead of answering, and Rosalind ran away from us back toward Cuckoo in the garden.

"Let me get you a drink," I babbled into the silence. I practically ran into the parlor, secured a glass, and poured Archie a small whisky. Racing back to his side, I said, "Here, this should help."

"Is it really so dire as that?" He shook his head at my efforts. "Do I look that desperate?"

"No, no," I hastened to assure him, although he did look rather terrible. "That's not what I meant at all. It's just your first day in a new position, and, and —" I struggled to think of another reason for my reaction. "I thought we'd have a toast to your job."

He drank down his whisky without even

touching his glass to mine. "I'm not certain that this role is worthy of a toast, Agatha," he finally said.

Oh no, I thought, feeling heartsick. This position was meant to solve the problems that had plagued us since our return from the Empire Tour, when Archie had learned that Goldstein's no longer had employment for him, which was a bit of a surprise, as the tour itself had been a government project and we'd assumed that Goldstein's would treat him kindly as a result. I'd hoped that this new job, long sought after and won only after six months of humiliating interviews, would restore my husband from his depression and his anger, which he usually exacted upon me. How many nights had I refused to leave his side as he lay despondent in our bed or on the sofa, even though he'd muttered over and over that I was of no use to him? While I wondered where the man I'd married — the man who'd resurfaced on our Empire Tour trip — had gone.

And what had happened to his feelings for me? The more downhearted he became, the more I seemed to irritate him rather than comfort him. My voice, my words, my manner, my appearance, my weight, everything seemed designed for one purpose — to vex Archie. I wondered how the qualities that once captivated him now exasperated him, and I began to think that his feelings stemmed more from the fact that I saw him at his very lowest — both emotionally and financially — than actual dislike. *No man liked to be seen at his weakest,* Mummy was known to say. I was willing to give him the benefit of the doubt. After all, wasn't that what good wives did?

"What do you mean, dearest?" I said, keeping my tone as bright as I could muster.

"I'm not sure this concern is engaged in entirely legal work," he answered, raking his fingers through his hair. "Strictly speaking."

"Are you certain?" I asked, pouring him another whisky. Anything to keep his mood from slipping further.

Knocking back the drink, he walked away from me toward the window, leaving my question unanswered. *How had things come to this point?* I wondered. Had Archie and I really stood on those surfing boards atop the Pacific Ocean and rode the turquoise waves all the way to the sandy Hawaiian shore? Had we really embraced, euphoric over our triumph, as water dripped from our bathing costumes and the hot sun beat down on our burnt faces? I might not be able to reclaim those precious moments, but I had to do whatever I could to stave off further disaster.

"Perhaps, in time, you will learn that the work is more legitimate than it seems on your first day," I said into the void left by his veritable absence. He did not reply, and I knew better than to expect one.

I left him to his thoughts and another whisky and hurried to the kitchen to finish the preparations for supper. We could no longer afford help, aside from Cuckoo, whom I could not dismiss without abandoning all hope of an income from my writing, so I cleaned, cooked, shopped, and undertook the washing. Ashfield and Mummy had done little in the way of preparing me for these tasks, and each night, I prayed for no catastrophe. Order and order alone might restore Archie's spirits, and that order was my job.

China laid out on linen, silver gleaming in the low candlelight, a presentable roast chicken at the table's center, I sat across from Archie, momentarily pleased with my handiwork. Would tonight's dinner offering suffice? It was the question I had asked myself every night since we returned to London. I watched expectantly as he cut into a serving of the chicken and placed a bite in his mouth. While he chewed the meat, his mouth slowed, and I realized that

I'd failed at yet another meal.

"How did you find the people at work?" I asked, hoping to prompt him to speak. If I couldn't mention the work, maybe I could talk about his colleagues. Perhaps they were a shade better than the work itself.

"Not much improvement there," he answered briskly, making clear that additional questions on the topic of his employment would be unwelcome. And then he settled into a silence, interrupted only by the sound of his silverware scraping the china and his chewing.

I didn't think I could face another meal in silence; we'd had so many since we settled into the London flat we'd found after returning from the Empire Tour. Short of dancing on the dining room table, I'd run out of ways to fill the quiet, so I decided to take a risk and broach a topic Archie typically didn't welcome — my writing. On occasion, when it appeared as though Archie might be receptive, I raised my latest book and the attendant business matters over our evening dinner, although I was never entirely certain he listened or remembered.

"Well, I received some good news today," I announced, making certain to keep my voice low at first. Archie loathed jarring sounds.

Archie glanced up from his plate, but that was the extent of it. Pretending that he'd inquired after my news, I continued, "Well, after an exchange of letters and two meetings, Mr. Edmund Cork of the Hughes Massie literary agency officially agreed to take me on as a client earlier this week." When he didn't respond, I prompted him to answer. I wanted to make certain he understood the magnitude of my news. "Do you remember me mentioning Mr. Cork a few weeks ago?"

Archie half nodded, which was more than the usual encouragement, and I chose to interpret it as a sign that he recalled the earlier conversation. I continued, "Having Mr. Cork as an agent means that he's helped extricate me from that onerous contract with my publisher, the Bodley Head. In the week since he's taken me on as a client, his letters to the Bodley Head have led to an understanding that the contract will end once I deliver one final book — instead of the three they were pushing for. Isn't that wonderful?"

I didn't wait for Archie to respond; I knew the most I could expect was a grunt of acknowledgment. I hoped for more reaction with my big development. "That isn't even the best news, Archie. Given that Mr. Cork secured a clear end date for the termination of my contract with the Bodley Head, he was able to informally shop my recent project, *The Man in the Brown Suit.* You know, the one that's based on our trip?"

I received another half nod. I'd certainly described the setting and the plot of the mystery enough. "Well," I said, pausing for effect, "the *Evening News* has made a sizable offer for the serialization of *The Man in the Brown Suit* today. Five hundred pounds, if you can believe it. I'm hoping the money will come in handy." I couldn't contain my excitement over this potential contribution to our dwindling resources and our mounting household expenses. The development had temporarily released me from the worry that we'd end up near penniless like my own mother after my father squandered the once-plentiful Miller fortune, and I assumed Archie would feel the same relief. I hoped to lift the burden he shouldered, if only a little.

The reaction I received was not the one I'd expected.

"You mean because I haven't been able to help with the finances as of late?" he asked rhetorically, no joy in his voice, just ice. He was incredibly sensitive to this topic, despite the fact that I never mentioned the long months he hadn't worked and the consequent burden on our finances. The only thing he could hear in my news was judgment.

I should have been more careful. I should have slipped the money into our bank account without a word. Why had I thought he might change?

"That's not what I meant at all, Archie. I've just felt so useless since we returned home, and I wanted to take some pressure off you," I rushed to say.

"Do you really think one book — one payment — can restore our position, Agatha? Somehow make up for our year-long holiday? We have much to do to atone for our self-indulgence."

CHAPTER TWENTY-EIGHT:
DAY SIX AFTER
THE DISAPPEARANCE

Thursday, December 9, 1926
Styles, Sunningdale, England

"Do you mind repeating your statement, Colonel Christie? I want to make absolutely certain that I copy it down verbatim."

"Not at all," Archie tells the reporter.

The young fellow from the *Daily Mail,* Jim Barnes, is not what he expected. He planned on having a cautious conversation with the reporter — outside the purview of the police, of course — to ensure that his position makes the papers once and for all. He thought he'd lay out his general perspective of the events so the public could see his reasonable nature, perhaps even hinting that whatever the police maintained, Agatha's disappearance is, in part, her choice. In this way, he hoped to soften public perception of him while still staying within the strict parameters of the letter. If he has to advance these ideas defensively while sidestepping any traps laid for him — a likelihood given the press's treatment of him this far — then so be it.

But when he meets the affable, civilized chap from the *Daily Mail,* he turns out to be quite a different sort of fellow than the riffraff who stake out Styles morning, noon, and night. Well-spoken and immaculately dressed, the chap seems familiar, not unlike his fellow members at Sunningdale golf club. Quite against his inclination and planning, he takes to the fellow the moment they sit down in the forgettable little pub. *Finally,* he thinks, *I've encountered a sympathetic soul.* And he lets down his guard.

"I'm happy to do so." Lifting up the stationery upon which he's written a formal statement for the press, he sets forth his prepared position: that he's terribly worried about his wife, that she has been suffering from nerves as of late, that they often made separate weekend plans according to their interests, which he planned to keep private, and that he's doing all he can to aid the police investigation.

"Thank you, Colonel Christie. Very well said," Jim says as he finishes scribbling on his notepaper. "Are you ready for a few questions?"

"Of course. There has been a bloody awful lot of unfavorable coverage about me and my friends in the papers, and I look forward to the opportunity to present my truth."

"That's my hope as well. Let's begin." The young man smiles and checks his notes. "What are the possible explanations for your wife's disappearance as you and the police see it?"

"There could be three possible explanations for her disappearance: it could be voluntary, it could stem from loss of memory, and hopefully not, but it could be the result of suicide. My instinct tells me it is one of the first two. I definitely don't believe it is a matter of suicide. It is my understanding that if someone is considering ending his or her life, he or she would threaten it at some point in time — which she never did. Moreover, would a person planning on ending their life drive miles away, remove a heavy coat, and then walk off into the blue before doing so? I don't think so; it simply doesn't make sense. Anyway, if my wife had ever considered suicide, my guess is that she would have planned on poison. Given her years as a wartime nurse and working in a dispensary, she was very knowledgeable in the area of poisons and often used them in her stories. So that would have been the method she'd select, rather than some mysterious suicide in a remote wooded area, but still, I don't think that's what happened." He was rambling a bit, but there you had it.

"So you are more inclined to believe Mrs. Christie's disappearance stems from a voluntary act or her loss of memory?"

Archie thinks back on the letter and answers, "Indeed, and I lean heavily toward loss of memory."

"Can you tell me a bit more about the day she disappeared?"

"I've gone over all this with the police time and time again, but I'll do so again here for your edification. I left home for work at 9:15 a.m. in the ordinary way, and that was the last time I saw my wife. I knew she'd arranged to go to Yorkshire for the weekend, and that was all I knew about her plans when I left for work on Friday. I have since learned that she went motoring in the morning and then lunched alone. In the afternoon, she took our daughter to visit my mother at Dorking. She returned here in time for dinner, which she took alone." Archie grows quiet. Should he broach the rest of the day?

Jim asks, "Do you know what transpired then?"

231

He's uncertain how to best articulate his position on what occurred next. "I don't know for certain what happened after that, as we were in different locations. I can only guess that she must have worked herself into such a nervous state — for some reason not known to me — and couldn't settle down enough to read or write. That has certainly happened to me in the past, and when it does, I head out for a rambling walk to clear my mind and calm my nerves. But my wife isn't much of a walker, and when she wants to clear her mind, she goes out for a drive."

"Why the suitcase then?"

"Well, she had intended on going to Yorkshire, so perhaps she planned to head there after her drive." Archie knows this fact doesn't fit precisely into his narrative, but it's the best he can do.

"Did she take any money with her? That might be an indicator of the disappearance being planned or prompted by injury or loss of memory instead?"

"Neither of her bank accounts — the one at Sunningdale for household purposes, nor the one at Dorking for private purposes — has been drawn upon before or after her disappearance, which suggests this wasn't planned. In fact, both of her checkbooks are still at home."

"In your view, the facts seem to support either a voluntary departure or a loss of memory?"

"I think I've been clear that I believe loss of memory is in play here."

"But just for argument's sake, if her departure was voluntary, do you have any idea what prompted it?" He does not meet Archie's gaze but keeps his eyes fixed on his list of questions.

Archie's hackles begin to rise. So this is where the chap was headed all along. How stupid he'd been to think this reporter might be more sympathetically inclined. They are all alike after all in their quest for the incendiary. But he refuses to let his mounting anger throw him from his course.

Careful to use a firm, even tone, Archie says, "I cannot fathom what would have prompted a voluntary departure. Contrary to newspaper reports, we did not have an argument or tiff of any sort the Friday morning before her disappearance, and she had been perfectly well in the months leading up to it, although she did lose her beloved mother recently, of course. In response to other salacious rumors I've seen in the press, she knew where I was going away for the weekend and who would be present. She knew and liked all my friends, and at no time did she indicate displeasure. The gossip and rumormongering that goes on in the papers is reprehensible and will not help me find my wife. And that is my objective."

"Again only for the sake of discussion, if she has voluntarily left, do you have any idea where she might be now?"

"If I knew, I would have rushed there straightaway several days ago. But I don't. The only hint we've received is from a rather curious letter she sent to my brother about retreating to a spa. I gather that the members of the press have taken it upon themselves to investigate all the spas and hotels in the region mentioned and found nothing." He finishes, "So you see, her disappearance remains a mystery. But I will do whatever it takes to find her."

CHAPTER TWENTY-NINE:
THE MANUSCRIPT

March 20, 1924, to December 10, 1925
London, England, and Surrey, England

I took Archie at his word. If more work was needed to atone for the selfishness of our Empire Tour year, then I would do that work. I finished *The Man in the Brown Suit* and submitted it for publication; I signed a three-book contract with Collins for an advance of two hundred pounds per book and improved royalties; I delivered my final book under the Bodley Head contract, *The Secret of Chimneys;* I wrote lucrative stories for magazines: *Sketch, Grand, Novel, Flynn's Weekly,* and *Royal.* I was determined to care for my family financially, to ensure our home was run efficiently and with taste, to limit our social calendar so Archie could have the quiet routines he preferred, and to provide proper care for Rosalind. Whatever formula Archie required for the success of our marriage, whatever alterations to my demeanor, whatever elixir that would bring back the Archie I once knew — the man I married as he marched off to the Great War, the man who emerged in glimpses on the Empire Tour — I would undertake. While I enjoyed, of course, the mounting popularity of my books and short stories, my primary focus in writing remained the happiness of my husband and daughter.

This was what I told myself as I plowed through stories, puzzling through them as I organized the meals and shopping schedule, met with the housekeeper we were finally able to afford, oversaw Cuckoo's schedule and Rosalind's schooling. But was this a lie? That everything I did, I did for Archie? In truth, the only time I felt like myself was when I was writing. No matter how I tried to anticipate his needs, I couldn't please Archie, and all the qualities he used to adore — my spontaneity, my love of drama and adventure, and my desire to discuss feelings and events with him — now irritated him. But why was Archie frustrated so often? Was it that he wasn't the only center of attention? That I was busy with my career? It didn't seem to matter that I was doing it for our family. My efforts to connect with Rosalind not only failed but angered Archie, time away from him and all that. But when I closed the door to my study and disappeared into the worlds of my stories, where I had complete control as I invented puzzles that the readers couldn't unpuzzle, as Madge had once challenged me to do, I delighted in the order I created and thrilled with the surge in my own power. And I suddenly understood my husband's craving for order and control.

But all the understanding in the world and all my hard work did not bring us closer. While driving through the countryside in my gray Morris Cowley — my one indulgence with my income from my first novel, *The Mysterious Affair at Styles* — I had an epiphany. What Archie and I needed to bond us back together was a shared activity, a beloved hobby much like surfing had been on the Empire Tour. My lack of athleticism provided an impediment to several options, but then I remembered lazy summer afternoons in Torquay playing golf with Reggie and East Croydon golf weekends early in our marriage. *Yes, golf was the ticket,* I told myself.

"What about this house?" I asked with a twirl of my overcoat. Did I see a hint of a smile on his face? *How long has it been since he found me engaging?* I wondered. These past months on any golf course nearby London where we could get a tee time had been a labor for me as I wasn't a natural sportswoman, and while I'd relished every moment with my husband, I wasn't certain he felt the same. While the hours chasing after tiny white balls on the rolling greens — and oftentimes, in my case, amid the high grasses — hadn't exactly brought the same squeals of delight as surfing, they had become a weekend routine we both looked forward to. So much so that Archie had suggested we consider moving from London to a home commutable to the city but nearby his favorite course, Sunningdale, and we'd spent several weekends examining houses to let. To me, the Surrey-Berkshire area didn't have the same allure as the sparkling Devon seaside of my youth — it felt too contrived and chock-full of business types whose sole focus was chasing money — but it was more compatible with Archie's job.

We wandered through the manicured yew hedges bordering the available property, past two well-planned ponds, until we reached two orchestrated flower beds sweeping out in either direction, although the blooms lay dormant for the winter season. These well-tended gardens belonged to a mock Tudor with gables springing up in every direction like a child's uncombed hair, with leaded windows that were small and mean, almost like squinting eyes. The house and its grounds were relatively new but built with a veneer of oldness, as if a newly wealthy city person had constructed their notion of a well-established country home. But I'd grown up in and around the world of authentic country life, where villas and their gardens sprang up organically in the Devon hills. To me, this house and the golf club life around which it revolved like a miniature solar system felt forced, even false, and the house's dark interiors reflected the darkness within this seemingly bright community. But I knew Archie wouldn't see it that way; in fact, for him, this was stepping into a world he'd always longed for but could never find. And his happiness was paramount.

"It is wonderfully close to the golf club." His eyes brightened a bit at the thought of proximity to the course. Did I even see them twinkle? "More so than the others we looked at. We could even walk to the course with our clubs from this house."

I smiled at him from the shade of my hat brim, and he grabbed me by the shoulders and drew me close. My heart raced at this unusual display of emotion.

"I think this is the one," he whispered into my ear. "We might build a lovely life for ourselves here, Agatha."

"Really?" I asked, lifting my face to his. Had I finally gotten something right? I said a silent prayer that this move and long weekends spent golfing might return the original Archie to me. The recent change of jobs to the more reputable Austral Limited, facilitated by Archie's friend Clive Baillieu, had boosted his mood a touch, but the depressive state still settled upon him with regularity.

"Really," he assured me. Then, to my great astonishment, a mischievous glint surfaced in his eyes, a madcap expression I hadn't seen since he returned from the war. "I'd need my own car."

"Oh, I think that would be brilliant, Archie. You know how I've adored motoring about in my Morris Cowley. Nothing beats the feel of the wind in your hair as you zoom through the countryside with utter freedom of movement." I remembered well the first time I got behind the wheel of my vehicle and realized that I was no longer limited by bus schedules and times or the distance walking could take me. "Have you an idea about what sort of car you might get?"

"I was thinking of a sporty little Delage."

"That's a fine idea, Archie."

He squeezed my hand. "Shall I put an offer on the house? We'll have to change the name, of course. Yew Lodge is perfectly awful. Sounds a bit like a disease."

I giggled. I couldn't even think of the last time Archie had ventured a joke. "I have a mad idea."

"What's that?"

"What if we named it after the country house in my first book. Styles."

He paused, and I suddenly worried that I'd ruined this perfect moment by referring to my work. Instead, he smiled. Then, stooping down, he kissed me on the cheek, and my heart soared.

Finally, he spoke. "Styles it is."

CHAPTER THIRTY:
DAY SIX AFTER
THE DISAPPEARANCE

Thursday, December 9, 1926
Styles, Sunningdale, England

The day passes with excruciating slowness. Police officers filter in and out of his study, reviewing the latest sightings. If the reports are to be believed, Agatha has been traversing the length of England, with stops at nearly every village along several train lines. Yet for all her public sightings, she remains elusive to those hunting for her.

His every move within Styles is monitored and recorded by a pair of junior policemen, even trips to the bathroom. He can no longer pretend, even to himself, that he isn't a primary suspect in the investigation, if not *the* primary one. He can only be thankful that he managed his interview with the *Daily Mail* without interference from all this constant surveillance. Perhaps it will sway public and private opinion alike.

He is at loose ends. He should probably

call Agatha's sister, Madge, to give her an update, as he has promised to do. But he cannot stomach the thought of talking to the condescending, judgmental Madge, and he shudders to think what he might let slip if anger took hold of him. *No,* he thinks, *I'll wait until she calls me and suffer her fury.*

As he watches the mantelpiece clock tick slowly and smokes a steady stream of cigarettes, he hears the front door slam, awakening him from his thoughts. Hearing Charlotte and Rosalind rustling about in the front hallway, he walks out to greet them. He could use a lift in spirits, and his daughter can usually make him smile. They share a quiet, dry sense of humor, a quality that sets them apart from the ebullient, overly emotional Agatha.

When he walks into the front hallway, Rosalind's back is to him. Charlotte's arms are enveloped around his little girl, and the nanny is whispering words in his daughter's ear. He hears a sniffle.

"Is everything all right, Rosalind?" he calls out. They turn toward him in unison, startled at his appearance. Rosalind's cheeks are wet with tears, and he asks, "What is it, darling?"

Charlotte usually allows the articulate Rosalind to answer his questions, unlike many nannies who shush their charges in the presence of parents. But not today. Today, Charlotte answers for Rosalind. "It's nothing, sir. Just a bit of childish nonsense at school." Her Scottish accent is thick, which happens in moments of high stress.

What is she hiding? What does she know?

"They said Mama was dead," Rosalind blurts out.

"Dead?" He feels like screaming at the thought that even school-children are speculating about the fate of his wife, but instead he shakes his head as if the very notion is ridiculous. "Well, you and I know that's simply preposterous, don't we?"

She sniffles again and stares into his eyes, seeking the truth. "Do we?"

Rosalind's eyes unsettle him, and he wonders if Charlotte has told her something. He's been relying on Charlotte's discretion in the face of relentless police inquiry until now, but can her circumspection continue to hold, particularly given that she knows Agatha left him a letter? This is a question he cannot ask. Certainly the presence of her sister Mary has served as a support and a distraction for her and Rosalind, as he has hoped, but how long can that last?

He turns his attention back to Rosalind's question. "Of course, darling. Mama has gone away to work on one of her books. She's just forgotten to tell us where that is. That's why all these police are about. They're trying to help us find her."

With her bare hand, she wipes under her eyes and under her nose, and Archie recoils. Why isn't Charlotte ready with a handkerchief? And more instructive with the manners? Isn't that her job? He opens his mouth to offer a critique but shuts it. He needs Charlotte's allegiance.

"So you didn't kill Mama?" she asks him, her blue eyes boring into his.

Charlotte's hand flies to her mouth, and Archie reels at Rosalind's words. Before he can stop himself, he screams, "Where did you hear that?" His tone is irate, and he chastises himself for his lack of control. How will Charlotte react to his fury? Hasn't his daughter suffered enough without being spoken to in that manner? Won't she be enduring even more in the days to come? In most ways, it really doesn't matter where she heard this awful information; it could have come from anywhere.

Rosalind runs behind Charlotte's legs, cowering in fright. "The children at school were chanting it, Papa. Over and over and over," she squeaks, burying her face in the nanny's back. Charlotte's expression is part apology and part horror.

No one speaks. Not even Rosalind, who is too terrified to cry. Archie knows he should embrace and comfort his daughter, but he can't. It seems as though some invisible breach has been crossed, and they now tread on unfamiliar ground.

Archie feels unbalanced, as though he's stepped off a ship after a long, rocky sea voyage. Steadying himself with the wall, he walks back into his study, his only place of refuge. Or so he thought until now. Styles is no longer his home — an orderly place where he can retire in peace after the onslaught of the unpredictable world of business — but a prison from which he cannot escape.

CHAPTER THIRTY-ONE:
THE MANUSCRIPT

April 5, 1926
Styles, Sunningdale, England

"Carlo!" I called out to Charlotte Fisher, whom we'd employed to look after Rosalind and also to serve as my secretary. The arrangement worked out well, as Rosalind attended the Oakfield school in Sunningdale, leaving Carlo, as Rosalind had taken to calling Charlotte, largely free during the day to assist me. When Rosalind returned from school, Carlo tended to her so I could finish my work and focus on Archie. Her no-nonsense Scottish demeanor and fierce intellect combined with her patience and humor to make her excellent in both roles, a far cry from the irritating Cuckoo, whom I couldn't wait to let go.

While I waited, I returned to my typewriter. Deep in the final proofread of my latest book, slated for a May publication, I was pleased with the device I'd chosen for

The Murder of Roger Ackroyd. In this story, I'd taken the challenge Madge gave me all those years ago — to construct a mystery that no reader could solve — to the next level. The entire premise of the book rested on an unexpected twist, that the unassuming doctor who narrated the book was actually the murderer. Once I decided upon this quintessential yet unique unreliable narrator, I found it easy to write with the simple language that allowed the reader to focus on the labyrinthine puzzle of a plot. It was the first book under my new Collins contract, and I wanted it to dazzle. As I reread it for a final time, it occurred to me that we are all unreliable narrators of our own lives, crafting stories about ourselves that omit unsavory truths and highlight our invented identities.

After marking up the last page, I glanced around my study, a wood-lined room that, like the rest of Styles, didn't have enough sunlight, but at least it had abundant bookshelves. *How pleasant our lives were,* I thought. Archie's work at Austral Limited, with a boss who was his friend, was remunerative and satisfying, and my writing was an unexpected success, providing not only financial support for our family but creative contentment. Rosalind was an even-tempered, energetic little girl, if a little serious and stubborn. It was true that our weekends had been overtaken by golf; he played two rounds of eighteen holes both Saturday and Sunday, admittedly accompanied by a group of club friends instead of me, except when I invited my old friend Nan Watts and her husband to make a foursome. But Archie seemed happy, and wasn't that the point of living in Sunningdale? Perhaps that *frisson* we shared in our early days was missing, but wasn't that only natural? For the first time in the course of our marriage, I wasn't plagued by doubts and worries.

I suddenly remembered Charlotte, and I wondered how long ago I'd called for her. Fifteen minutes? An hour? It seemed an age, but I lost track of time while writing. Glancing up at the clock, I guessed that I'd summoned her three-quarters of an hour ago.

"Charlotte!" I called out again. She might be in Rosalind's bedroom, as she tidied my daughter's belongings and did her laundry when she wasn't undertaking projects for me. Charlotte didn't trust Lilly, our housemaid, with Rosalind's delicate things.

The staccato step of my secretary's shoes on Styles's wooden floors echoed down the hallway to my study. She must have finally heard my call. The door creaked open, and I reminded myself to have Lilly oil its hinges.

"Yes, Mrs. Christie?" Charlotte asked.

Holding up the manuscript like a trophy, I said, "I'm ready to have you post the very final version of *The Murder of Roger Ackroyd.*"

Charlotte's face broke out in a wide grin. She knew how I'd labored on this particular mystery, not because it was unusually challenging but because I wanted it to be unusually perfect. "Congratulations, ma'am. What a relief it must be to complete it."

"It is, Carlo." My secretary winced a bit at the nickname, but I couldn't seem to stop using it. Rosalind had dubbed her "Carlo" on her very first day, and somehow, it stuck. "Shall we have a small sherry and toast to its completion?" I asked.

I wanted to celebrate this small victory, and I knew Archie would not be the appropriate partner for the occasion, even if he hadn't been traveling for work in Spain. More and more, he found my writing a nuisance, which I attributed to his success at Austral and his increased salary. What seemed acceptable to him when we needed money was becoming a bother when we had more cushion. So I tried not to discuss it too much.

Charlotte hesitated. "I do have to pick up Miss Rosalind in an hour, Mrs. Christie. I wouldn't want to appear out of sorts to her schoolteacher."

"I hardly think one small sherry will cause you to appear out of sorts, Charlotte." I forced myself to use her proper name. It would hardly be a celebration if I drank my sherry alone.

She nodded, and I poured sherry into two small crystal glasses. We clinked them together and sipped.

"Ah, I almost forgot. A letter came for you," Charlotte said.

"Is it from my mother?" After I received a troubling letter in shaky handwriting from Mummy in February, I traveled home to Ashfield, where I discovered that she'd been laid low with a virulent bronchitis that taxed her already straining heart. She was living in only two of the many rooms at Ashfield, as she'd become fairly immobile, with her belongings heaped high along the walls so she could access her clothes and books. Only one elderly maid, one of the two Marys, remained to help her keep house. I spent two weeks feeding her nourishing soups and ensuring that she rested to regain her strength while I cleaned the spare rooms, trimmed the border in the brisk sea

251

air, stocked the larder, and arranged for a gardener to undertake the heavier yard work when the weather turned from winter. I only left because Mummy insisted, but I'd wept on the train because I longed to stay and care for my lovely, fading mother.

Charlotte's dark eyes grew darker. "I would have brought it to you immediately if it had been, Mrs. Christie. Surely you know that?"

"Of course, Charlotte. My apologies." How could I doubt that Charlotte would have delivered Mummy's letter posthaste? She knew how I fretted over her and her condition. If Mummy herself hadn't admonished me to stay by Archie's side and banished me to return home to Styles during my last visit, I'd be in Ashfield now. Instead, Madge shipped Mummy for a stay at Abney Hall, under her care.

Examining the envelope, I saw it bore the return address of Abney Hall. I should have instructed Charlotte to bring these letters to me with the same urgency as those penned by Mummy, especially since our phone service had been erratic as of late. A delay in reading Madge's letters could be catastrophic, but Charlotte wouldn't necessarily have associated a letter from Abney Hall with my mother, even though Charlotte should have noticed that this letter was delivered by special courier.

Slicing it open, I saw a single page with only two sentences in Madge's hand spilled out. *Come at once, Agatha. Mummy is failing.*

CHAPTER THIRTY-TWO:
DAY SIX AFTER
THE DISAPPEARANCE

Thursday, December 9, 1926
Styles, Sunningdale, England

"Why did you do it, Archie?" his mother asks when he picks up the telephone after dinner. Her voice is tight and small, almost unrecognizable from the demanding, certain tone that echoes throughout his memories of his childhood and early adult years.

It isn't the question he expected. Not from her at least. From the police perhaps, but not his own mother. And he is unprepared to answer.

"Are you there, Archie? I heard you pick up the phone."

"Yes, Mother, I'm here."

"Then why don't you answer me? Why did you agree to this terrible interview with the *Daily Mail*?"

His body, which had been frozen into place by her query, relaxes. *She's only referencing the article,* he thinks. Nothing more, certainly not Nancy. At the thought of her name, he wonders how his beloved is bearing up. "I wanted to give my side of the story, Mother. The press had been painting me in an unfavorable light, and I hoped to correct that depiction."

"Oh really? That was your goal? Well, you certainly went about it in a very peculiar way." His mother's familiar tone returns.

"What do you mean?" Why is his mother talking in circles? His head is already spinning from his exchange with Rosalind, and he's not certain he can take much more today.

"Did you think that telling people that you and your wife routinely spend the weekend apart would paint a pretty picture of your marriage, Archie?" She doesn't wait for him to answer before continuing. "And did you think that announcing you didn't want to bother with the press and all the — I quote — 'relentless' phone calls you receive would endear you to readers?"

"Yes?" he answers quizzically. Hopefully.

"Can't you see that makes you sound heartless and unfeeling? A man who cares about the whereabouts of his missing wife would take *every* phone call and *every* tip and be grateful for it. Don't you understand?" He hears his mother inhale deeply, as if forestalling tears. "And to raise the newspaper gossip about possible arguments between you and Agatha is damnably foolish. It gives credence to the rumors about the state of your marriage where no credence should be due. If you weren't worried about that gossip, you wouldn't have mentioned it."

Has he ever heard his mother swear before? He doesn't know what to do — apologize, rationalize his behavior, yell — so he says, "That wasn't what I intended."

She is quiet, an unnatural state for a woman brimming with opinions. After a long, silent pause, she says, "If anyone was considering whether or not you were guilty of your wife's disappearance and unsure, Archie, you went and convinced them in the *Daily Mail*."

Those scathing words are the last thing he remembers. He must have signed off on his conversation with his mother at some point, because when Kenward and Goddard seek him out, he's sitting at the telephone table with the receiver in his hand and the line is dead. But when he checks the clock, an hour has passed, and he has no recollection of what he did with that time.

"Colonel Christie?" Goddard says with a note of concern in his voice.

256

"Yes?"

Kenward answers; no such worry is evident in his tone. "We have some questions for you."

"We can retire to my study," Archie offers, rising from the chair. He is weary.

"No, I think we will have this discussion in the kitchen," Kenward says.

Why the kitchen? Archie thinks but does not ask. From Kenward's demeanor, he knows better than to critique or argue.

As they walk toward the kitchen, they pass Charlotte and her sister Mary in the hallway. The women — so alike with their unattractive bobs but so different in the appearance of their eyes, Charlotte's inclined toward merriment and Mary's naturally downcast — are whispering. Although they stop talking upon spotting him, Archie catches the tail end of a phrase: "tell them." What are they discussing?

The officers must have instructed the staff to vacate the kitchen, because it is empty when they arrive. After they settle into three of the four mismatched chairs that surround the simple wooden table where the staff eats their meals, Kenward says, "Your *Daily News* article was certainly a surprise."

"So I hear," Archie says with a sigh.

Goddard raises an eyebrow, but Kenward

plows forward. "You do realize how you appear in that piece, don't you?" He can't resist a nasty smile.

Archie doesn't answer. He doesn't want to dignify Kenward's query and certainly doesn't want to encourage questions along those lines. He's had quite enough on that topic from his mother and realizes now that he has made a major misstep.

"You galvanized otherwise silent players with that article, Colonel Christie. Good for us, of course, though I'm certain that wasn't your intention," Goddard says, much to Archie's surprise. He'd assumed that this particular interrogation was Kenward's idea and, as such, his to control. But Goddard seems to be in the thick of it as well.

"No, it wasn't."

Goddard pulls a pad of paper from his pocket and consults it for a moment. "After reading your *Daily Mail* interview, a maid in the employ of the James family of Hurtmore Cottage has stepped forward. She says — and I quote — she felt compelled to divulge the truth in the face of your lies." He glances at Archie, who is stunned. What had he said or done at the Jameses' home for which he'll now be accountable? Rifling through his memories of the weekend, he wonders what was overheard or seen. He has no particular memory of a maid, but then, why would he? The servant's role was to *avoid* notice.

Kenward leaps into the fray. He's almost giddy. "Do you know what she told us?"

Archie says nothing. He's too terrified to speak.

"No? It's a fact that we've long suspected but did not have any confirmation. Until now. And boy, what confirmation we received!" He exchanges a glance with Goddard, which to Archie seems to say *Should you tell him or shall I?*

In the end, Kenward can't restrain himself, and he blurts out, "The maid told us your weekend at Hurtmore Cottage was no ordinary golf weekend. Its main purpose was to celebrate your engagement to your mistress, Miss Nancy Neele."

A surge of vertigo overtakes Archie, and he feels as though he's fallen backward from a great height, when in fact, he is still sitting on the kitchen chair. Details from his evening at Hurtmore Cottage take hold of his mind — whispered conversations between him and Nancy, the toast given by Sam James, and the late-night visit to Nancy's room — and he knows it would be futile to deny the maid's assertions outright. But he'll be damned if he'll admit anything beyond the maid's claims. Nancy Neele is the woman he loves, the one he plans on marrying, and he will do whatever it takes to protect her good name.

Goddard takes a turn, looking at Kenward as if this exchange is rehearsed. "But what we can't help but wonder, Colonel Christie, is this. How can you be engaged to Miss Neele when you are still very much married to Mrs. Christie?"

Kenward answers, "Unless, of course, you know that Mrs. Christie is dead."

CHAPTER THIRTY-THREE: THE MANUSCRIPT

April 18, 1926
Styles, Sunningdale, England

I would never forgive myself for failing to reach Mummy's side in time to say goodbye. Although I raced to the train upon receiving Madge's letter, leaving Rosalind in Charlotte's capable care, barely even stopping to bring anything other than my large handbag, I was too late. Mummy died at Abney Hall while I was on the train to Manchester. She wasn't Mummy by the time I reached her side; she was gone, a pale, lifeless shadow of her former self. I didn't remember much of the days that followed — the funeral planning, the travel from Abney to Ashfield, the arrival of family members, the service. Perhaps the gaps in my recollection were a godsend, as by all accounts, I became a howling, sobbing animal.

All I remember was wanting Archie. His warm enveloping arms, his lips upon the top of my head, his words telling me that all would be well in time. I yearned for the comfort I hoped he'd provide, comfort I hadn't actually received for many years but still believed in. He didn't come. My eyes bleary from crying, Madge read aloud Archie's telegram saying that he could not travel home from Spain in time for the funeral. I dissolved at the news, remembering only then his great dislike of emotion and grief. And I wondered, for the first time, about his absence.

Only one clear image from the day of the funeral remained with me. Rosalind and I stood with our fingers gripped around each other's as we listened to the parson deliver a final prayer over Mummy's gravesite. Hand in hand with my darkly dressed daughter, we walked from the parson's side to the front of the newly dug grave. Glancing into her somber eyes, I nodded, and together we tossed a bouquet of bluebells and primroses onto the top of Mummy's casket. I wanted her to be surrounded by the fragrance of her favorite blooms as she left this world.

How could my beloved mother be gone? I could not envision my life without her constant, reassuring presence, whether in person or in word. I'd involved her in every one of my decisions, events, and ideas; how could I proceed without her guiding hand? It was then that I realized the comfort I'd longed for from Archie was actually the solace that only my mother could have provided.

Even from my study, I heard his footsteps in the hallway before his key sounded in the lock. Could he really be home? It had only been a little over two weeks since he'd been on a work trip to Spain, but it seemed an eon since I'd seen his vivid blue eyes. My world had utterly upended in the passage of those days.

I sprang to my feet, dropping my notepad and pen on the floor. After I'd put Rosalind to bed, I'd been unsuccessfully trying to distract myself by outlining a new book for my Collins contract, but it didn't matter now. Archie was home. Running to the door, I embraced my husband before he could even cross the threshold.

Half laughing, he said, "Can a man even take off his hat before he's accosted by his wife?"

I laughed at his rare joke, a mad cackle that I knew was a mistake the moment it escaped my lips. It sounded brash and over-reactive, and Archie wouldn't like it. It smacked of disorderly emotions.

I swallowed the laughter and simply said, "I'm so glad you're home."

He slipped out of my embrace, placed his coat on the stand and his hat on the front table, and then put his suitcase down in the hallway near the stairs. Then, as if it was any other evening after a long day at the office, he entered the parlor to pour himself a whisky and sat down on the sage-green sofa. I settled at his side.

"The trip was long, of course," he commented as he sipped his drink. "Although rather smooth."

"I'm relieved to hear it," I answered, thinking that surely we'd race through these preliminaries to discuss the heart of things.

"The train a bit more reliable than the ship," he continued on the topic of his travel home.

I struggled with a response and settled on saying, "I guess that's not a surprise."

"No, I suppose you're right." He finished his drink. "The business went quite well, though. I think I've just about wrapped up a new contract for Austral."

"That's wonderful news, Archie." I tried to muster the appropriate enthusiasm.

How strange, I thought. Was he ever going to ask about the funeral? Mummy? My grief? We'd exchanged a few cursory letters since it happened, but I hadn't been in a state of mind to pen any details. Nor, it seemed from the brevity of his missives, had he. Were we going to sit here and act as though a monumental loss hadn't just occurred?

I waited. The house seemed unnaturally still and silent. Rosalind was asleep in her room, and the small sounds that Charlotte normally made were absent as she was still in Edinburgh tending to her ill father. Would Archie fill in the silence with meaningful conversation? Or would we continue to share niceties like two perfect strangers?

Pushing himself off the couch with a weary sigh, he walked over to the drinks area and poured himself a double whisky without even asking me if I'd like one. Instead of sitting back down next to me on the sofa or even near me on the adjacent armchair, he chose a stiff, wingback chair all the way across the room. Normal banter tempted me — I sorely yearned for a return to normality with my husband — but I resisted. I needed to see if he'd ever ask about my mother.

Finally, he spoke. "Everything all right?"

Was this meant to be his inquiry about the death of my mother? This simple question that could just as well be about the weather? For the first time, instead of concern over how he perceived me, I began to feel deep disappointment in Archie. Even anger. "Is *what* all right?" I needed to make him say the words aloud, to stop pretending.

"The funeral. All that about your mother."

Tears began to well in my eyes. Not the tears of grief and sadness that had overtaken me since Mummy died but tears of fury that the loss of my mother should be belittled by his minimizing treatment. I pushed back the tears and, with as much dignity as I could muster, said, "No, Archie, it is not all right. I've been terribly despondent, and I've needed my husband. I need him now."

He froze at my words; although he'd become accustomed to my displays of emotion, he was ill-used to any tone other than the passivity that he'd cultivated in me. But he said nothing. No condolences. No apologies. No professions of love. No embrace.

His mouth opened and closed several times as he tried on different phrases for size. I held my tongue until he spoke. "Time heals, Agatha. You'll see."

The suppressed tears broke free and spilled down my cheeks. "Time? I should just sit by stoically, waiting for time to heal my grief? Without the comfort of my hus-

266

band? Not even an embrace?"

Archie suddenly stood up, spilling a bit of his drink on his pants. This normally would have upset him and necessitated an immediate trip to our bedroom for a change of attire. Yet he didn't seem to notice in his haste to make his proposal. "Here's an idea, Agatha. I've got to go back to Spain next week to conclude my business. Why don't you come with me? It'll take your mind off all this."

He hadn't answered my question about his ability to comfort me directly, I noticed. He hadn't moved toward me and wrapped his arms around me in the manner I craved. He'd merely offered a temporary distraction, no real acknowledgment of my loss. Despite my disappointment, despite my sense of having been abandoned in my time of extreme need, I decided to respect the limitations of Archie's nature — his discomfort with all this emotion — and forgive him. I reminded myself that a good wife would indulge him no matter her own situation, and I wanted desperately to be a good wife.

Chapter Thirty-Four:
Day Seven after
the Disappearance

Friday, December 10, 1926
Styles, Sunningdale, England

Archie swears that Charlotte will not look him in the eye.

"You have a good day at school, darling, all right?" he calls out to his daughter from the hallway. His daughter and the governess are readying for Rosalind's police-escorted school day, a necessity to avoid the surge of press around Styles and Rosalind's school.

"Yes, Papa," Rosalind answers, giving him a hesitant smile. Her demeanor toward him has been skittish since his harsh behavior yesterday afternoon, and he desperately wishes that he could take back his words. Isn't it enough that she has to ride to school in a police vehicle so she isn't mobbed by reporters and photographers, only to be greeted once there by swarms of bratty children taunting her? What sort of father is short-tempered with his child in such circumstances? He has inflicted enough harm upon her, and he knows that damage has hardly reached its end.

"Take good care of her en route, Charlotte," he says. The statement is unnecessary, as no one watches out for Rosalind with the hawkeyed vigilance of the governess, but he needs an excuse to connect with her and gauge her reaction. Is Charlotte actually avoiding his gaze, or is he imagining it?

"Yes, sir," she answers with unusual formality and a quick bob. And no eye contact. Why? Is she scared after his outburst at Rosalind? Or is it something else entirely?

As he watches his poor daughter navigate the throngs of reporters who've made camp in his garden, he spies Kenward and Goddard striding toward the front door. All manner of police inhabit his house at every hour of the day and night — plainclothes detectives, uniformed officers from two different forces, and even young officers in training — and they all enter Styles through the back entrance. Why are the constable and superintendent approaching the house with such formality?

No sense pretending he cannot see them, he thinks. He opens the door as they near it. "Morning, gentlemen."

"Good morning, Colonel Christie," God-dard — of course — responds politely.

"Would you like to come in?" Archie offers.

"No, sir," Kenward replies. "We need you to come with us."

Where do they want him to go? What have they found? "I'm sorry, I don't understand," he whispers.

"To the police station."

Archie is perplexed. He's sat through countless meetings with the police, and none have required an official visit to a police station. What has changed? Why now? What have they learned? "Come with you? Whatever f-for? Why can't we just talk in my study . . . or the kitchen as we always do?" A slight stammer has taken hold of his tongue.

"We will need you to make an official statement," Goddard says softly.

"Isn't that what I've been doing every day for the p-past week?"

"No, Colonel Christie," Kenward answers, taking one step closer to Archie so they are nearly face-to-face. "No, you haven't. You've been interviewed about your wife's disappearance. That is a very different matter from a formal police statement. Please get your coat and hat and come with us."

With Kenward's and Goddard's gazes fixed on him, he pulls on his gray wool overcoat and trilby and steps out through the front door. Even though he walks behind the police officers and the brim of his hat is pulled low, the flashes of light from photographers' bulbs are nearly blinding. For most of the press, this is the first time they've encountered him in close proximity, and the questions ring out in a deafening roar. Inquiries turn into accusations, and they mesh with one another, becoming indistinguishable denunciations for what seems like a walk to the gallows. Archie guesses that is precisely Kenward and Goddard's intent with this parade, particularly when they seat him in the back of the police vehicle.

During the ride to the Bagshot police station, everyone is quiet. Silence is normally a comfortable state for Archie, but in this context, with the typically verbose Kenward rendered mute, he feels unsettled. And why isn't anyone talking about this formal police statement, explaining the necessity for this ceremony? Wouldn't any number of his previous statements on record have sufficed? Should he summon his solicitor, or would that signal guilt on his part? Without Kenward's usual jeers — which would be strangely welcoming — Archie feels an

271

increasing sense of doom.

The two men exit the vehicle first and escort him into the station. A line of junior officers has assembled to watch the procession into what Kenward dubs the interrogation room. With the condemnatory stares of the police on him, this march is worse than the walk from Styles to the police car. Archie's thoughts go wild. Has this been his last day at Styles? Should he have given Rosalind a more fitting farewell?

No offer of a glass of water or a cup of tea is forthcoming as Archie sits down on a chair facing the other men in the tiny, windowless room. No one speaks. They seem to be waiting, but for what? Both officers are present.

The interrogation room door slams open with a bang, startling even Kenward. A slight, balding man in a fastidious suit enters the room. He sits in the empty fourth chair, lays out papers and pens on the table, and then selects a particular writing utensil, placing its tip onto a page. The stenographer then nods to Kenward and Goddard.

"We spent the better part of last evening interviewing Mr. and Mrs. Sam James as well as Miss Nancy Neele," Kenward announces. "Again."

Oh my God, why didn't Nancy or Sam

phone him? Forget the communication blockade. This qualifies as an emergency. Archie feels sick at the thought of his friends and his beloved being subjected to Kenward's antics — and even sicker at what they might have divulged — but he refuses to show it. He wills his face to remain impassive in the face of Kenward's taunts and reminds himself to abide by the terms of the letter, no matter how horribly worried he is about Nancy and the Jameses.

"This time, we finally got around to the truth. They confirmed that last weekend was no ordinary golf weekend but a celebration of your engagement to Miss Neele. Just as the maid reported to us and the press." Kenward continues, "Apparently, the two of you have been conducting an affair for the past six months. At least."

"The Jameses told you that? Miss Neele told you that?" Archie could not fathom his demure, supportive love confessing to their transgression.

"Well, not Miss Neele. She refused to comment unless we had a court order. But the Jameses did concede a knowledge of your relationship." A smug smile appears on Kenward's face. "And Sam James alluded to a connection between your affair and your wife's disappearance."

Archie cannot quite believe that Sam would give him up, and he wonders if Kenward is just trying to bait him into disclosure. But the locked gates have opened, and he cannot stop himself from speaking the truth. Perhaps for the first time since this nightmare commenced. "Even if it is true — that I was engaged in a relationship with Miss Neele, which I do not admit — then the only connection between that and my wife's disappearance is that Mrs. Christie drove off in a fit of pique."

Goddard speaks for the first time since they entered the interrogation room. "Then why did you burn the letter your wife left you?"

The question flattens him. How did they find out about the letter? It dawns on him — too late — that the damnable letter is the real reason he's in the police station, that his statements yesterday about his relationship with Nancy would be sufficient.

"I see that you're surprised, Colonel Christie. That's perfectly understandable. After all, the existence of the letter has stayed quiet until now, as has your burning of that letter. But remember what I told you about your *Daily Mail* interview? It loosened people's lips," Goddard says.

Archie still doesn't speak. Why should he?

He's damned if he does and damned if he doesn't. He knows exactly how his burning of Agatha's last missive to him before her disappearance appears. It is only open to one interpretation.

"I'll ask you again, Colonel Christie. Why did you burn the letter from your wife?"

He grasps on to one last gambit. "You're presuming the existence of such a letter."

"Ah, you're going to play the literal game with us." Goddard shoots a glance at Kenward. "That's fine. We can play at that too. Someone saw the envelope that your wife left for you on the entryway table before she disappeared. That same someone remembered your letter because it sat alongside the one your wife left for her."

Ah, that's how they know. Charlotte finally broke. He should have guessed from her skittish behavior this morning. Did he push her to the edge by his *Daily Mail* interview? Was it his treatment of Rosalind yesterday? Or did her sister Mary push her to do it?

No sense denying it now, he thinks. "I didn't disclose the letter because it referred to a purely personal matter that has no bearing on the events transpiring afterward."

"So the letter did exist?" Kenward cannot help but ask.

"Yes," Archie answers. How can he insist

otherwise?

Goddard takes charge of the questioning again. "You expect us to believe that you burned that letter because its contents contained some personal matter that has no relationship to your wife's disappearance?"

"That's right." He clings to this explanation, even though he knows it's thin and paltry at best.

"Could that personal matter be your affair with Miss Neele? Surely you realize *that* sort of personal matter could have an enormous bearing on the investigation into your wife's disappearance."

"I know nothing of the sort. And I am not prepared to elaborate on the topic of my wife's letter." He has no choice. If he is to survive this catastrophe intact, he must stay the course on the letter. In fact, the letter itself mandates that he remain silent on its contents.

Kenward stands and walks to Archie's side, leaning down so that their faces are level. "I must say, burning the last letter left by your wife mere moments after the police found her abandoned car isn't the behavior of an innocent man. It isn't the act of a man with nothing to hide, a man who's upset about his wife's disappearance. It's the destruction of evidence by a guilty man."

CHAPTER THIRTY-FIVE:
THE MANUSCRIPT

August 3–5, 1926
Ashfield, Torquay, England

Spring turned into summer, and still Archie and I remained apart. His business trip to Spain had stretched from days to weeks, and duty obliged me to travel to Ashfield during that time. Mummy's death meant that the future of our family home must be determined — to sell, rent, or keep, because we couldn't work out the death taxes otherwise — and that required the sorting of her belongings. Madge couldn't leave Abney Hall until August, so I labored in Ashfield largely alone but for Rosalind, Peter, our new dog, and the occasional temporary maid from town, as Charlotte remained in Scotland with her ailing father. Even when Archie returned from Spain in June and we made plans for him to stay in his London club during the week with jaunts to Ashfield on weekends, I did not see him. One excuse or another kept him from visiting us.

I stayed ensconced in Ashfield, which had become a repository of memories, a museum of the lives once lived here rather than a house brimming with life itself. Every one of its five bedrooms, the library, the study, the dining room, and the sunroom brimmed with boxes of remembrances, some of which had been locked away for years as the space Mummy inhabited at Ashfield dwindled. Only the two sad rooms in which she'd existed in her final months were free of the detritus of bygone times. In the weeks after her passing, as we decided what to do with our family home, I became the cataloguer and caretaker of Ashfield's past.

I never knew what a box might contain. It might be stacked with letters between Mummy and Papa from their courtship days. It could be crammed with moth-eaten evening gowns Mummy had worn on balmy Torquay evenings. It might be stuffed with old board games and the Album of Confessions that recorded years of our family pastimes. It could be heaped with Auntie-Grannie's possessions, including lengths of silk she'd been saving for some long-past ball. With each fresh opening, I was assaulted by the past.

But I continued, burying my tears for

Rosalind's benefit. I plowed through the piles and the trunks and boxes without comfort from anyone, not even my husband. I tried to bolster my dark moments and growing disappointment over Archie with my mother's words — *if you put aside unworthy thoughts about your husband and cast your eyes upon him lovingly, you will earn his love* — but then I remembered that the sage advice came from my mother, and I was plunged back into my grief. Yet I persevered.

Although the smell of mold was everpresent at Ashfield, the scent was magnified by the day's storms. I tried to ignore it as I worked my way through the trunks in the dining room and the serving items stashed in sideboards and cupboards, but it became overwhelming, and I had to avoid certain hallways and back rooms as the rainwater started to trickle down the walls. I had to retire to the kitchen, because there, the aroma of cooking masked some of the smell of decay.

Rosalind was holed up in the corner, using pencils and a sketchbook on the rough wooden kitchen table in front of her. "Will it ever be sunny again?" she asked.

I sat across from her and held her small hands tightly. "Of course, darling," I reassured her, but I wondered myself. The Torquay of my childhood seemed an endless blur of bright days and sparkling waves, but Torquay now seemed plagued by endless rain instead. Rosalind had been confined to the house for days, and even though she was a serious child who busied herself with projects of her own making, it was becoming tedious. "I think we shall have sun tomorrow. And we will play on the beach, I promise."

She sighed and returned to her drawing. "All right, Mama."

"Thank you for being such a good girl while I'm occupied with this work, Rosalind."

"You're welcome," she said without glancing up from her sketch. "I just wish Papa was here to play with me on the weekends."

I thought she hadn't noticed Archie's ongoing absence. *How perceptive she is,* I thought. "Me too, but I'm enjoying our summer together, Rosalind," I said. While this unexpected time alone with my daughter hadn't exactly bonded us as I'd been bonded to Mummy, the absence of Charlotte and Archie had yielded a certain understanding and camaraderie between us.

She gifted me with a small smile, and I felt a surge of triumph. Perhaps this period wasn't all mourning and black thoughts. Perhaps a strong connection had indeed been forged.

Peter interrupted this notion with his barking, and when it didn't cease, I wondered what rodent he was chasing now. Rosalind and I had found him staring down any number of squirrels and badgers over the course of the summer. I rose from the table and stared out the kitchen window, wondering if I'd have to hire a gardener to help with the pests and the overgrown lawn.

But Peter wasn't hunting down an animal. He was barking at the arrival of my sister, who'd just pulled into Ashfield's drive in her silver Rolls-Royce. For all the jealousies and rivalries that had passed between us over the years, all I felt in that moment was love and relief.

I ran out of the house. "Madge, you're finally here!" I cried and embraced her as soon as she stepped out of her automobile.

"What a welcome, Agatha! I must say I hadn't expected such a warm one after leaving you here on your own to sort out this mess over the summer."

I closed the door for her and linked my arm through hers, and we strode into the house together, each carrying one of her suitcases. "You're here now. That's all that matters."

Despite her long drive and the August heat, Madge was impeccably dressed as always, in a sleeveless silk drop-waist dress with a navy cardigan slung over her shoulders like a scarf.

"Of course I'm here. Haven't I agreed to stay with Rosalind while you and Archie holiday in Italy? Did you forget?" Madge looked at me, a concerned expression in her eyes.

When Archie had repeatedly offered up excuses for not coming to Ashfield — either that the general strike kept him working on weekends or that the travel expense was a waste of money as we'd see each other soon — he'd vowed to organize a trip to Italy for the two of us, and Madge and I had arranged for her to come the day before Rosalind's seventh birthday. Archie promised to come to Ashfield to celebrate the birthday, then together, he and I would leave for Italy while Madge watched Rosalind and took over the chore of sorting through Ashfield.

How had I forgotten today was the day? I wondered. I'd lost track of time as I'd become more and more immersed in Ashfield's past, and I hadn't realized until she pulled up that the date for Madge's arrival had come. Not that the time had passed quickly, mind. There were many afternoons I thought would never end and several long nights where I sobbed until dawn. But time didn't feel exactly linear when I was knee-deep in years gone by, and I'd quite forgotten the calendar, even this journey.

Despite having stayed up late, sharing with Madge the treasures I'd discovered, I arose the next morning before dawn, my stomach churning with anticipation. To pass the hours until I heard the sound of Archie's car wheels on gravel, I prepared breakfast, tidied the areas of the house I'd cleared of boxes, and then, while Madge played with Rosalind in the garden, I began wrapping her birthday presents. I almost didn't notice when the Delage pulled up in front of Ashfield, but I jumped up in time to meet Archie at the door.

Mindful of his reaction when he returned to Styles from Spain after Mummy's funeral, I greeted him with a light kiss on the cheek instead of a powerful embrace. But even this mild welcome seemed to overwhelm him. He recoiled from my touch.

"Hello, Agatha," he said in a stilted voice, almost as if he were greeting a business colleague he'd never met instead of his wife whom he hadn't seen in months. It was as if we were strangers.

As footsteps clipped down the hallway behind me, I realized something was terribly wrong. I didn't have the opportunity to inquire, because Rosalind came rushing into the entryway. "Papa, Papa!" she cried, making clear that her allegiances hadn't changed over these summer months.

Archie swung her around, suddenly warm and loving. This sea change in his attitude telegraphed an important message to me, but I couldn't yet work out the lettering. I reached for Madge's hand, and she gripped it tight, sensing my alarm.

Gently, he placed Rosalind back down on the floor and turned to me. "Agatha, may we talk in private?" he asked.

"Of course," I answered, although I thought his request was strange and disconcerting. What did he need to discuss that he couldn't reveal in front of Rosalind or Madge? And why must the discussion be undertaken the moment he walked into Ashfield?

He followed me into the library, and I closed the door behind us. I'd forgotten that this room, once a favorite where I spent long, lazy afternoons pulling books at random from the bursting shelves, was now devoid of furniture. We were forced to stand and converse.

He looked at me with his bright-blue eyes. "I haven't done anything about organizing a holiday for us in Italy. I don't feel like going abroad."

I felt momentarily relieved. Perhaps this was the source of his strange behavior: he was worried how I might react to this failure in planning. I rushed to reassure him. "It doesn't matter, Archie. It'll be just as nice for the two of us to holiday in England. Or even stay here at Ashfield with Rosalind. It's been so long since we've been together as a family."

"I don't think you quite understand." Beads of sweat formed on his forehead, and I gathered this perspiration wasn't due to the heat. My own back started to sweat as nerves began to assume control. Something was wrong. "You know that dark girl who used to be Belcher's secretary? We had her down to Styles once with Belcher, about a year ago, and we've seen her in London once or twice."

Why was he mentioning this inconsequential girl? Someone we'd only met a few times? She was pleasant enough — dark hair and eyes, midtwenties perhaps — but rather bland overall. She'd once served as secretary to Major Belcher of the Empire Tour fame, and she'd been part of a large group we'd invited to a party at Styles. "Yes, I know who you're talking about. I can't remember her name. She visited Styles with a crowd."

"Nancy Neele," he said, his cheeks flaming red. "Her name is Nancy Neele."

"Yes, that's it," I said, but I wondered what she could possibly have to do with whatever unpleasant news he was about to deliver. I simultaneously wanted and didn't want him to make his terrible announcement.

"Well, I've spent quite a lot of time with her during my summer in London." His voice dropped to a near whisper, and his eyes were focused upon the black-and-white marble parquet floor.

"Well, why shouldn't you? Some company to share the occasional meal while you're on your own." Was this flirtation his awful news? A guileless dalliance was certainly better than the cancer or the firing I'd envisioned. I wasn't delighted that my husband was carrying on innocent tête-à-têtes with a girl of twenty-five when his own wife of twelve years had suffered the greatest loss of her life all alone. Anger flared in me, but I knew better than to express it. His news could have been far worse.

"I don't think you understand, Agatha. This isn't some innocent friendship. I've fallen in love with Nancy." Finally, he looked at me directly. In those vivid blue eyes, I saw his disgust in me. His disappointment in my aging looks and heavier body, different from Nancy's sweet, youthful visage and curvaceous but thin physique. His revulsion at my wild mourning for Mummy when Nancy was discreet and quiet in her manner. In an instant, I saw how the two of them fell in love over hushed, intense candlelit meals in London and on the golf course in Sunningdale. "I did tell you once that I hate it when people are ill or unhappy. It spoils everything for me. It spoiled us, Agatha."

Was this meant to be his apology for an affair? I wondered, horrified and shocked at his words. *If so, it was a poor one indeed.* But then I realized from his expression and his tone that this was no apology; it was barely an explanation. If anything, it was an announcement.

"I want a divorce as soon as possible." His tone brooked no hesitation.

With those words, I crumbled to the library floor, and my existence crumbled along with me.

CHAPTER THIRTY-SIX:
DAY EIGHT AFTER
THE DISAPPEARANCE

Saturday, December 11, 1926
Styles, Sunningdale, England

The laughter in the kitchen draws Archie's attention. Since the police turned it into their central command, much to the cook's chagrin, since she must still prepare meals there, it has hardly been a place of merriment. What on earth could be raucously amusing to ten policemen? Particularly after they'd just been chastised by Home Secretary Joynson-Hicks for not making faster progress?

He is supposed to be preparing a verbatim reconstruction of Agatha's last letter to him — a task he will never undertake — but curiosity gets the better of him. He pads away from his study down the hallway toward the kitchen. Standing behind a thick wall near the butler's pantry, he listens to the exchange.

"Come on, guv," a youthful-sounding

policeman with a particularly thick accent says. "You've got to be jokin' us."

Kenward's familiar voice booms back. "Mind your p's and q's, Stevens. We might not be in police headquarters, but that doesn't give you liberty to forget your rank and manners. Not to mention we're operating out of someone's home, so you should be especially mindful. There are children within earshot."

"Sorry, sir. Your announcement made me forget myself," the young policeman apologizes.

Kenward resumes where he must have left off. "I am deadly serious. We got a public scolding from the home secretary yesterday. He's telling everyone we're dragging our heels with this investigation, which, as we know all too well, couldn't be further from the truth. You boys have been working around the clock, and some of you haven't seen your families for days. But Joynson-Hicks has called for those London bluebottles — damn Scotland Yard — to step in if we don't get results soon. So it's all hands on deck to find this woman. But in the meantime, if Joynson-Hicks thinks Conan Doyle should be one of the hands on deck, it's not our job to question his decision."

Kenward couldn't possibly be talking

about Sir Arthur Conan Doyle, Archie thinks. Why on earth would the home secretary think that Sherlock Holmes's creator could help find Agatha? The very idea was preposterous. There must be some *other* Conan Doyle.

The kitchen grows loud with the buzz of the police officers chatting among themselves. Archie can hear a few men chuckling and one bold fellow call out "Sherlock Holmes" until Kenward yells, "Pipe down now, men. We've got work to do, and the pressure is on. Today, we start planning the largest manhunt England has ever seen. We launch the Great Sunday Hunt tomorrow, and we'll mobilize not only the police from all neighboring counties but also any volunteer who wishes to pitch in. We expect thousands to show up."

One bold officer ventures a question. "Um, sir, before we begin planning our manhunt, do you mind telling us what Sir Arthur Conan Doyle said? If he made any important contributions, I'm sure we'd all like to know." His voice is hesitant; he knows he's risking Kenward's ire.

The detective chief constable lets out an audible sigh and then says, "I've been told that the home secretary contacted the famous writer through a mutual acquaintance. I believe Joynson-Hicks thought the writer might share the same skills as his famous detective. But when the home secretary asked the writer for his aid, Conan Doyle — who seems to be some sort of occultist — offered to consult a psychic friend on Mrs. Christie's whereabouts. This psychic person, a fellow by the name of Horace Leaf, held one of Mrs. Christie's gloves —"

One of the men interrupts, "One of the gloves we found in the Morris Cowley?"

"Now, what did I just tell you men about your p's and q's? You interrupted me, Sergeant." Kenward's voice is angry again.

"Sorry, sir," the chastened policeman says.

"Yes, it was one of the gloves we found in her automobile," Kenward says. "Where was I? Ah, yes. Without being told anything about the person who'd owned the glove, this Mr. Leaf said that the person who owns that glove is not dead but is half-dazed. According to the psychic, she'll surface next Wednesday. For whatever that's worth."

Ironic, Archie thinks, *that the esteemed Sir Arthur Conan Doyle has been called in to assist in locating Agatha, given her adoration of the author.*

Kenward clears his throat. "Now back to business. Planning this manhunt. Cooper and Stevens, I want you two on flyers —"

Archie hears the clatter of shoes and turns around. Rosalind has arrived home after a walk with Charlotte and her sister Mary. His daughter's cheeks are ruddy from the cold, and she has a smile on her lips that disappears when she sees him. He doesn't want them to know that he's been eavesdropping or that he's worried about the investigation in any way, so he tries to explain away his presence near the kitchen. "Have any idea where Cook is, Charlotte? I'd welcome another cup of tea this morning, and I can't seem to find Lilly."

"I believe Cook's gone to the market, Colonel Christie. She's altered her usual schedule and now does her shopping while the police hold their morning meeting. Less disruptive, I think. And less upsetting," Charlotte says, not meeting his eyes.

Archie hasn't thought about the staff being upset by Agatha's disappearance; he's been too focused on his own standing in the investigation to muse upon other people's reactions other than Rosalind. Are they indeed worried about her? Should he say a few words to the staff? There is no protocol for this sort of thing, but he wants to behave in a manner befitting a man anxious about his wife. He must.

Charlotte stares at him, as do her sister

292

and Rosalind. He forgot them as he mused on the other staff members. They are waiting for him to respond, and he needs to say something. "I'm sorry to hear that."

Rosalind pulls on Charlotte's hand, and she looks over at his daughter in relief. She can't wait to get away from him, he sees, and from the sour expression on her face, neither can her sister. How he wishes he never invited Mary to Styles. But he can't dwell on that now, as he must discuss something with Charlotte.

"Charlotte, might I have a word?" he asks.

Her forehead creases with worry as she says, "Of course, sir." She directs her sister to take Rosalind upstairs to the nursery and then turns her attention to him. "What can I help you with?"

"Let's talk in the study," he says and leads her down the hallway.

They are silent as they walk. Only after they enter the study and he closes the door behind them does he speak. "I understand that you told the police about the letter Mrs. Christie left for me."

Her face is ashen, and the stoic Charlotte appears as though she might burst into tears. "I'm sorry, sir. I know you didn't want me to inform them, but they quizzed me on it particularly. And it's illegal to lie to the police."

"I understand, Charlotte. I don't want you to think that I'm angry with you. The only reason I'm raising this with you is that I'm curious about their questions."

"I didn't tell them anything, sir. Only that you'd been left a letter as well."

"I know, but what did they ask you about it?"

She takes a deep breath and says, "Detective Chief Constable Kenward asked repeatedly whether I knew what was written in your letter. Superintendent Goddard kept fairly quiet."

"Did Kenward venture any guesses as to what might be in the letter?"

"No, sir."

"Did he ask *you* to venture any guesses?"

Her ashen face turns crimson, telegraphing the answer to his question. "Yes."

"What did you say?"

"I said that, if I had to guess — and I didn't like to do so — that I thought your letter was likely to be similar to my own. My letter focused on the weekend's change of plans — she'd asked me to cancel the Yorkshire reservations and said she'd contact me when she'd decided where she was staying instead — and I supposed yours was

294

the same."

Perfect, Archie thinks. This will aid in his reconstruction of the letter Agatha left him. *Although,* he reconsiders, *he'd told the police that the letter had nothing to do with her disappearance, so Charlotte's statements might not be entirely helpful.*

"Did he ask you about how things stood between me and Mrs. Christie?" Since learning that Charlotte had divulged the existence of his letter to the police, despite his request to the contrary, he's supposed she might have shared even more with the police. This query is the real purpose of bringing Charlotte into his study.

Her crimson cheeks turn ever redder, and he fears that she'll be scared into silence. He needs to know what she's told Kenward and Goddard to prepare for the questions they're sure to ask him next about Nancy. He walks toward her, placing what he hopes is a comforting hand upon her shoulder. When she flinches, he realizes that his actions have the opposite effect than he intended.

"I sh-shouldn't like to say, sir."

"Please. Don't worry about sparing my feelings."

When she inhales deeply before she speaks, her breath is shaky. "I told them that

295

I'd become aware of a great divide between you and Mrs. Christie, one that had driven you from Styles most nights since the fall. I also told them that you'd had your worst row ever on the morning of the day she disappeared. But when I called from London that evening — she'd given me leave to keep my planned day trip to London — she sounded perfectly fine and even encouraged me to stay and enjoy the city for the evening."

"Anything more?" He wills his voice to remain calm. He needs to know what she knows — and what she's revealed.

She hesitates for an eternal beat and then answers his question. "Only that I suspected that something — or someone — had come between you."

CHAPTER THIRTY-SEVEN:
THE MANUSCRIPT

August 5, 1926
Ashfield, Torquay, England

The seven candles glowed brightly. They illuminated the otherwise dark dining room, turning Rosalind's birthday cake from a traditional white vanilla dessert to an orange-red confection. Madge, Archie, and I gathered in a semicircle around our small charge in a false attempt at birthday cheer. I only prayed that Rosalind didn't notice the wetness of my cheeks and the redness of my eyes.

Archie had planned on leaving for London — and for Nancy — as soon as he'd dropped his devastating news upon me. Precision bombing, they called this sort of accurate target attack during the Great War, and it felt no less explosive now. I'd begged him to at least stay for the day, his daughter's birthday no less, and he'd begrudgingly agreed. While Nancy's pull on him seemed urgent, one that trumped even the gentle tug Rosalind had on her father, I was heartened to learn that propriety and duty still maintained a limited hold upon him.

"Happy birthday, dear Rosalind," we sang in unison. Madge's hand clutched mine tightly as my voice wobbled and threatened to crack. I hadn't yet told her what Archie had revealed in the privacy of the library, but she sensed something had gone horribly awry.

"Blow out the candles, dear one!" Madge called to Rosalind in a merry voice. I appreciated her efforts to lift the black mood that had settled upon our desultory group and to make this a celebratory occasion. I couldn't bear to look at Archie directly. How could he want to leave me? I knew that relations between us hadn't been idyllic for some time, but how could he want to break up our family and our home? After all, we'd only just gotten settled into our lives at Styles, created a rhythm as it were, and we had chosen Sunningdale for him. For his happiness.

Rosalind smiled at her aunt Punkie, as she liked to call her, and blew with all her might. One by one, the candles' flames flickered, then disappeared.

"What did you wish for?" Madge teased.

"You know I can't tell you, Auntie Punkie," Rosalind answered with a big grin. She and Madge shared an easy banter and lighthearted taunting that I could never achieve with my otherwise somber daughter. Thinking on our connection — or lack thereof — I blamed Archie, with his insistence that I always keep him first in my mind. That admonition had made me cautious in my treatment of my daughter for years. At what cost?

"Just tell us the subject of your wishes. You don't have to divulge the details," Madge said with a conspiratorial wink.

"All right," Rosalind agreed, and the smile abandoned her face when she continued. "All my seven wishes are about Mama and Papa."

"That is very kind of you to share your wishes with your parents, Rosalind," Madge said with a little squeeze of Rosalind's hand.

A sudden panic overtook me. My daughter's words yielded quite a different reaction in me than in Madge. Had Rosalind overheard the awful conversation between Archie and me in the library? Was that why *all* her wishes were for Archie and me instead of, say, a pie-in-the-sky hope for a pony? I didn't think I could stand it if she had. Sobs threatened to overwhelm me, and I left the dining room for the kitchen. Moments before a cry escaped, I managed to call back, "Just fetching your gifts, darling."

The clip of Madge's heels echoed behind me as she followed me into the kitchen where she found me leaning against the rough plaster wall, trying to calm my breath. "What is going on, Agatha?"

"It's nothing. I'm fine." I didn't think I could keep up the facade for the duration of Rosalind's birthday if I told Madge the truth. A look of pity would certainly well up in her eyes, and I simply couldn't tolerate it without breaking.

"Don't nothing me, Agatha. You are obviously upset about something, and Archie is acting very queer too, as if he's ill or something. And there was all that cloak and dagger in the library."

I couldn't say the words aloud. Sending the terrible words Archie had spoken to me back into the world might turn them into reality. If I could keep them secret, maybe they would disappear.

"Agatha." Madge took hold of my shoulders and stared me in the eyes. "Did you hear me? What on earth is going on here?"

"You won't need to stay with Rosalind at Ashfield," I said. This was all I could manage and as close to the truth as I dared go.

"What are you talking about? Why are you talking in riddles?" My usually composed sister's nerves were starting to frazzle. "What the hell happened in that library? I'll be forced to go ask Archie if you don't tell me yourself."

No, not that, I thought. I couldn't bear Madge hearing about my rejection from its source, and anyway, perhaps there was a chance he'd change his mind. The more frequently he spoke aloud the terrible words he'd said to me in the library, the more wedded to them he was likely to become.

Left without options, I vocalized the unthinkable. "Archie wants to leave me."

Chapter Thirty-Eight:
Day Eight after
the Disappearance

Saturday, December 11, 1926
Styles, Sunningdale, England

Archie fumbles through the dresser and wardrobe in the master bedroom. Socks spill out from open drawers, and boxes lie upturned on the floor. He's already made hay of the upstairs; he supposes he'll have to reassemble it all before he turns his attention back downstairs, where he's already searched once. He can allow no one to see what he's doing.

Where are the papers? He believed that he'd destroyed each letter and each memento from Nancy. In fact, it was his practice to do so as soon as a missive was received and read. But now, he is not sure that he did indeed destroy the items. And much depends on the lack of evidence of his affair. He knows that Nancy's notes, brimming with affection and plans, would give Kenward the motive he seeks.

Archie scrambles to return undergarments to the dresser, clothing to the wardrobe, and shoeboxes to their stack in the closet. Seconds after he's finished, he hears Charlotte calling his name. What can she want now?

Not bothering to feign a smile, he walks to the top of the staircase. He looks down the steps to see her panicked face staring up at him.

"Yes, Charlotte?" he asks.

"Apologies, sir. I never expected you'd be upstairs or I'd have walked up to fetch you rather than yelling out."

"Not to worry. What do you need?"

"It's the phone, sir. You have a call."

"Ah. Thank you," he says, walking downstairs and striding toward the tiny table where the phone rests. Perhaps it is his secretary from Austral or even his boss, Clive, he thinks, welcoming the distraction. But then he recalls that it is Saturday, and dread takes hold instead. Who on earth would be calling? In the first days of Agatha's disappearance, he received a flood of calls, but as the days progressed and he made known his desire for quiet, the calls nearly ceased, aside from his mother, of course, and Agatha's family members.

"Hello?"

"Archie, it's Madge." His sister-in-law's authoritative voice rings out on the line, and he flinches. He's always shied away from the self-confident, affluent woman, always felt the gaze of her judgment upon him. *Not successful enough, not wealthy enough, not high enough social standing* — he could almost hear Madge's thoughts aloud when he was in her presence. Agatha had maintained that he was imagining this unfavorable assessment, but Archie knew better. He knows Madge's type all too well.

"Hello, Madge," he says, his tone guarded.

"I'm calling for an update. We had agreed that you'd call me twice a day, every day, with news, but I haven't heard from you since yesterday morning," she barks at him.

"I didn't call you because there was no news."

"Our agreement was for two phone calls a day regardless."

Anger threatens to take hold of him. Why does she think he needs to answer to her? But he knows the rage will not serve him well, so he simply apologizes.

Madge turns to the real reason for her call. "I'm thinking I'll drive down to Surrey today so I can assist in the search tomorrow. I understand it will be a massive undertaking, and I'd like to be there to represent Agatha's family."

"I don't think that's wise, Madge. As soon as the press learns who you are — which they undoubtedly would from any number of townsfolk — you'd be under siege from reporters. Especially because they're hyping it as the Great Sunday Hunt and they expect thousands of volunteers."

"Thousands are good. I can hide in plain sight among thousands," she says, although her confidence has waned.

"The locals will identify you, and you will be swarmed by reporters. I don't think you'd relish being the focus of a *Daily Mail* article," he says. His assertion is true, but it isn't the real reason for Archie's resistance. He could not stand to have the overbearing Madge underfoot at Styles, and he'd do anything to deter her.

The line grows quiet as she considers his warning. "At least let me take Rosalind for a while. She must be beside herself with worry, and she shouldn't be exposed to this circus. I could drive down and fetch her. I'll bring her back to stay at Abney Hall until we locate Agatha."

Archie knows there's a strong bond between his daughter and Madge, and in his mind, that relationship is Madge's one redeeming quality. But he doesn't think he could bear having Madge at Styles even for an hour, even assuming that what Agatha told him was true — that she hadn't told Madge about their marital troubles. Anyway, what would he do with Charlotte and her sister Mary in Rosalind's absence? Without his daughter to focus upon, the Fisher sisters would be mooning about Styles, unnerving him with their presence and their fussing. No, Rosalind would stay at her own home.

"I don't think that's for the best, Madge. She really doesn't understand what's happening. She thinks Agatha is away on a writing trip and that the police are overreacting because they're horribly mistaken about her whereabouts," he says.

Madge is uncharacteristically quiet, and he can hear her inhale one of her constant cigarettes. "Let me talk to her. I'll judge for myself."

"Madge, there is no need. She is my daughter, and I know what's best for her."

"Oh really?" She laughs, a caustic, horrible chortle that sends shivers up his spine. "Just like you knew what was best for my sister? When you had an affair and broke her heart?"

CHAPTER THIRTY-NINE: THE MANUSCRIPT

August 7, 1926, and October 14, 1926
Surrey, England, and Guéthary, France

A curious calm settled upon me when Rosalind and I returned to Styles. To be sure, during the days at Ashfield after Archie departed for London, I surrendered to my devastation. Madge sat by my childhood bed, holding my hand and letting me sob, when she wasn't tending to Rosalind. As I lay in that bed, more bereft than I'd thought possible, I replayed the few times I'd seen Nancy and Archie together over the past two years since we'd moved to Sunningdale, hunting for any sign of their tryst and wallowing in my husband's betrayal. But once I decided to leave Ashfield and take the train to Styles — a place I could no longer think of as home but only as a way station — I squared my shoulders and determined that I would do whatever necessary to rebuild my family.

As the train chugged past the bucolic, sunlit countryside, which seemed to mock me with its verdancy and hopefulness, I realized that Archie wasn't the man I'd believed him to be. I'd conjured up that man. On some level, I'd always known he didn't fully embody the characteristics of his fictional character in *The Man in the Brown Suit* — Harry Rayburn — but was he entirely different from the brave, moral man I'd created in my mind and on the page? *No matter,* I told myself. *Archie is my husband, and I will accept him in his truest self, even if that is not what I'd hoped.* Anyway, it was likely my fault that he'd become fascinated with Nancy. Hadn't Mummy always warned me never to leave my husband alone for too long? And hadn't I emotionally and physically abandoned him this summer in my grief? Even when he was in Spain, he knew my heart and mind weren't with him but lost to my sorrow over Mummy.

With this mindset, I left Rosalind with Charlotte, who'd just returned to Styles on the heels of her father's recovery, and I hopped in my Morris Cowley. Archie would be finishing his workday at Austral Limited, and I would meet him as he exited. I would whisk him off to a lavish dinner and beg him to return to his family.

Archie had agreed to my entreaties. But his agreement came with great reluctance and an abundance of conditions. Over my tears and several shared drinks at an out-of-the-way London pub — Archie didn't want anyone from his office to see our emotional exchange — he consented to a three-month trial reconciliation as well as a holiday away for just us two. I thought the Pyrenees might prove the perfect setting for a reunion.

The snow-capped backdrop of the Pyrenees village of Guéthary was even more breathtaking by moonlight than by day. I'd considered planning our trip for Cauterets, another village at the foot of the Pyrenees that I'd visited with my parents as a child. Over the years, my memories of that trip — our hikes along paths lined with pine trees and vivid sprigs of wildflowers and the sound of my parents' laughter echoing through the forest as they strolled hand in hand — had not faded. But I had worried that no matter how successful my trip with Archie could be, it would never compare to that perfect summer. Now, given how Archie was behaving, I was pleased that I hadn't spoiled my vision of Cauterets and had chosen Guéthary instead.

To get a better view through the window, I stood on my tippy-toes by our hotel bed, which we'd slept in but hadn't shared, to see the small mountain village in the Pyrenees, famous for its spas, now illuminated by hundreds of flickering candlelights. I opened my mouth to call out to Archie so he could see this spectacular view, then I thought the better of it. He'd grown silent over dinner in the lodge, and even a second bottle of cabernet and the warmth of the fire hadn't loosened his tongue.

What had I done wrong this time?

Initially, I'd interpreted Archie's willingness to take this Pyrenees trip as an indicator of his commitment to leave behind his mad idea of abandoning us for Nancy. But since we'd arrived in this picturesque mountain range in the Iberian Peninsula between Biarritz and the border of Spain, he'd grown more recalcitrant by the day. The first few afternoons, he'd been willing to undertake hikes, and he'd engaged in conversations over our meals, desultory exchanges though they were. But by the fifth day, his voice had seemingly disappeared, and aside from a series of terse yeses and nos, he stopped engaging in any communication or undertaking any activity with me other than meals.

I glanced around the hotel suite, with its connected bedroom and sitting room. Where was Archie? As the holiday had progressed, he'd taken to quietly leaving our suite and settling into the public areas of the hotel with a book. Reading alone had become his refuge and his rebellion.

Opening our door, I peeked out and down to the lobby below, but Archie wasn't there. As I glanced back around the two-room suite, I wondered where on earth he could have retreated to in the short span of time since dinner. Was I so repulsive that he would have left the hotel altogether and fled to the town pub? I then realized I hadn't checked the balcony, largely because I couldn't imagine that my company was so abhorrent that he'd brave the frigid night air.

Pulling open the heavy oak and glass door, I stepped onto the balcony. Archie's back faced me, and I called out in what I thought was a bright voice, "Archie?"

My handsome husband, a hat pulled low on his forehead and a plaid scarf wrapped around his neck and chin to ward off the chill, turned around. He dropped the pipe he'd been smoking and yelled, "Can't a man be left alone for one second? I just wanted a bit of peace and quiet away from your endless chatter." His face twisted and became ugly.

I felt as though he'd slapped me. Walking

sideways away from him, I hit the wooden slats of the balcony balustrade. "I'm — I'm sorry."

Archie approached me at a steady clip until his face loomed over me. "Do you think I like being here with you? Listening to you drone on about culture, music, silly book ideas, your mother, and your . . . your desperation."

Was this really Archie talking to me in this awful way? I'd grown used to his coldness, but he'd usually wounded me with silence, not words. This was a new weapon, and it stung.

His face mutated again, forming a sick, self-satisfied smile. "Finally rendered speechless, are you? Well, I'll answer the question for you. I don't want to be here with you. I don't want to be anywhere with you." He was so close to my face I could feel his spittle freeze upon my cheeks. He raised his hand, and for a moment, I thought he'd strike me or push me. But then he abruptly dropped it.

A rogue thought passed through my mind, and I suddenly felt very afraid. What if he'd agreed to the three-month reconciliation with no intention of actually reuniting? He'd hardly been back to Styles except for the odd family dinner and a few golf club events. What if he'd agreed to the reconciliation for the sole purpose of bringing me to this isolated mountain town where he could get rid of me once and for all so he could marry Nancy Neele? I glanced down, realizing that with one shove, Archie could push me off this balcony forty feet to the icy, rocky ground below.

After all, that sort of thing didn't happen only in my books. It could very well happen in real life.

CHAPTER FORTY:
DAYS EIGHT AND NINE AFTER THE DISAPPEARANCE

Saturday, December 11, through Sunday,
*   December 12, 1926*
Styles, Sunningdale, England

The press wants to hang me on innuendo and inference alone. A burned letter, a weekend away from one's wife, a maid's gossip about an affair. The reporters and readers of daily rags and esteemed newspapers alike seize upon these unverified facts and stitch them together to conjure up a philandering husband turned murderer.

But they don't have a body, not yet anyway, and they don't have any proof of infidelity, he tells himself. So, like a pitchforked mob, they clamor for a definitive end to the search for his wife and the justice they're certain it will yield. Lambasting both the Berkshire and Surrey police, they cry for Scotland Yard to enter the fray. *Woman Novelist's Disappearance Goes Unsolved, Local Police Need Yard's Expertise,* the headlines demand.

When Scotland Yard refuses to get involved in the investigation on the same grounds it offered Archie nearly a week ago, newspapers offer up their own resolutions. After dredging up retired police, judges, and authors to give their interpretations of the events, the *Daily News* trumps the other publications by soliciting the insights of detective novelist Dorothy Sayers, a mystery writer whom Agatha has admired. While she claims that firm resolution of the disappearance — whether voluntary, suicide, spurred by memory loss, or the result of foul play — is impossible based on newspaper reports alone, she poses several questions, the answers to which, she asserts, might point to Mrs. Christie's whereabouts. Inflamed by the possibility that the noted writer might solve this mystery, she is invited to the Great Sunday Hunt.

Sickened by all the speculation and accusations and terrified about where they might lead, Archie throws the stack of newspapers on the study floor. Lighting a cigarette, he stands and starts pacing the small room. By God, he wishes he could speak, but he is bound by the clever, clever shackles of the letter and its author. So now he waits, but not for tomorrow's Great Sunday Hunt.

■ ■ ■ ■

"You missed a spot, Papa." Rosalind giggles, scrubbing a tiny smudge of dirt with her damp rag. Desperate for a distraction and restless with anticipation, he's asked his daughter if she'd like to clean the Delage with him. It is his Sunday ritual, one he prefers to undertake alone, but he needs to mend the rift between them. Anyway, Charlotte and her sister are off at church, and Rosalind is in his care.

Rosalind adores having routines and a firm schedule, too, and even though this particular chore is a deviation from her usual quiet Sunday, it's part of his routine, so she welcomes it. Like him, Rosalind understands the need for order. It is something Agatha never comprehended or embraced, even for him.

He smiles at the diminutive child, grateful for the moment of peace. He made the right choice by refusing to let Madge take her to Abney Hall. The deluge will arrive soon. It is the one thing about which he's certain. The timeline has always been clear, from the very moment he sliced open that envelope with his silver letter opener.

The sound of gravel crunching underfoot

316

intensifies, and Archie peeks around the bend to see who is approaching the back of Styles. Police guard the perimeter, so he doesn't worry about a stray intruder or reporter, but he isn't expecting a soul until Charlotte and Mary return in an hour.

When he spies a familiar young man of about twenty with ginger hair ambling toward them, Archie sighs in relief. It is only the gardener's son, who assists with the property upkeep from time to time. Archie raises his hand in farewell and returns to Rosalind and the car washing.

As Robert nears the side of the garage where the garden tools are stored, he greets them. "Colonel Christie, Miss Rosalind, I must say I'm surprised to see you here. Dad and I figured you'd be off at the Great Sunday Hunt, so we thought it might be a fine time to finish up some of the work preparing for winter."

Archie doesn't know what to think. Is it possible that Robert is oblivious to the suspicion cast upon Archie? Why else would he think that Archie would actually be welcome at the Great Sunday Hunt, as everyone seems to be calling it? The boy seems too earnest to be baiting him into some damning statement.

Reading a refusal into Archie's hesitation,

Robert steps backward. "But I can come back another time, sir, if I'd be bothering you."

"No, no, don't be silly, Robert. Rosalind and I are just finishing up with the Delage, aren't we, dear?" He smiles at his daughter, who's preoccupied with a small dent on the driver's side of the vehicle. She scrubs the dent as if her effort could somehow return the door to its original, pristine condition.

"All right then, if you're certain, sir?"

Archie nods and picks up his buffing cloth again, giving the Delage a satisfying sheen. *If only I could prolong this moment,* he thinks. But the clang of metal startles him, interrupting his wistful thoughts until he realizes that it's just Robert assembling his tools in the wheelbarrow.

The wheelbarrow creaks as Robert approaches them. *Why doesn't he head out back?* Archie thinks. *Why won't he leave them alone to enjoy this brief respite?* Soon, too soon, all would be lost.

"You should see the scene down by Newlands Corner, sir. They say that there are fifty-three search parties, with thirty to forty people each! Can you imagine it, upward of two thousand people looking for Mrs. Christie all at the same time? With all those folks hunting, I'm sure they'll find her, sir."

Archie wants nothing more than to silence this young man but knows that any commentary on his part will either encourage the lad or be reported to others or both. Anyway, the young man is only trying to give him comfort. So he nods in Robert's direction to signal the end of the conversation and then returns to his project.

But the gardener's son misses the hint entirely and blathers on. "I mean, more folks keep coming, even though some are only spectating or eating, what with Alfred Luland setting up a makeshift refreshment kiosk to serve the volunteers. A woman who breeds award-winning bloodhounds brought her dogs on the hunt, and they're sure to sniff Mrs. Christie out if she's there. Oh, and that writer woman Mrs. Sayers came to the site too. Took one look at the Silent Pool and announced your wife wasn't there. Not a lot of help she offered, huh?"

"Why don't the people know that Mama is away writing, Papa?" Rosalind pipes in with her small, high-pitched voice. When had she started listening to this conversation? Archie hadn't heard her approach. He thought she was still engrossed in that dent. "Didn't you tell them?"

Robert stares at the child, agog at her ignorance of her mother's disappearance.

Or perhaps agog at Archie's fostering of that ignorance. Either way, the gardener's son finally takes his leave and pushes his wheelbarrow to the farthest reaching corner of the property.

"Papa, you didn't answer my question," Rosalind notes. Then, in case he's forgotten her query, she repeats it. "Why didn't you tell everyone that Mama is just away writing a book and that she'll be back when she's done?"

Archie turns toward Rosalind, kneeling down and gazing directly into her dark eyes. "Darling, please don't worry. The resolution of this terrible situation is very nearly at hand."

CHAPTER FORTY-ONE:
THE MANUSCRIPT

December 3, 1926
Styles, Sunningdale, England

Three months. Ninety days. Two thousand, one hundred and sixty hours. This was what Archie had allotted me to save our marriage, and when I returned to Styles after the debacle of the Pyrenees, I realized that I had only forty-five days left to convince Archie to stay. Only one thousand and eighty of those original hours remained, and the mere thought of the dwindling minutes was enough to start my heart racing. But how could I win my husband back when he was rarely to be seen?

Over the preceding forty-five of those ninety days, there had been times when I felt like giving up. There had been entire days when I felt like relinquishing him to Nancy and losing myself in my writing, my family, and my daughter. *Would it really be so terrible?* I asked myself. After all, if I were honest with myself, our marriage had been empty for some time; golf seemed to play a more robust role in Archie's life than I did. Yet when I thought about Rosalind, I knew I had to stay the course. I couldn't let the stain of divorce taint my beautiful daughter and strain our relationship.

I resolved to wait for him to return. This waiting was different from all the waiting I'd undertaken before. Somehow, waiting for him for leaves during his military training, waiting for him to come home from the Great War, even waiting for him to appear on our London doorstep from Spain after Mummy died did not compare to waiting for him to return my love.

I felt the clock ticking constantly, and more and more, I took walks around the Silent Pool to calm my nerves. Despite the macabre history of the place — legends about dead maidens and rumors about the odd suicide — I found the still body of emerald water and the quiet woods surrounding it strangely soothing. Not to mention that it was the one place where I could indulge in my sobs without a witness.

By the time December arrived, the days left to attempt reconciliation were numbered, and I was in a frenzied state. When Archie was absent — he frequently stayed at his London club on weekdays — I would worry about whether Nancy was with him despite his promise, and Charlotte would have to urge me to stay at Ashfield and not drive into the city to surprise him. When he made his brief, unannounced visits to Styles on weekends and rare weekday evenings, primarily to see Rosalind, my nerves would shred even further as the pressure mounted to be charming and lighthearted in an effort to make Styles — and me — appealing to him.

I worked on my new book, *The Mystery of the Blue Train,* at a feverish pace. My publisher, Collins, was desperate for a new Hercule Poirot book and wielded my contract as the means to insist. The recently released *The Murder of Roger Ackroyd* had not only been critically well received but had sold well, and they hoped to ride that success with an immediate follow-up publication, along with the release of a collection of short Hercule Poirot stories that I'd serialized in magazine and newspaper publications. But every time I sat down at my typewriter, my mind clouded with emotion, and even the internal pressure to produce out of financial necessity should my marriage implode didn't clear my thoughts. More than anything, more even than Mummy's comforting and sage presence, I wished for more time.

Archie and I stared at each other across the breakfast table. *How ordinary the room looked,* I thought for an unreal second, *for such an extraordinary morning.* The sunlight filtered through the curtain, dappling the tablecloth with an attractive pattern. The table gleamed with Mummy's sweet rosebud china, and a perfect semicircle of toasted bread spread across the silver serving tray. Tiny puffs of steam rose from our teacups, and a jar of ruby-red jam sat at the center of it all. It could be any regular morning in any regular home of any regular family. But it wasn't.

"Please," I begged, "please don't do this. Let's talk about it this weekend, after dinner tonight. I made a reservation for us at a lovely inn in Yorkshire where we can discuss the future in privacy."

"There is no sense begging, Agatha. It only makes you appear less attractive than you already are, and that doesn't help your cause. I will not be joining you in Yorkshire this weekend. I will be spending the weekend with the Jameses," Archie answered, his tone firm and his posture erect such that his suit had not a single crease. He spoke as dismissively as he did when responding to

Rosalind's endless requests for a pony.

"And Nancy will be there as well, I'm guessing? She's good friends with Madge James, isn't she?" I asked, and although it was certainly true, I immediately regretted my words. Archie's face darkened with anger, and I knew I wouldn't win him back like that. "Please listen, Archie." I reached for his hand, but he pulled it away and stepped backward. I proceeded with my case, although I could hear Charlotte's voice in my head, cautioning me against pleading. She believed it only brought out a cruel streak in him, and she'd implored me not to beg him after she witnessed an unpleasant altercation. "You promised me three months. Three months of reconciliation before deciding. But we barely saw you. You just need more time, that's all — Christmas at Abney Hall, a New Year's trip to Portugal with our neighborhood friends, the full three months that we discussed."

"I don't need any more time to make my decision, and I do not want to keep up this charade any longer. I am finished." His voice didn't waver, and neither did his gaze. *Had he practiced this composure in the mirror?* I wondered.

"How can you say you're finished with our family when you haven't even tried?" I asked, my voice cracking.

He didn't bother to answer my question. Instead, he repeated the hateful words he had first uttered back in Ashfield. "I want a divorce."

"I don't want a divorce, Archie. I want our family and our marriage back." The tears came, and I began to sob. "Rosalind loves you. I still love you. When you were fighting in the Great War, you used to write that you'd do anything to keep me. How has it come to this?"

"Agatha, I will be meeting with a lawyer to begin the divorce proceedings. My marriage to Nancy will happen as soon as the divorce is finalized." He sounded as if he were conducting a business meeting for Austral Limited, not ending his marriage and ruining his family.

For the very first time, rage instead of desperation took hold of me. How dare he? How could he talk of marriage to Nancy in the same breath as he spoke of our divorce? *By God,* I thought, *if he wants this shameful divorce, I will get what I want as well.* I will make him give me the very thing he wants to protect. Otherwise, it will be the undoing of me.

Pulling a handkerchief from the pocket of my silk dressing gown, I dabbed at my eyes and nose in an effort to compose myself. "I will only agree to a divorce if you name Nancy Neele as your adulteress and the reason for the dissolution of our marriage." I kept my tone as unruffled and business-like as he'd been all morning, repressing the fury kindling within me.

With this statement, his carefully assembled countenance of calm and determination cracked. His eyes widened in disbelief at my request, and in that moment, I knew that I had struck him in his very core, a heart that I thought he no longer had. "I will not name Nancy in the divorce. Under no circumstances."

How dare he refuse me? Who did he think he was to deny me this request? My incredulity and my volume rose alongside my anger. "Can you really believe that I would agree to a divorce in which the reason isn't explicitly articulated? So everyone would fill in that gap with *me* as the cause? They'll think I was an unreasonable wife. Or that *I* was the unfaithful one! Imagine what Rosalind would think one day." I straightened my dressing gown and robe, tucked a curl behind my ear, and very slowly and very distinctly said, "I want Nancy Neele named as the reason for our divorce. Or I will not grant you one."

327

His eyes narrowed, and he walked toward me for the first time that morning. "Nancy is the woman I love, and I plan on marrying her. I will not besmirch her name."

I laughed, not caring for the first time in months how loud or unladylike my guffaw sounded. Because in that moment, I did not care about his opinion of me. "That's rich, Archie. You won't besmirch the reputation of your mistress, but you find it perfectly acceptable to betray your wife and drag her name through the mud?" I stared at him right in the eyes. "No Nancy, no divorce."

A menacing expression, familiar from our trip to Guéthary, appeared on his face. He grabbed my shoulders — as if he wanted to shake *his* sense into me — and as I pulled away, my hand swung across the breakfast table, sending Mummy's rosebud teapot crashing to the floor and me along with it. When I tried to stand up, he pushed me back down, grinding my leg into a shard of shattered china. The next thing I remembered was the sound of his footsteps storming out of the dining room and out of Styles. I felt the vibration of those footsteps across the floor, followed in quick succession by the rapid clip of Charlotte's no-nonsense step and Rosalind's patter.

Rosalind shrieked at the sight of me on

the floor amid the broken china as Charlotte raced to my side. As she kneeled down to help me up, she asked, "Mrs. Christie, are you quite all right?"

"It's nothing, Carlo." I tried to muster up a smile. "Clumsy, that's all."

"You're not clumsy, Mama," Rosalind's high-pitched voice chirped. "You and Papa were having a row. We heard it."

"It was nothing to concern yourself with, Rosalind," I said as I struggled to my feet with Charlotte's aid. "It's nothing to do with you. Not to worry."

"Oh, I know that, Mama," she answered, all confidence and assurance. "After all, Papa likes me, but he doesn't much like you."

CHAPTER FORTY-TWO:
DAY TEN AFTER
THE DISAPPEARANCE

Monday, December 13, 1926
Styles, Sunningdale, England

The newspaper is spread wide on his study desk: *Biggest Manhunt in History Yields Nothing. Is Foul Play to Blame in Novelist's Strange Disappearance?* He does not need to read the full article to know who is being suspected of that foul play. There is and has always been only one suspect.

It doesn't matter that he's heard the odd policeman mutter that Agatha went missing on purpose for reasons of her own design. It's unimportant that the *Liverpool Weekly Post*'s recent serialization of *The Murder of Roger Ackroyd* has prompted some pundits to speculate whether Agatha staged her own disappearance as a publicity stunt for her latest book. None of this really affects the fact that the public at large — and the detectives in charge — thinks he's a philanderer who's killed his wife to be free to marry his lover, particularly with the recent evidence.

Archie thinks that he has made peace with his fate. But he knows his state of mind makes no difference. The end is at hand, regardless of how he feels about it. A mere glance at the newspaper article and, alongside it on his desk, the sheaf of paper entitled *The Manuscript* that was recently delivered to Styles reminds him of the inevitability of the outcome.

There's only ever been one path through this intricate web. His only recourse has always been to follow the sticky silken thread right to the web's center, and only then does he stand a chance of being unwound — as if he were Theseus clutching at Ariadne's red thread through King Minos's deadly labyrinth. But who knows what really awaits him at the labyrinth's center? After all, Agatha is no Ariadne, and he is no one's Theseus.

Still, in his darker, private moments, he cannot believe the turn his life has taken. His existence used to be normal and ordered, and he is just an ordinary man. How has it come to this? Is he really to blame for it all, as he's read?

A loud, determined knock sounds at the study door, not the demure rap of any of the Styles servants. For a fleeting moment, he considers not answering it. The door is bolted tight from the inside, after all. He's kept it locked since this most recent bout of madness began. With the number of police in and about Styles, the effort at resistance will be futile, he knows, and will only forestall the inescapable. He rubs his wrists as if he can already feel the grip of the steel handcuffs upon them.

"Colonel Christie," a deep male voice calls to him. It is unfamiliar, and that surprises him. He's been expecting Kenward or Goddard to deliver this final blow and to do it with a certain amount of glee and smugness.

"Open up, Colonel Christie," the voice booms. "We know you're inside. Miss Fisher already informed us. And we have a police guard outside the study window, so don't think of doing a runner."

The sound of Charlotte's voice drifts into his erstwhile fortress. "Sorry, Colonel Christie." She sounds meek although not terribly apologetic. With each passing day since Agatha's disappearance, she's grown more inhospitable to him, and he's begun to worry that she's sharing her feelings with Rosalind. Their most recent conversations only cement that suspicion.

He is frozen. Unable to answer. Unable to move. For all the inevitability of this next step, now that it has arrived, he feels incapable of moving forward to meet it head-on. Still, if he retreats and refuses to play the role penned for him in that damnable letter, then any chance of freedom, any chance of a life with Nancy — however slim — will elude him forever.

The door shudders with a hammer-like thumping. A voice he knows all too well reverberates through the air. "Colonel Christie, it's Detective Chief Constable Kenward here, and I've got Superintendent Goddard by my side. Open the door of your own free will, or we *will* break it down."

So this is it, he thinks. He is standing at the center of the web, and there is only one direction to go, one laid out for him step-by-step in the parcel he's received. He walks to the study door and unbolts the lock. Throwing open the creaky door to the crowded hallway that awaits him, he surrenders to them — and to his fate.

Chapter Forty-Three:
The Manuscript

December 3, 1926
Styles, Sunningdale, England

I had eaten many meals alone in my life. Tea as a young child with elderly parents and two older siblings busy with their own lives. Breakfast as a young nurse with an early shift whose husband was away fighting the Great War. Lunch over the desk in my Styles study as I worked away on a detective story on my typewriter. But I had never suffered through a meal as lonely as this one.

Earlier that day, I'd instructed the cook to make a formal dinner for two and asked the housemaid, Lilly, to set the dining room table accordingly. I hadn't spoken to Archie since our horrific argument that morning with its terrible exchange of ultimatums, but I still had hope that he'd return home for dinner as we had arranged before our row. Archie was a man of order and routine, and I counted upon that quality for his attendance at dinner. I kept myself busy during the day by planning a perfect evening meal and taking a drive through the countryside, and when Rosalind came home from school, she and I visited Archie's mother as we had planned. Throughout the visit, I kept turning our fight around and around in my mind and saying silent prayers that Archie would return home come twilight. If he came, perhaps the weekend in Yorkshire could be saved, and when we got back to Styles, I packed my suitcase for the excursion in preparation. Then, after she'd had her tea, I tucked Rosalind into her bed, ensuring that her favorite blue teddy lay beside her on her pillow, and kissed her good night.

I had dressed for dinner with care. Selecting a green knitted suit, I'd turned this way and that in the mirror. *Did the outfit make me look any slimmer?* I wondered. Archie had complained about my weight over the past few years, but once, he'd complimented me while I was wearing this particular ensemble. I hoped he'd find it pleasing, or at least not objectionable.

I settled into my seat in the dining room. As I waited for Lilly to serve the first dinner course, I kept my eyes averted from the empty chair that faced me. Instead, I studied the room. On the shelves and on the sideboard were silver-framed photographs of me, Archie, and Rosalind, interspersed with images of my family and a lone portrait of Archie; his brother, Campbell; Peg; and their late father. Scattered among the frames were china figurines and a vase that Mummy had adored; I'd brought them from Ashfield to Styles in the hopes of turning this artifice of a house on a carefully orchestrated street into a warm, natural home like Ashfield.

The mantelpiece clock ticked loudly, or so it seemed, as I waited for him. I studied the steaming bowl of clear consommé that the cook prepared as a first course, a dish that always soothed Archie's troublesome stomach. The minute hand passed the one, then two, then three. When it hovered between the three and four, I noticed that the soup was no longer steaming. Even though I was not planning on eating until Archie's arrival, I decided to have the soup, as it would soon be chilled.

With the sound of the clattering spoon, Lilly reappeared. Her expression was somewhat anxious, and I realized that this situation fell outside her training. *Should she clear the table or wait for the master?* I could almost see the question pass through her consciousness.

"You may remove both soup bowls, Lilly. Mr. Christie seems to be running late, so I think you can tell Cook that we will move on to the second course." I reached down to pet Peter, who'd settled at my feet. The gentle pup seemed to sense the despair that had overtaken me since Archie's betrayal and rarely left my side these days.

When I glanced up, Lilly was still looking at me, although her expression had changed from perplexity over the soup bowls to pity over my excuse for Archie's late arrival. *My god,* I thought with a start. *Not even the staff believes that my husband will return home to me.* I wondered if I really even wanted him back. Had the events of this morning changed my mind, but I'd become so accustomed to waiting for him that I hadn't let that feeling register? Shouldn't they have changed my mind?

In a few moments, Lilly reappeared with plates of venison for the second course, and after a suitable interval, she entered the dining room again, carrying the third course. She hesitated before placing the plates of Dover sole down on the table, given that the second course hadn't been touched. I guided her with a gentle nod; while it was unconventional to serve a third course when the prior course had not been eaten, on this occasion, it was fine.

I resolved not to eat from either of the two courses Lilly delivered. I wasn't hungry, but as the minutes continued to pass, refraining almost became a superstitious obsession. If only I could wait until I heard the sound of his car crunching over the gravel, then all would be well. If I took even the smallest nibble of the venison or sole, then Archie would never come home at all. But sometimes, I would look down at my hand, and the fork would be in it, hovering over the food, and I realized that I was vacillating over what I really wanted.

The road outside Styles grew quiet as the neighbors returned home for their evening meals and settled in behind closed doors with their families and friends. Still, I waited in the dining room as if I'd become one of Mummy's china figurines awaiting animation. But when the minute hand reached the twelve, I knew. Archie was not coming home to Styles. Perhaps he would never pass through its doors again.

A swell of sadness overtook me, and I choked down a sob that I didn't want Lilly or the cook to hear. I'd given Charlotte the night off to visit a friend in London, so I didn't need to worry about alarming her. I didn't think I could withstand the wellspring of emotion. All this sorrow, all this pain, it was too much, even if it was tinged with relief. If only I could disappear.

Then the phone rang, shattering my lonely vigil. When I picked it up, I nearly cried in relief to hear a familiar voice. But then the voice spoke. And in that moment, I knew that everything had changed.

PART TWO

PART TWO

CHAPTER FORTY-FOUR

Tuesday, December 14, 1926
Harrogate Hydro, Harrogate, England

I stare at the evening dresses hanging in the wardrobe. Like a pastel-colored rainbow, they shimmer against the dark, burnished wood, and I can't resist running a finger along their silken lengths. Each gown is lovely in its way and newly purchased from the local dress shops in Harrogate and Leeds. But which to wear? I want to look especially nice. *No, that's not right,* I think. I want to look perfect tonight, but only for myself.

My gaze rests on a salmon-colored georgette gown. With its drop-waist silhouette and its alternating lace panels with subtle pearlescent beading, it is particularly flattering, or so the salesgirl at the exclusive Harrogate store told me. She'd sounded sincere, but was she simply trying to lure me into a purchase? *Let's see,* I think as I pull it out of the wardrobe and twirl it around on its hanger.

I slide the gown on over my new ivory satin slip. I walk over to the full-length mirror in the corner of the hotel room, avoiding my image until the very last second. It's been quite some time since I enjoyed my reflection. Opening my eyes, I almost gasp. Could that really be me? The gown skims my newly slim figure, and the salmon color gives my complexion a healthy, dare I say younger, glow. For the first time in a very long time, I feel attractive.

I brush my hair until it has a sheen, tucking a wayward curl behind my ear and arranging another curl to mask the small cut and bruise that are fading on my forehead. I add a sheer coat of apricot-shaded lipstick and dab cologne behind my ear. Strapping my delicate silver heels on around my ankles, I turn this way and that in front of the mirror. *A shawl around the shoulders will be the final touch,* I think as I drape a finely embroidered swath of fabric around me. A last glance in the mirror confirms that I am ready. This is indeed the perfect gown for this evening.

The crystal handle feels heavy in my hand as I turn it to swing open the door to my room. An unusually loud din sounds on the hotel's ground floor, just below the staircase outside my room. Unused to the noise, I shut the door closed, returning to the safety of my room. I've grown used to the quiet ebb and flow of the hotel over the past week; I can predict a bustle of activity around breakfast, teatime, and the cocktail hour but a gentle lull in the hours in between. I always choose this hushed hour — the gap between cocktails and dinner — to enter unobtrusively into the hotel's evening fray and settle down to dinner with one of the books I've selected from the Harrogate library for company. Or perhaps a crossword.

On instinct, I pull aside the heavy brocade curtains covering the main window of my room. The glass looks out at the manicured gardens that serve as the entryway to the hotel, resplendent even in winter with viburnum, holly, and laurel interspersed with flowering hellebore, otherwise known as Christmas rose. I notice that the lot is full of automobiles and that three small groupings of people are outlined against the gaslit lamps that line the gardens. *Ah*, I think. *Here is my explanation for the unexpected racket: a party is assembling in the hotel's ballroom, perhaps an early Christmas gathering.* Or perhaps it is something else entirely, something as well planned as a holiday soiree. Either way, I feel prepared. I have been planning for this moment for some time.

I open my door once again. My heels make a satisfying clip as I cross the hallway from my room to the wide, impressive staircase that leads down to the lobby. The crimson-red and golden-yellow Persian carpet that lines the stairs muffles my step but not the drama of my entrance. A sea of faces stares up at me as I descend.

I nod at Mrs. Robson, with whom I've shared a cup of tea and a lively discussion about gardening. Mr. Wollesley, with whom I've played several jolly rounds of billiards while discussing the spa's various services, gives me a wave. I smile at the sweet waitress, Rose, who serves at breakfast and dinner but returns home during the lunch shift to care for her elderly grandmother. What a lovely array of folks I've met here at the Harrogate Hydro, I think. In this place, with these people, outside normal time, I feel safe. I am in a cocoon of my own making, in a protected realm that hovers beside reality, and I wish I could stay here longer. Sometimes I long to stay here forever.

But then I see him, as I knew I would. There, at the base of the staircase, to the side of the column that separates the lobby from the tearoom, stands a man. He looks so small and insubstantial, so different from my memories that, for a moment, I almost don't recognize him. But then he steps under a pool of light, and suddenly, it is absolutely him. And I know that it is time.

CHAPTER FORTY-FIVE

Tuesday, December 14, 1926
Harrogate Hydro, Harrogate, England

The man takes a step toward me. I pause, uncertain whether I should ignore him and continue onward toward my dinner reservation. What is the right course at this precise moment in the narrative? As he opens his mouth to speak, I notice that two other gentlemen, one in a rumpled coat and a battered trilby and the other in a perfectly pressed charcoal suit with a black overcoat, which they haven't bothered to remove indoors, move out of the shadows cast by the eaves of the staircase in my direction. Something about their demeanor makes me uncomfortable, and I step away from all three of them.

Turning toward these gentlemen, the man holds a hand up, as if keeping them at bay. Disregarding his gesture, to some extent at least, they continue to approach, but they only proceed so far. I glance at them quizzically, but they will not meet my eyes.

I draw my shawl tightly around my shoulders — as if the delicate, embroidered fabric could serve as a protective shield — as the man takes a step toward me. "Might we have a private word over a drink?" he asks in a voice loud enough for the other gentlemen to hear.

His request disturbs the peacefulness I've enjoyed here at the Harrogate Hydro, and I desperately want to refuse. I know that if I acquiesce, my cocoon will be compromised. But I also know that if I decline, I cannot continue to cling to this unreal world. This is the moment to which I have been building.

"Just for a moment?" he asks, his blue eyes pleading.

I nod and lead him in the direction of the leather wingback chairs that are scattered around the lobby fireplace in sets of two. As we walk, I hear the clatter of heels, not only those belonging to me and the man but also the other two gentlemen. They are trailing behind us.

I purposefully stop midstep, causing one of them to nearly collide with me. The role I'm playing requires that I call them out.

349

Pivoting, I face them and ask, "May I help you?"

They glance at each other and then at the man, who nods. The heavier-set one says, "Please allow me to introduce myself, ma'am. My name is Detective Chief Constable Kenward of Surrey."

"And you are?" I say into the awkward pause to the other, more meticulously dressed gentleman.

"I am Superintendent Goddard of Berkshire. It's a pleasure to meet you, ma'am."

"While it is nice to make your acquaintance" — I hesitate as I try to recall their names and titles exactly — "Detective Chief Constable Kenward and Superintendent Goddard, I must say, I am puzzled by your presence. You are both a long way from home, after all, and yet, you are uncomfortably close to me." I force a giggle, as if the question I was about to ask was preposterous. "Am I in some sort of trouble?"

Kenward clears his throat and answers for both of them. "Not at all, ma'am. I think that perhaps once you two" — he gestures to the man with the blue eyes — "have had a chance to chat, the reason for our presence will become clearer. Are you comfortable being alone in the presence of this man while we wait over here?" The bulky police officer gestures to a lobby area that is near but not within earshot of the wingback chairs near the fireplace where the man and I had been heading before our little collision.

I nod after a brief, hesitant pause.

Before the officers sidle off, a familiar face inserts itself into our strange group. "What do we have here?" The elderly gentleman wags his finger at me as he glances at the three men in turn. "Are these ringers?"

The men give me a confused stare. Despite the odd tension between me and these men, I can't help but laugh. Earlier today, over breakfast, I'd promised Mr. Wollesley a round of billiards after dinner. He has grown used to winning these nightly rounds, and I guess that the unexpected appearance of three rather burly men has him worried about his chances of success.

"Not to worry, Mr. Wollesley. Our billiards round will be as usual. Just you and I," I reassure him with a broad smile. "And possibly Mrs. Robson." I reference another hotel guest who joins us occasionally.

He returns my grin. "Well, that is a relief. I thought that perhaps you'd brought in the cavalry."

"Not a chance. If I win tonight, it'll be fair and square. Not that I'm expecting to win, mind you."

"I'm relieved to hear it." Mr. Wollesley looks at the gentlemen expectantly. Courtesy demands that I introduce them, a rule I have no intention of following.

"Will you please excuse us, Mr. Wollesley? My unexpected guests are here from out of town, and we may squeeze in a drink before dining."

"Of course." He gives us a little bow and then says, "Enjoy your dinner, Mrs. Neele."

CHAPTER FORTY-SIX

Tuesday, December 14, 1926
Harrogate Hydro, Harrogate, England

Carefully choosing the seat that faces outward, I sit down, allowing the wingback chair to envelop me. I smooth the skirt of my georgette dress, tuck a curl behind my ear, and force a pleasant, expectant expression on my face. *I hope I look attractive,* I think, then chastise myself for the thought, as it shouldn't matter what anyone but me thinks about my appearance. Then I wait for him to speak. I can hardly wait to hear what he has to say.

But he is speechless, it seems. His mouth opens and closes as if words are cycling through his mind but can't quite decide whether they should form on his lips. I hold my tongue for a few long moments, but ultimately, it seems that nothing will emanate from his mouth. I am forced to take the helm, and I'm ready.

"Aren't you happy to see me, Archie?" I ask my slack-jawed husband.

"Mrs. N-Neele? You're calling yourself M-Mrs. Neele?" he stutters. Then his voice begins to rise. "What the devil are you on about, Agatha?"

"Do you mean by calling myself Mrs. Neele or in general?" I ask with a small smile. I know I shouldn't bait him, but I cannot help myself. This moment has been long in coming. Keeping my tone even and light, I say, "You might want to wipe that anger from your face and replace it with a smile, Archie, or at least a look of concern. We may be out of the direct spotlight, but there are eyes everywhere." I nod at a passing waitress and back at the police. "A man who misses his wife, a man who has been worried for eleven long days that she was dead, would be delighted and relieved when she resurfaced. He might even hold her hand or give her an embrace. *If* he had nothing to do with her disappearance, that is."

Archie's fists clench and unclench at his side, and anyone watching would see his fury mount rather than dissipate. As he works to manage his anger, I continue, "I'm certain you realize that photographers and journalists encircle the hotel? I saw them gather from my hotel room window before I came downstairs. And of course, there are police cars stationed outside from the local authorities as well as Kenward and Goddard's men. I'm guessing that you are aware of this, despite the fact that they've sounded no alarms? So if you allow yourself to get angry, it will play right into everyone's preconceptions about you."

He doesn't respond, and I didn't expect that he would. My goal is simply to warn him against releasing the outburst clearly brewing within him. Not because I have any desire to protect him but because delaying his anger is important for the rest of my plan.

Instead, he says, "How could you?" The words are heavy with accusation.

His expression is incredulous, and I find his discomfort quite delicious.

"How could I? How could *you*? How could *you* have an affair with Nancy Neele? How could *you* leave me to my grief over my mother without a shred of emotion and then use that grief as an excuse for your affair? How could *you* abandon your family after asking so much of me?" I ask all of this quite calmly, making plain the irony of his comment.

His mouth opens and closes again as he considers and rejects any number of replies.

I use his muteness as an opportunity to continue. I've been voiceless for far too long as it is.

"Perhaps I've misunderstood you, Archie. Are you asking not how could I use Nancy Neele's name but how could I orchestrate my disappearance?" I pretend that he's nodded. "Ah, well, that *is* an interesting question, isn't it? But before I tell you the how, aren't you curious about the why? Let's reframe your question: *Why* did I orchestrate my disappearance?"

I pause, pretending to give him the opportunity to comment, but instead, I rush ahead. "You may think you know why, Archie. You may believe that I disappeared to punish you. But that would be incredibly narrow-minded and, unsurprisingly, very self-focused. The real why began the precise moment that you committed murder."

"Murder?!" he practically shrieks, and I glance over to see if Kenward and Goddard have heard. They're too busy whispering to each other. "Me, commit murder? What the hell are you talking about, Agatha? It's you that's been framing me for a murder I didn't commit, and your presence here today proves I didn't harm you."

Keeping my voice even and my face placid, I say, "You killed the innocent woman I once was — the one who believed she had a contented marriage and pleasant family life, the one who molded her entire existence around you and your happiness — just as surely as if you committed murder."

"That's, that's not fair, Ag—"

As I speak to Archie, I've been keeping Kenward and Goddard in my peripheral vision. They've been hovering on the edge of the tearoom carpet, always respectfully far enough away that we can't be overheard, engrossed in their own conversation. But now, they stop talking and begin to walk toward us.

I interrupt Archie. "Your detective friends will be here in a moment. I want you to tell them that we need more time alone, that I'm still suffering from amnesia. Just as I laid out in my letter to you. Follow the steps. All along, the timing and the actions you are meant to take — and not take — have been very clear."

"Why should I? Now that you've reappeared, I won't be a suspect in your death. And anyway, those bastards aren't my friends."

"Do you think I've reached the limit of my power? Do you imagine that my reemergence absolves you from all responsibility,

357

that I don't have another plan?"

Archie's eyes narrow as he assesses me, seeing me — with all my capabilities and all my determination — for the first time. I'm not surprised by his reaction. Only recently have I come to understand the breadth of my power myself. Why would I expect Archie — with his narrow worldview — to be aware of my capacity sooner than I was?

"All right," he agrees. "For now anyway, I'll do as you've asked."

Kenward's heavy step thunders across the floor as he gets closer to us. I glance up as if noticing him for the first time. "Why, Detective Kenward and Superintendent Goddard, you've returned."

"It's Detective Chief Constable Kenward." Kenward is quick to correct me.

"My apologies," I say.

Goddard jumps in, his eagerness evident. "How are you two doing here?"

"I think we might go on to dinner alone. My wife and I need some more time to talk," Archie answers for us both.

I force myself to go wide-eyed at the word *wife* and watch as Kenward and Goddard take note.

As if on cue, Archie continues, "You see, we need a bit more time to get re-acquainted."

CHAPTER FORTY-SEVEN

Tuesday, December 14, 1926
Harrogate Hydro, Harrogate, England

"A table for two, please," I hear Archie say to the maître d'hôtel, who glances at me quizzically. The little man in his fastidious evening attire, who reminds me of my fictional Hercule Poirot in some ways, has grown quite used to me dining alone over the past week with a book or a crossword puzzle for company and seems confused by this change in my habits. Only after dinner do I typically join other guests for a congenial turn at the piano or billiards.

I nod to indicate my assent.

"Right this way, Mrs. Neele," he says, and I watch as Archie's back stiffens at the name.

We don't get very far. Just as we cross the threshold into the dining room — a formal cream-and-sage-green affair with a lovely glass ceiling — I feel a hand on my arm. "Mrs. Neele, you have a dinner guest. How very nice for you."

It is Mrs. Robson, always nosy about the comings and goings of the hotel guests. Before I can answer or explain, she asks, "Does this mean you won't be joining us for billiards?" I'd discussed a round of billiards with her and Mr. Wollesley for this evening.

"I'm afraid I won't be able to play with you tonight," I say and begin following the maître d'hôtel again. But she doesn't leave.

"Is your guest visiting from South Africa as well?" she persists.

Archie glances at me as I answer, "No, I'm afraid not. Enjoy your evening, Mrs. Robson." She finally accepts this signal of farewell and departs for her own dinner.

The maître d'hôtel leads us to a small table in the back corner, flanked by columns. It is discrete, and I couldn't have chosen it better myself. From a distance, I see that Kenward and Goddard have positioned themselves in lobby chairs that have a view of the restaurant's entrance. *Are they watching to collect evidence or to ensure that neither of us escapes?* I wonder.

As I sit in the upholstered dining chair that the maître d'hôtel pulls out for me, he asks, "Shall I bring you and your guest glasses of the red wine you've been enjoying, Mrs. Neele?"

"Yes, please," I answer, watching Archie wince at the name.

We don't speak as the waiter arrives and pours us each a glass of garnet-colored wine in the crystal glasses already set out on the table. As he busies himself at our table, I glance at the diners around us, well-heeled men and women here for the spa waters and treatments who are engrossed in themselves and each other. I must take care that they stay preoccupied and do not become drawn up in the exchange Archie and I are about to have.

When the waiter finally leaves, I take a long sip, and just as I'm about to launch into my prepared speech, I suddenly feel bashful, even wistful. A deep surge of longing for my daughter surfaces in Archie's familiar company. "How's Rosalind?" I ask.

"She doesn't know anything about what's happened, aside from a few snarky remarks by classmates, so she is fine," he answers with surprising warmth. But then, I suppose he's always cared more about Rosalind than me, even though he forbade me from feeling that way.

"Thank God."

"Well, it's certainly no thanks to you." The warmth disappears from his voice, and bitter coldness takes hold again.

I catch myself about to apologize and launch into a long rationale for my behavior, and I stop. I mustn't backslide into sentiment and old patterns of behavior with Archie. Instead, I allow the same iciness I hear in his tone to pervade my heart and voice. And I begin.

"Let's return to the why of my disappearance before we turn to the how, shall we? Although in truth, the two are inextricably intertwined," I say.

When he doesn't speak but only glowers at me, I continue with my speech, one I've practiced over and over in the solitude of my hotel room. I've been building to this moment for much, much longer than the eleven days I've been missing, but now that it's here, I must steel myself against my feelings and my years of pliability and softness for Archie.

"*Why* did I disappear, Archie? I told you earlier because it was the necessary consequence of your murder of me. This must sound confusing to you, because here I sit across from you, alive and in person. But the murder of which I speak is the murder of my authentic self — that vivacious, creative spirit you first met at Ugbrooke House all those years ago. You killed her bit by bit, over days and weeks and months and years of tiny injuries, until she'd grown so small and weak as to almost vanish. That person clung to life, however, in some far cavernous reach within me until you delivered your final savage blow on Rosalind's birthday at Ashfield."

"You're not making a bit of sense, Agatha. Maybe your sanity went missing along with you," he says with a rueful laugh.

I ignore his snide remark. "The story of that murder lies in the manuscript I sent you. Did you read it?"

He gives me a begrudging nod. "I had no choice. Your letter threatened dire consequences if I didn't familiarize myself with those pages. And if I didn't follow your instructions about how to handle your disappearance — which I did."

"Good. I won't ask if you enjoyed it, as I know it's hard to read about oneself, if you are even self-aware enough to see yourself in those pages. I suppose some might call that manuscript an autobiography, although you and I know there's a bit of fiction in there. Not in the way you are depicted, of course. No, not there. Although I suppose you fought against your portrayal when you read it; none of us like to see our unflattering truths laid bare."

I see from his countenance precisely how distasteful he found my manuscript, but I note that he's not arguing about his characterization. Not yet at least. "In those pages, I revealed myself — from the girl I'd been to the woman I changed into, as well as the wife and mother I became — and I demonstrated how that woman grew increasingly unpleasant to you. How you shrank from my emotions, how you flinched at my animated conversations, how your eyes glazed over in boredom over my books, how you recoiled at my touch. And I showed you how the parts you found distasteful were killed off, one by one, until there was almost nothing of me left. I sacrificed my relationship with Rosalind most of all, because you couldn't stand to have any competition for your attention. Not that I blame you entirely, mind. Mummy always told me that you and your needs came first — before those of my child and before my own. And for a long time, I believed her.

"Imagine my surprise when the ideal wife I'd molded myself into — what you told me was ideal, anyway — wasn't good enough. Imagine my astonishment when, even though I'd shed every real part of myself and transformed into your perfect woman — except the weight you tortured me about shedding, as I couldn't — I was still intolerable to you. Then imagine the deadly shock you delivered when you informed me that, in fact, there was an idyllic companion for you out there, and it wasn't me but a younger, prettier, meeker, more 'appropriate' woman named Nancy Neele.

"So you see, you murdered that pure Agatha, just as many people out there believed that you murdered the physical Agatha. Your affair was just the final blow in a murder that took place over a long, long time."

"This is madness, Agatha. Pure fiction. Just like one of your silly books." His voice is quiet, but his face reveals a thunderous rage.

"Is it, Archie? As you changed, you wanted someone who suited the newly confident and successful you. When it became clear that I couldn't be that person — I was too familiar with your failings, your dark disappointments, and your history — you were drawn to Nancy. You wanted to become your own unreliable narrator, rewriting your past and your present history to suit the story you told yourself and Nancy. But I couldn't let you do that."

Archie doesn't move, doesn't argue, barely even blinks. Are my words resonating with him in a way that my manuscript didn't?

"Why?" he suddenly blurts out. "Why did you have to do this? Why couldn't you just let me quietly divorce you?"

Anger begins to replace my calm resignation. "Have you been listening to me at all, Archie? Did you listen that Friday morning you announced you were leaving? Didn't you read about this in the pages of my manuscript? If I let you do what you wanted — write me out of your story altogether after altering me and my relationships to such a vast extent, without any accountability to the truth about your actions and your affair with Nancy — I never could have arisen from my deathbed into the new, stronger person I've become these past months. You would have taken not only my truest self, but you would have taken my reputation and, most importantly, my daughter from me."

"What the hell are you talking about, Agatha? I never insisted on taking Rosalind from you in the divorce, and anyway, the tender years doctrine favors maternal custody until a child is sixteen. I don't think I could get custody if I tried." He sounds exasperated and confused.

It is my turn to laugh. Is he being intentionally obtuse to thwart me, or is he really this thick? How had I ever thought the world of this selfish, literal-minded man? Without him weighing me down like an anchor, my mind and my pen will be free to soar. But first, I must slice the anchor rope, and there is only one way to do it.

"You don't understand anything, Archie, no matter my efforts at illumination. I'm not talking about the legal loss of my daughter. I'm talking about the emotional loss, beyond the estrangement you've already wreaked by insisting that she come second in my life and by my idiocy in listening. If I had allowed you to divorce me without naming Nancy as your adulteress — and we both know that the Matrimonial Causes Act requires some form of adultery to be cited — then Rosalind, and the world, would have forever thought I was to blame. And given how she currently favors you, I would lose her forever. I've already lost so much to you; I will not lose Rosalind. In order to avoid that, I needed everyone to know that you are the cause of our problems and that I did everything I could to save our marriage and our family."

"That's why you staged this charade of a disappearance?"

"If you'd been listening to me, you would see that's only part of the reason. But yes, I had to very carefully arrange my disappearance so that my whereabouts would be mysterious and the reason behind my departure ominous, but also so that you would eventually be implicated and your affair revealed as part of the investigation. *Because* you wouldn't come clean on your own. In the months before I vanished, I made certain our estrangement wasn't a secret; friends, family, and staff all knew you'd been staying in the city, away from Styles, because of a rift between us. The few times we reconnected at Styles were awkward at best. I went missing the evening after our biggest fight — one in which you refused to go away with me for the weekend, opting instead for a house party at the Jameses *with Nancy* — an argument witnessed by several people. My car was found in the early hours of the dawn, the morning after that terrible fight; the headlights shone out of an otherwise desolate area onto passersby as they went to work. When the police located my Morris Cowley, it rested on the edge of a precipice, stopped from crashing to the ground below by a fortuitous tangle of bushes. My car, which was packed with items for the Yorkshire trip I'd hoped to take with you, had been abandoned there, near the Silent Pool, a notorious place for suicides. But I was nowhere to be found, and the clues I left behind for you and the police — my heavy coat in the Morris Cowley's back seat despite the coldness of the night, my weekend bag despite the cancelled plans, the car teetering on the edge of a cliff but no body to be found, the strange letter to your brother that raised the specter of some nebulous illness, the late-night call that seemingly precipitated my departure although it was only a check-in call from Charlotte — were open to multiple interpretations, all of them ominous and most of them pointing to you. How long did you think it would take for the police to connect the dots that led to you? And from you to Nancy? And from that time forward, how long did you think it would take for the authorities to shade in the blank areas of that image with my murder or suicide, prompted by you in either case?"

He crosses his arms and leans back in his chair, a self-satisfied smile spreading across his face. "You think you're so smart, Agatha, but you've forgotten something important. You've lost your leverage against me. You've reappeared."

For a brief, inexplicable moment, the image of Reggie Lucy flashes through my mind. How different my life would have been had I married that kindly man instead of Archie. Never would my life have devolved in this way. But I may never have transformed into the strong, talented woman I've had to become.

I can't afford any weakness, so I banish the thought of Reggie from my mind. Instead, I harden myself and smile right back at Archie. "You've forgotten that I am gifted in the complex plotting of mysteries. Did you think that the little manuscript I sent you was simply for your edification? To elicit some sympathy for me? No, Archie, that's not its primary purpose at all. It's a copy of a document that will be sent to Kenward and Goddard if you do not follow my instructions to the letter. In that case, it will become evidence in a different crime."

"You're bluffing, Agatha. The only crime at issue here was your suspected murder, and that's been solved by your very alive presence here at the Harrogate Hydro. So if you'll excuse me —" He pushes himself up as if to leave.

"Think about it, Archie. Think about the story my manuscript tells. Think about the picture it paints of you."

Reluctantly, he sits back down. He knows he must listen, but he still has a spark of defiance in his eyes. I hope to snuff out that spark forever.

I continue, "The coldness over my mother's death. The affair and the businesslike announcement of your abandonment. The debilitating affect it had on me. The threatening behavior on the terrace in the Pyrenees. The violence over breakfast on that last day."

"None of that's true, Agatha," he seethes.

"Really, Archie? I'll admit to a certain amount of fiction in the manuscript, but only exaggeration in the area of your threatening behavior in the Pyrenees and at breakfast — and in the ongoing desire I felt to remain your wife and in the emotional demeanor with which I faced that final meal on Friday night. Otherwise, the fiction came in elsewhere, primarily in the form of omission. Obviously, I omitted all the planning I undertook in the months before my disappearance. It took patience and time to lay the groundwork — and a certain amount of dramatic skill when I was with you, admittedly — but I couldn't share that in my manuscript, could I?" I say with a little chuckle.

"I also omitted certain feelings I had about motherhood, an ambivalence that grew from the distance you imposed between me and Rosalind and the irritation I occasionally felt when her needs overlapped with my work demands. I needed to depict myself favorably in the manuscript so I left that out, of course. The same rubric applied to my ambitions for my writing. I describe my writing as primarily undertaken for the benefit of our family, and that's true only in part. I mostly write because I adore creating worlds and puzzles, and I want to succeed at it wildly. But ambition is a dirty word when it's used by women; it's decidedly unladylike, in fact. Consequently, I had to jettison that piece of information as well."

The light of understanding begins to illuminate Archie's eyes as the flicker of resistance starts to die out. Does he finally understand? I pause to give him space to comment, but he doesn't speak. I need to ensure that he comprehends my meaning, so I must speak more plainly than I'd like.

"For all intents and purposes, the manuscript is the story of my life, and it's one I'll share with the police if necessary. In their hands, it will become evidence of your *attempted* murder that night near the Silent Pool, an attempt that I barely escaped after you called me to lure me there. An attempt that forced me into hiding at the Harrogate Hydro."

"What? Attempted murder? Hiding? I won't stand for this, Agatha. You'll give me the divorce I want, and I'll expose you to the world in the process," Archie announces, standing up. His sudden motion causes his chair to clatter to the floor. The diners around us look over in alarm, and I see Kenward and Goddard rise from their carefully positioned seats and approach the entrance to the restaurant. Are they planning on protecting me from Archie — or vice versa?

Chapter Forty-Eight

"Sit down, Archie," I insist with a sharp whisper as I slide my shawl down to show him the bruises on my arm, and I lift up my bangs to reveal the deep laceration and bruise on my forehead. "I don't think you want me to show these to the police."

After he sits, I raise my hand to Kenward and Goddard to show that all is well and tell Archie that he must do the same. Only then do I slide the shawl back over my shoulders and continue, "Taken together with my injuries — which the hotel maids, not to mention three massage therapists, have serendipitously seen on several occasions, beginning with the first night of my arrival here — the manuscript will establish a pattern of threatening behavior on your part, one that culminated on the night of my disappearance. That morning, I refused to give you the quiet divorce you sought, and as a result, that evening, you lured me to the Silent Pool where you would ensure you were free to marry Nancy by ending my life. But I escaped. Fearing for my life, I fled and went into hiding until the threat was over and your misdeeds became known."

"You're mad, Agatha." He remains seated but doesn't bother to quieten his voice. "Aside from the fiction of your manuscript and your self-inflicted injuries, it's your word against mine. No one will believe you."

I lean across the table, sliding a black-smeared envelope toward him. Recognizing the handwriting, he lunges for it. Opening the flap, he feels around inside. "There's nothing in here. What the hell do you think you can do with an envelope from Nancy to me? You still have no evidence of my relationship with her, which means that there's no hard evidence for your far-fetched allegation of assault," he jeers.

"I have the letter that was within the envelope, of course. It's a love note from Nancy to you." I think about my devastation when I initially found the love letter. The details about their trysts in London and their plans for the future nearly broke me, but now, I'm happy I discovered it and two other similar ones. They gave me the strength to take this step instead of continuing to fight for a marriage and a man I'd never have. A man who never really existed. "And I'm fairly certain the letter talks about the importance of divorce so you can marry her."

Archie blanches, all bravado draining from his face. "How did you get this? I burned all the letters."

"Not all of them. I have a nice collection of three that will serve as corroboration for the affair and the motivation for the assault on me at the Silent Pool."

He is very quiet and very still. "You've won, Agatha. I expect you'll get what you want now. Whatever that is."

Rage kindles within me. How could he think that I *want* the events that have transpired, the outcome that will surely follow? "You couldn't be more wrong. What I want is my old life and old self back. I want to be that trusting, optimistic person I once was, who believed in the happiness of her marriage and family. But you made getting what I want impossible."

"Then what do you want? What was this all for?"

"Most of what I *need,* I've now achieved. I needed you to be seen for who and what you are so my relationship with Rosalind wouldn't be ruined. Along with my reputation."

"Your reputation?" he practically snorts. "If anything, you're more famous now than ever, and that will only help your popularity as a mystery writer."

"That wasn't part of my original plan, Archie. I hadn't anticipated that the public would take hold of this story the way it has. I also hadn't planned on it lasting exactly this long. Who knows how much longer it would have gone on if I hadn't started carrying the newspaper face out around the Harrogate Hydro so someone would finally notice the resemblance between me and the woman on the front page? It was almost a relief to finally be identified and have the police contacted. I wanted this charade to end nearly as much as you."

Archie smiles for the first time; it seems he finds amusing the manner in which I hastened my discovery here at the hotel. The crinkling around his blue eyes and the flash of his white teeth remind me of happier times, but I steel myself against it, against him. I cannot betray myself with these residual emotions. How can I still have a shred of feeling for him after everything we've been through? I chastise myself for my rogue emotions.

"But if that name recognition comes in handy selling books, well then, I'll take it. I'm going to have to support myself as a novelist going forward after all," I say.

His eyes brighten when I say "support myself." Because of course, the notion of divorce is implicit in the phrase.

"Please understand that I have no wish to remain your wife after all this. Not too long ago, that would have been my greatest desire in the world, but no more. But I do need you to maintain your status as my husband, in name only, for a while longer. If I'm going to succeed with my story that I suffered from amnesia as to my identity instead of claiming that you attempted murder and I disappeared to protect myself, which is the only other option, then I need your full public support. You'll need to hire a doctor to confirm my amnesia, convey information about my condition to the press as I pretend to recover, and only then, after you've made clear to Rosalind what everyone else now understands — that you are to blame for our separation and my disappearance — will I agree to the divorce. Our daughter must know with utter certainty that I did everything I could to make our marriage work."

"Why couldn't we have come to this arrangement in the first place? When I first asked for the divorce?"

I laugh at his conveniently selective memory. "I should have thought that was abundantly clear by this point, Archie. It seems you have a case of memory loss yourself. Have you forgotten your insistence that Nancy Neele's name remain pristine in a divorce, which would have led to unacceptable implications about me? No, Archie, there's only ever been one way through the devastating wreckage you've made of our lives and my long-held myopic perspective on you, and it's been by following the path that I mapped out for you and that you followed, the one that began with the letter I left you on the day I disappeared."

THE ENDING,
OR ANOTHER BEGINNING

Wednesday, December 15, 1926
Harrogate Hydro, Harrogate, England

I pull up the collar of my coat as if its soft wool fabric could somehow shield me from the cameras and journalists and members of the public who wait outside the heavy oak doors like a military onslaught. I reach behind me for Madge's hand. I don't think I could take the necessary step outside the cocoon of the Harrogate Hydro and into the real world again without my sister, who's been both my rival — prompting me onward to better, higher versions of myself, whether or not that was her intent — and my dearest friend. Madge knows, without explanation, without discussion, what has transpired over these past eleven days, and I will have her unwavering support and counsel as I rebuild myself into the woman I am meant to become, as I have begun to forge, in the days ahead.

I could have never become that person as Archie's wife. The man I believed him to be, the man who could have fostered my strengths and talent into being, never existed. I wrote him into being on the first night we met, on the dance floor at Chudleigh Hall, just as I had the characters of my detective novels. But I could never get him quite right because I was an unreliable narrator of my own life, with only the vaguest sense of myself. In any event, even if he had been the man I'd hoped for, he could have never been *my Fate* as I understood that notion while still a girl. Because each of us, man or woman, has our *own Fate*, less fate than hard work and circumstance, I've come to believe.

I wish there could have been another way; I truly do. When it became clear that societal mores and Mummy's advice — which I'd clung to throughout my adult life like gospel — were fatally flawed, I wish that I'd been able to rewrite my story there and then. But I wasn't yet ready; I was still waiting for someone else to author my narrative, still hopeful that another ending was in store for me. Only when Archie killed that still-innocent woman did I finally accept that I had no other choice but to pick up the pen to save myself.

Madge's hand squeezes mine, and I know I'm as prepared as I'll ever be. Kenward and Goddard glance at me, and I nod. They lead our group, consisting of me, Madge, Madge's husband, and Archie, through the Harrogate Hydro lobby, and the two policemen together fling open the hotel's front doors. The bulbs of a hundred journalists' cameras flash, and I am momentarily blinded. When the bright lights stop and my eyes refocus, a sea of blinking eyes stares up at me, waiting for my story.

I stare back at them, wishing that I hadn't needed to create an unsolvable mystery in order to solve the mystery of myself. But I promise myself — and them — now that I have authored an authentic self into existence, I will write a perfect ending.

AUTHOR'S NOTE

I am a writer on a mission. I love nothing more than to excavate an important, complex woman from history and bring her into the light of the present day where we can finally perceive the breadth of her contributions as well as the insights she brings to modern-day issues. It is this desire to rediscover historical women, their stories, and to write their legacy back into the narrative that inspired this book. But as you may now know, the woman at the heart of this novel is different from anyone else I've written about, and consequently, so is this book.

Unlike many of the women I champion, the heroine of this book is certainly known. In fact, she's famous. I have been reading her stories since I was a teenager. She is the most successful novelist of all time — more than two billion copies of her books have been sold worldwide — and she's credited with both creating many of the essential tenets of the modern mystery novel and defying those tenets to deliver some of the most compelling, unorthodox mysteries ever. Decades after her death, her books still sell, versions of them continue to be made into blockbuster movies, and her puzzles often remain unsolvable.

The very fact of Agatha Christie's fame nearly deterred me from writing about her. I kept asking myself whether I should focus instead on a woman whose legacy we benefit from every day but whose identity is entirely hidden. But then I learned that a compelling, unsolved mystery surrounds Agatha the real-life woman, and I had a sense that the resolution of that mystery might help explain how she became the most successful writer in the world. I knew I had to turn to her story next.

When I learned about her 1926 disappearance — seemingly torn from the pages of one of her own books — I became even more fascinated with the bestselling writer. I couldn't help but wonder: What happened to her during the eleven days she was missing? Did she disappear by her own hand or someone else's? Was she running from her life or creating an entirely new one? I couldn't shake the question of what role

Agatha might have played in her own disappearance and why.

After all, even though she was not yet the famous Agatha Christie we know now, she was a mystery novelist on the rise who had just published her groundbreaking *The Murder of Roger Ackroyd.* As I reread this mystery, I was struck by the mastery of its plotting, especially the deft use of an unreliable narrator. Surely a writer this talented in the art of plotting could not have been a victim in her own vanishing. How could she have suffered from amnesia or gotten herself into some sort of fugue state, as some have theorized? She *had* to have crafted her disappearance as skillfully as she crafted her mysteries, as a vehicle to serve her own ends.

This speculation about Agatha Christie, the writer and the woman, was the genesis of *The Mystery of Mrs. Christie.* To my way of thinking, Agatha was that rare example of a woman who used her skill and talent and moxie to escape from the confines of her era — with the limitations it placed on women — and wrest control of her life. So, instead of writing a forgotten woman back into history, as my other books have done, this book explores one strong woman's successful endeavor to take her history into her own hands and write herself back into the narrative.

READING GROUP GUIDE

1. Agatha Christie is one of the most cele-
   brated mystery writers of all time. What
   did you know about her personal history
   before you read *The Mystery of Mrs. Christie*? Did the book challenge any of your
   preconceived notions about her life?

2. Agatha Christie was a successful writer
   within her lifetime, quite unusual for a
   woman of her time. How did her desire
   for independence shape the course of the
   story, both obviously and more subtly?

3. Do you think Agatha Christie is a good
   representative of the issues that women
   faced in her era? Did she have any privi-
   leges or responsibilities that set her apart
   from other women of her period?

4. Describe the night Archie and Agatha
   first met. How did their relationship

change over time, and why? Do you think Agatha's manuscript told the full story? What details do you think she changed or left out? Why do you think she might have altered the "truth"?

5. Archie spends much of the story trying to protect his reputation. Do you think that would be the case if the story took place today? Would it be easier or more difficult for him to deflect guilt in the modern news cycle?

6. What differences did you see between the Agatha within the manuscript and the Agatha who appears at the end of the book? What creative licenses did she take with her own personality and story? Were they justified?

7. Toward the end of the book, Agatha mourns the mother she could not be for Rosalind. What forces dominated their relationship? Do you think Agatha's struggle to balance husband and child was common in her historical period? How do you expect her relationship with Rosalind to evolve after the events of the book? How does this compare with parental struggles mothers face now?

8. Which characters, if any, did you find to be most relatable? Did you connect with Agatha? Were there any characters you wished you knew more about?

9. Agatha left an enormous mark on the mystery community and on the world of books more generally. Do you think her marriage had an effect on her success? Or her disappearance? If so, what was it? How would you characterize her personal and professional legacies?

A CONVERSATION
WITH THE AUTHOR

Unlike a few of your previous heroines, many readers are familiar with Agatha Christie. What prompted you to look into her less public life?

Actually, the very fact that Agatha Christie is so famous and successful — she's sold more books than any other writer! — nearly stopped me from writing *The Mystery of Mrs. Christie*. I questioned whether I should focus on excavating from the past a lesser-known woman who has made important contributions. But when I started to research the circumstances and history around her 1926 disappearance, I had the uncanny sense that it played a key role in her journey to becoming the most successful writer in the world, and I felt compelled to explore that idea. One of the questions I like to explore in each of my books is how a woman at the story's core transformed into the person who made such an extraordinary bequest, one that continues into modern times.

What were the most surprising details you uncovered in your research process? Was there anything you found particularly fascinating that didn't make it into the final book?

Oh, there are so many astonishing facts I learned about Agatha! I particularly loved the fact that she was one of the first Europeans to learn surfing, and I *had* to include that little nugget in the book, even though it wasn't really necessary for the story! The same applies to her extensive knowledge of poisons, which she acquired from her World War I work in a hospital dispensary; I knew I needed to find a home for that in the story, as that experience turned out to be useful in many of her mysteries. Some of the intriguing particulars that did *not* make it to the page are, of course, the many hypotheses proposed about her disappearances, ranging from amnesia to a fugue state to a plot against her husband's alleged mistress, among many suppositions. That, and the fact that Agatha wrote a series of romance novels under the pseudonym Mary Westmacott.

At what point in the research process do you decide who will be your supporting cast? How do you develop characters like Detective Chief Inspector Kenward or Agatha's mother?

In writing historical fiction, I am constantly encountering fascinating period details and people that I would adore adding to my books. But I always have to pause and ask myself whether the detail or person is important to either creating the setting or moving the story forward. In the case of Agatha's mother, I knew that Agatha's attachment to her was key not only to the development of her personality but also to her emotional state around the time of her disappearance, and thus really needed to be included. As for Detective Chief Inspector Kenward, I believed that Archie needed an antagonist to propel forward Agatha's version of her disappearance, even though Kenward did not realize he was doing so.

How did you balance the dual timelines of the manhunt and the manuscript? Was it difficult to write about the early blushes of Agatha and Archie's attraction knowing where the two were headed?

Crafting the dual stories of the manhunt

and the manuscript certainly meant that my office was papered with timelines and lists of dates and flow charts! And I certainly experienced some painful moments knowing what history had in store for Agatha and Archie — and what Agatha had in store for Archie! But I thoroughly enjoyed the plotting and the intricacy of writing this unusual sort of historical fiction. I'll never be as masterful at suspense and mystery as Agatha, but it was fun to try, and I viewed it as an homage to her.

Agatha's manuscript is critical for her to triumph over Archie. Did she ever write a manuscript that bore such a resemblance to her own life?

In terms of writing her own life story, Agatha did publish her autobiography, which was enormously helpful in my own research and an inspiration for her voice. It provided some interesting insights into her upbringing and her early writing, but it says *nothing* about the disappearance. *Nothing.* She skips over it entirely, much as she refused to talk about those eleven days for the rest of her life. So her autobiography shares only selective pieces of her past.

How did you feel investigating the soci-

etal expectations that Agatha's mother continuously flung her way? Do you think the demands of husband and child are still at odds in the modern day?

I really felt for Agatha when I learned about the sort of messages her mother imparted over and over again about the sort of relationship she needed to foster with her husband — namely, putting her husband first above all else. Given the closeness of the mother-daughter relationship they shared, I knew that advice would have an enormous impact on Agatha's relationship with Archie — and consequently on Agatha's relationship with her own daughter — and would affect Agatha's feelings about pursuing her career. While I think modern women struggle with the demands of balancing work and family, I do not think it necessarily stems from the sense that women must put their husbands first, but that women still bear much of the burden of both work and home.

What advice do you have for other historical fiction writers, especially those who are just starting out?

I would suggest that, as with all writing, aspiring writers focus on topics for which they have a real and abiding passion, rather than pursue presumed fads in readers' tastes. The enthusiasm for their subject will be clear and appealing to the readers, and may even start its own trend!

How would you describe Agatha Christie's legacy, both for her contemporaries and for women today?

The most obvious aspect of her legacy is her role at the center of the Golden Age of mystery fiction, where she was central to the creation of the classic mystery novel. Her astounding skill and talent is such that her books continue to sell today, stemming in part from the elusive nature of her puzzles. Those enigmas, coupled with her morally ambiguous characters and the alluring settings often placed in that critical but sometimes overlooked period between the two world wars, make the books compelling and justifiably bestselling. But in order to achieve that success, Agatha had to overcome the limitations imposed upon women of her era, and it is her act of leaping over that hurdle that I explore in *The Mystery of Mrs. Christie.*

ACKNOWLEDGMENTS

The Mystery of Mrs. Christie would have remained in the shadows without the efforts and encouragement of many, many people. As always, I must begin my thanks with Laura Dail, my incredible agent, whose wise counsel and unflagging support were critical in bringing this idea to the page. I am so appreciative of the talented folks at Sourcebooks, who have tirelessly championed this book, in particular my masterful, wonderful editor, Shana Drehs; Sourcebooks's inspiring leader, Dominique Raccah; not to mention the accomplished Todd Stocke, Valerie Pierce, Heidi Weiland, Molly Waxman, Cristina Arreola, Lizzie Lewandowski, Heather Hall, Michael Leali, Margaret Coffee, Beth Oleniczak, Tiffany Schultz, Ashlyn Keil, Heather VenHuizen, Heather Moore, Will Riley, Danielle McNaughton, and Travis Hasenour. And I am deeply grateful to all the remarkable booksellers and librarians and readers who have enjoyed *The Mystery of Mrs. Christie,* as well as my other books.

I am incredibly fortunate in my family and friends, especially my SISTAS, the Sewickley crew, Illana Raia, Kelly Close, Laura Hudak, Daniel McKenna, and Ponny Conomos Jahn. But it is Jim, Jack, and Ben — their love, confidence, and sacrifices — to whom I am most thankful.

If the life of the inimitable Agatha Christie is of further interest to you, beyond the fictional version of her life I've created in these pages, I can recommend the following books, among many wonderful choices: (1) *An Autobiography* by Agatha Christie; (2) *Come Tell Me How You Live: An Archaeological Memoir* by Agatha Christie Mallowan; (3) *The Grand Tour: Around the World with the Queen of Mystery* by Agatha Christie, edited by Mathew Prichard; (4) *Agatha Christie* by Laura Thompson; (5) *Agatha Christie: The Disappearing Novelist* by Andrew Norman; and (6) *Agatha Christie and the Eleven Missing Days* by Jared Cade. But for those intrigued by her legacy, nothing can compare with reading the actual mysteries written by Agatha Christie, those timeless puzzles and conundrums that have no parallel.

ABOUT THE AUTHOR

Marie Benedict is a lawyer with more than ten years' experience as a litigator at two of the country's premier law firms and Fortune 500 companies. She is a magna cum laude graduate of Boston College with a focus on history and a cum laude graduate of the Boston University School of Law. She is also the author of the *New York Times* bestseller *The Only Woman in the Room, Carnegie's Maid, The Other Einstein,* and *Lady Clementine.* She lives in Pittsburgh with her family.

The employees of Thorndike Press hope you have enjoyed this Large Print book. All our Thorndike, Wheeler, and Kennebec Large Print titles are designed for easy reading, and all our books are made to last. Other Thorndike Press Large Print books are available at your library, through selected bookstores, or directly from us.

For information about titles, please call:
(800) 223-1244

or visit our website at:
gale.com/thorndike

To share your comments, please write:

Publisher
Thorndike Press
10 Water St., Suite 310
Waterville, ME 04901